Also from Indigo Sea Press

by

Dorothy McMillan

The Gray Green Underground
Vile Acts
Soul Crossed

Deadly Urges

NEVER MISTAKE CHILDREN FOR ANGELS

By

Dorothy McMillan

Stiletto Books
Published by Indigo Sea Press
Winston-Salem

Stiletto Books
Indigo Sea Press
302 Ricks Drive
Winston-Salem, NC 27103

First Stiletto Books edition published
December, 2015
Stiletto Books, Moon Sailor and all production design are trademarks of Indigo Sea Press, used under license.

For information regarding bulk purchases of this book, digital purchase and special discounts, please contact the publisher at indigoseapress.com

Cover design by Stacy Castanedo

Manufactured in the United States of America
ISBN 978-1-63066-268-4

Dedicated to the love of my life, Al, and my three children, Debra, Kimberly, and Michael. And of course to all my grandchildren and great-grandchildren. Without all of you, I would never have continued to write. You are my inspiration, and the strength I need to face each day.

And to my dear Ray Bradbury, who would not let me give up.

ACKNOWLEDGEMENTS

My sincere thanks to all of my beta readers headed by Trina Williams, as well as to Al McMillan, Debra Harvey, Kimberly Harris, Ann Snow and Lauren and Billy Harris who have struggled through rough drafts without complaints.

PROLOGUE

An odd shiver hit Mick Sullivan as he stood on the beach looking at the weathered Cape Cod house. Although it was December, it felt colder than it should have, especially since hot Santa Ana winds had been blowing all day. He shivered again and goose bumps crawled over his skin, prickling like insect bites. Was he coming down with the flu? He considered abandoning his plan to rob the beach house.

A stocky man, Mick had bushy hair the color of rat's fur, and a bent nose, the result of numerous street fights. He shivered again and felt his heart jump and then it skipped a beat. He reached into his pocket and fingered his gun. Just the touch of it made him more comfortable. He knew that with his gun's silencer, he could walk into the house, put a bullet into the owners' brains, and walk out with anything he wanted. Even if he didn't feel so good, he could manage it.

All the lights were out in the old house. He moved toward the redwood deck. The back door, which was a large glass slider, would be easy to open. Just before he reached the deck, a painful, piercing chill, like wafts of Alaskan air, gripped his bones. It stabbed his legs and arms like spears of ice. Still determined, he stepped up on the redwood deck. With his Nikes whispering against the wood, he walked to the sliding door. When he reached out to test the door, a racking pain clawed at his back.

He leaned against the glass door for a moment waiting for the pain to stop. The way he felt, he would be lucky to find the occupants and pop a bullet into each of their heads. He'd have to take whatever he could grab and get the hell out of there before some insomniac son-of-a-bitch spotted the stolen van he'd parked in the alley behind the house.

He sucked in a deep breath. The sea air felt strangely thick, as if he was forcing wool into his lungs. Streams of moisture began to flow down the sides of his neck. Then his eyes began to burn and water. Tears, hot and coppery smelling, poured from them. He wiped them with the back of his hands. Even in the shadowy light, he could see something was drastically wrong. Christ! He was bleeding! He

1

touched his ears and felt blood flowing from there too. Had he burst something inside his head? Then his entire body began dripping blood. Blood seeped hot and wet out of every pore. It soaked his shirt and jeans. His heavy pea coat was sodden with the sticky stuff. It was then that his legs crumpled under him and he fell, smacking painfully against the splintery wood of the deck.

"Oh, my God!" he cried. "What's happening?" His heartbeat made a hollow sound, as if it had nothing left to pump. It echoed in his ears. He felt the growing pool of liquid around him, like some strange warm bath. He heard it weeping through the spaces between the redwood boards. His life force surged out of him like a tidal sea, and he could do nothing to stop it.

He made a desperate effort to find his cell phone. He fumbled in his blood-wet pockets. Then he remembered. He'd left it in the van he'd stolen! He tried to crawl closer to the sliding glass door. If he could make someone inside hear him, get someone to call 911, they could stop the bleeding. For a second, he almost laughed at the idea of begging help from people he'd planned to snuff. His fingers made little scratching noises against the wood. He could smell the metallic scent of his blood all around him. He could see it steaming in the night air, the way he'd seen a deer's blood steam when he'd shot one a few years before.

Why the fuck had he decided to rob the house tonight? Was this punishment for his past deeds, he wondered? His felt his veins begin to collapse, felt them twisting and urging others to flatten, like rows of dominos set in motion. His mouth tasted like bitter wine. He was in the grip of something squeezing and pressing the blood and the life from him, like someone squeezing an orange. Something he could only feel, but not see.

Deep, deep in his bones, he felt a slight tremor. Just the faintest movement. Then it stopped. In a spasm of agony, his heart began pounding itself to pieces against the inside of his chest. Then battered and bruised, it quit.

A December moon rose over the Saddleback mountains. Its silver light crept quietly along the beach, highlighting the phosphorus in the waves, but failed to reach the redwood deck. Two late-night lifeguards patrolling the beach saw nothing out of the ordinary. Not until several hours later when the sun came up.

CHAPTER ONE

Monday morning dawned bright, hot, and windy. Newport Beach Detective Ted Bearbower thought how odd it was that in Southern California it could be nippy one day and roasting the next. He'd removed his dark wool jacket, opting to work in rolled-up shirtsleeves. Even so, he felt sweat trickling in little rivulets down his back. Through the window beside his desk, he could see palm trees bending in the wind. A Santa Ana wind blowing in off the desert was uncommon during California's winter months, but not unheard of.

"I'd bet anything the damn air conditioning is down again," Ted grumbled to no one in particular.

"It's just confused," said Detective Mike Ajax, grinning at him from his desk across from him. "After all, we had the heat on the day before yesterday."

Sitting at his desk in the detective's room, Ted looked as inconspicuous as a polar bear at a child's tea party. He was not so much fat as behemoth; his two-hundred-sixty pounds had fortunately distributed themselves evenly over his six-foot-five frame. Sitting next to, Ajax, his latest partner, he resembled a mountain.

Ted gave Ajax a furtive look. In the span of twenty months, since a lunatic had murdered Steve Lock, Ted's longtime partner, he'd managed to go through four other partners. Each one of them had asked to be reassigned after working only two weeks with him. He wondered what he could do to shake off this latest one. Ajax had been with him almost three months now, and nothing seemed to discourage the little runt.

A dark-haired, dark-eyed young man in his late twenties, Ajax had a mat of thick black hair scattered across his body, which made him look remarkably like a tarantula to Ted. His reedy arms and legs did nothing to dispel this illusion. Ted hated the way the guy dressed. He wore baggy slacks, oversized polo shirts, a tweedy jacket in shades of brown, along with black Reeboks, and an opal pinkie ring.

Ted shrugged and looked away. He'd tried insulting the guy, made him do all the paper work, stuck him with late-night stakeouts, and used any flimsy excuse he could think of to bellow at him. Ajax just grinned and went along with it. Well, he'd find a way to get rid of this latest nuisance before long. He always did. He didn't need or want another partner. Losing Steve had caused him the most pain he'd ever felt. He didn't want to ever feel that way again.

The phone on Ajax's desk rang. He tuned out the conversation and turned his attention to the pile of folders on his desk. Nothing much there. Things had been quiet in the city for some time. The worst he'd seen was a drive-by shooting at Newport Harbor High School, a failed daylight robbery at Bank of America, and two car jackers. People, he mumbled to himself, should stop driving such expensive cars and ride the bus.

He reached for his thermos and poured a cup of Vienna Roast coffee. Then he opened the box of lemon bars he'd picked up at the bakery on his way in. It felt good, he thought, to have his old appetite back. After the death of his partner, he'd lost his enormous appetite for the first time in his life. Before that, he'd been a gourmand. Food was his love, his sedative, his companion. It had taken him until just a few months ago to get back to his normal eating habits, and his present weight.

A few months ago, he'd discovered a wonderful new bakery called A Little Bit of Heaven. The owner, a woman named Madeline, made the most delicious pastries he'd ever tasted. In his time, he'd tasted plenty. "Call me Maddy," the owner had said. "And I'll tempt you with delights you never thought possible." Maddy wasn't young, around fifty, close to his age, with sleek blond hair, and a soft full figure. The pristine white uniform she always wore was cut so he could see the smooth rounded tops of her large breasts. He wondered if he found her attractive, or was it her baking skills that excited him. He stopped at the bakery every morning now, including weekends, and Maddy gave him something new each time. Today lemon bars, yesterday cinnamon croissants, and Saturday cannolis. When she had time, they would sit together at one of the bakery's small tables and exchange recipes.

"Hey, Teddy Bear…." Ajax said, jerking Ted back to reality. "We've got something."

Ted felt himself cringe. No one else in the department had used his nickname since his partner had died. Leave it to the little tarantula to pick up on it.

"What?" Ted growled.

"Dead guy. Blood all over the place. We are assigned," Ajax said.

4

Ted looked out the window at the wind. It had to be blowing at least forty miles an hour. Shit! He hated the Santa Ana winds. At least it was winter and the chance of brush and forest fires were at a minimum. During the summer and fall, the winds could fan a tiny blaze into an inferno in seconds. He really didn't want to go out in the unseasonable heat and that damn wind.

"You cover it," he said.

Ajax put down the phone. "Nope. Chief emphasized both of us. Medical examiner's still there. Forensics too. They want us to see for ourselves."

"I've seen plenty of dead guys."

"Not like this you haven't. This guy bled to death, with no visible wounds."

The words bled to death jabbed at Ted. His last partner had bled to death. Actually, it had been worse than that. Far worse. Ted forced the thought of what happened out of his mind.

"Hemophiliac maybe?" he said.

"Maybe. Come on. Let's go." Ajax got up and picked up his awful plaid jacket from the back of his chair. "I'll drive."

"I drive. You drive like a buffalo in heat," Ted said. "Where to?"

"The end of the peninsula. Ocean side."

Ted's heart gave a painful lurch, and then thumped erratically. "Peninsula! Christ!" he growled. He had actively tried to avoid the peninsula since Steve's death.

"What? You don't love it down there? It's incredible, man, incredible! We should all be so lucky as to live in one of those million-dollar shacks. Watch the boats coming in and out of the harbor. White-water view. What more could you want?"

Ted tossed his wool jacket over his arm, lowered his head slightly, and looked at Ajax with penetrating eyes. "I hate the place. Okay?"

Ajax grinned. "Sure. One man's candy is another's poison I guess."

Ted felt grateful he didn't have to explain or rehash the terrible events that led to his partner's death. "Worst kind of poison," he muttered.

"Man, those lemon bars look great. Can you spare one?" Ajax looked at the box on Ted's desk. "I mean, you got a whole dozen."

Ten hesitated, then said, "Yeah, sure. Take one with you."

Ajax grinned like a second grader, spent a moment deciding on which lemon bar he wanted, chose the largest one, lifted it carefully, and took a bite.

"If we're going," Ted snarled, "let's go."

Ajax nodded with his mouth full. He wiped a yellow crumb off his lip. "Ummm," he said.

Ted led the way to the parking garage. By the time they reached the car, Ajax had finished the lemon bar and was dabbing at his mouth with a grungy white handkerchief.

"Boy that was great! Where did you get them?" Ajax asked.

"Found a little bakery over on Superior."

"I'll have to go over there. I could eat stuff like that all day."

"If you did, you'd be as big as I am."

"So, what's wrong with that, Teddy Bear?"

Again, Ted winced at the nickname. He knew his co-workers had, because of his girth, given him that name affectionately. He only wished they'd thought of something more dignified. Rocky, maybe, or Ted "The Giant" Bearbower.

Ted pulled the car out onto Pacific Coast Highway and headed north. Strong gusts of wind buffeted them. Traffic was light but he kept his speed slow. As they went over the Bay Bridge, Ted looked out at the harbor. It was dappled with whitecaps. Moored boats rocketed up and down in the wind-chopped water. The minute he turned onto Balboa Boulevard, he felt a shot of déjà vu. Christ! He didn't want to go down there. Not anywhere near the Balboa Pier, or the Point. Not after all that had happened there. Nevertheless, he pressed his lips together, mashed down on the accelerator, and increased his speed.

"Hey!" Ajax said. "Talk about driving like a buffalo in heat! What's with you? First, you crawl, and then you break speed records. If you're gonna drive like this all the way down the peninsula, turn on the fucking siren!"

"Sorry," Ted said, relaxing his pressure on the gas pedal. "Just thought we might as well get there and get it over with."

Ajax turned to study him. Ted felt his gaze and said, "What?"

Ajax shrugged, and gave a half grin. "The chief said this would be tough on you. He didn't know the half of it, did he?"

"Half of what?" Ted didn't want to discuss it. He wanted to investigate whatever had happened on the Peninsula and get the hell out of there as fast as possible.

"Whatever happened, you have to get back on the old horse and ride, buddy. Sometime or other you have to, or else give it up and put yourself out to pasture."

Shit, Ted thought, every damn cop in the city knew what happened. Probably held an orientation meeting for all the new guys. Filled them in on all the grisly details.

"What's the address," Ted asked in a low growl.

"Ahhh." His partner fumbled with his jacket pocket and pulled out a piece of paper. "Ocean front. Can't read the numbers. You know my scribbling. However, it's almost to the end of the point. Probably can't miss it, with black-and-whites all around the place."

As they passed the street that was the main turn-off to the Balboa Pier, Ted felt a hot trickle of fear in his belly. He quickly switched his mind to thinking about the bakery, the pastries, and the lady named Maddy. He wondered what kind of treats she would have baked for him tomorrow morning. Maybe some chocolate éclairs with vanilla custard pudding.

They pulled into the alley behind the row of houses that faced the ocean. Squad cars were parked all over the place. A row of gawkers had formed, lining the alley. People huddled together talking in low tones. Ted parked the car in front of someone's garage, pulled on his jacket, and he and Ajax snaked their way through the crowd and in-between two houses to the oceanfront. A hot blast of wind hit them, blowing bits of sand with it. Ted wished he'd left his jacket in the car. He felt the beginning of sweat beading up on his forehead.

"Hey, Ted. Glad you could make it." The medical examiner, Earl Gras, a pale man with wispy strands of graying hair buffeting about in the wind, motioned for him to join him on the redwood deck of a slightly weathered two-story house. "This one's a real puzzle."

"Why's that?" Ted asked as he made his way around a white patio table and chairs to where the dead man lay. He stood looking down at the body of a man crumpled on the deck. He wore a Navy pea coat and cords. All his clothing appeared to be soaked with dark blood. The medical examiner shifted the man's head so Ted could see. Even in death, it was a cruel face, Ted thought. Maybe that was because the person's pug-ugly nose looked as if it had been battered in a dozen fights. Or maybe it had something to do with the squinky little eyes, still open. A layer of dried blood coated the man's entire face.

"This poor bastard sprung a major leak," Earl said. "All over his

7

body. It looks as if he hemorrhaged from every pore."

"Maybe he had some sort of blood disease," Ajax offered, bending down to look at the body.

"I'm not aware of one that would cause something this massive or as fast as this seems to have been. We've got a deck soaked with blood, and it looks like a lot of it ran through the spaces between the boards."

Ted felt a surge of relief. This was completely different, he told himself. It wasn't the way his partner had died. Even though Ted himself had seen the killer die, he still had these moments of irrational fear that the serial killer, who'd mutilated so many people, including his partner, might have been reincarnated.

"Do we know if he lived here, or around here?" Ted asked.

"So far, no one knows him," Earl said.

"Time of death?"

"Can't be sure until we get him back and take a liver temp. But I'd guess it was maybe six or seven hours ago."

"I wonder what he was doing here in the middle of the night." Ted said.

Earl shrugged. "Best bet is, robbing the place. They found a stolen van parked in the alley. The patrolman ran a make on the plates. It was reported stolen last night."

Ajax pushed back the pea coat on the dead man. "Hey, will you look at this! What kind of gun is it? Never saw one like it before."

"A Ruger LCP, I think," Ted said. "With a handmade silencer. Nice little weapon. With the silencer, it's probably the closest to silent as you'll get."

"Has forensics come up with anything?" Ajax asked.

"Not that they've mentioned, but they just got started," Earl said.

"So, what do you think?" Ted asked.

Earl shrugged. "Sure as hell beats me. We need a complete autopsy. Drug tests. The works. This is the strangest thing I've ever seen. From the looks of it, it happened fast. With the sudden loss of blood, the guy's blood pressure dropped dramatically. I just hope it's not the effects of some new drug out on the street. Some of these guys would take rat poison if it gave 'em a high."

Ajax nodded and wandered off in the direction of one of the forensics men. Ted took in a deep breath and let it out slowly, feeling his pulse pounding against his temples. It's okay, he told himself. Not as bad as he thought it would be. He'd get through it. Ajax had been right. It was time to get back on that horse. The serial murders had been terrible, but he'd stopped them. That's what counted.

Ajax walked back to him; his mouth pursed forward, a frown on his forehead. He ran his fingers over his chin that was already beginning to show a five-o'clock shadow, even though it was only a little after nine in the morning. "The patrolmen got zip," he said. "Nada. They figure it was natural causes. Although only God knows what could cause a mess like this." Ajax stood looking down at the dead man and shook his head, and then leafed through his note pad. "The uniforms questioned most everyone around here that was home. No one saw or heard a thing. Should we re-question them?"

"No, not yet." Ted sighed. "Give them a little more time and maybe they'll recall something."

Ajax put his hand on Ted's arm. "This is good medicine, Teddy Bear. Sometimes it takes a little of one poison to counteract another."

Ted watched as two uniformed men pulled on rubber gloves and helped put the dead man into a body bag and onto a gurney. They rolled the gurney off the deck and with a lot of effort, pushed it through the sand, and disappeared around the side of the house.

"I'll get my report to you ASAP," Earl said. "But like I said, I'm afraid we may be looking at some kind of god-awful new drug here. Just what we need popping up on the streets. If that's it, let's hope to heaven the kids on campus don't latch on to it." Earl peeled off his rubber gloves, stuffed them into his bag, and left.

Ted gazed down at the dark stain on the deck. That will be hard to remove, he thought. A gust of hot wind hit him, spraying more bits of sand. He held his hand up to protect his eyes.

"Excuse me," someone said. A woman's voice.

Ted turned and looked into the bluest eyes he'd ever seen...eyes like two bright marbles glinting in sunlight. They blinked at him. He'd seen those eyes before! The hair too! Who could forget those swirls of long red hair? It blew about in the wind like licks of crimson flame, framing the woman's face. However, the most remarkable thing about her was the brilliant blue-white diamond set into one of her front teeth.

"Yes, ma'am," he said.

The woman's eyes narrowed slightly. It was obvious she too recalled their last meeting. "I live next door. May I ask what's

9

happened here?"

Ted hesitated for a moment. There's no reason people shouldn't know since it didn't appear to be foul play. "Lifeguards found a body here early this morning."

"Oh God!" the woman said, her blue eyes flashing brighter. "It's not…I mean, do you know who it is? My husband and I were gone early this morning and just got back. Are the people who live here okay?"

"Yes, ma'am," Ajax interjected. "The patrolmen questioned them earlier. So far no one around here can ID him. He was armed. Our guess is that he was attempting to rob the place."

"Maybe you should take a look," Ted said. "Perhaps you know him."

The woman shook her head. "My husband has already gone to the alley where they took the body. I'm sure he'll identify him if he can. I was just worried about my friends who live in the house where he was found."

"May I have your name?" Ted asked, getting out his notepad.

"Have you forgotten it already, Detective Bearbower? I'm surprised. It's Tyree Rattigan. My husband is Beauregard. Boo for short. We live in the Art Deco next door."

Ted lowered his pad. Of course he hadn't forgotten. He was only being formal. Tyree Rattigan had been a central figure in the serial killer case. Not that she'd done anything wrong, except not coming forward with information when she should have.

Just the sound of her name made him break out in more hot little beads of sweat across his forehead and upper lip. He dabbed at his lip with the back of his hand. Some of the sweat ran into his mouth, sweet and salty. He wanted to take his coat off, but it would have to wait until they were back in the car.

"No, I hadn't forgotten. Just wanted to get it right. We may be around to talk with you again later," he said. "But as of now, it looks like unusual, but natural causes." He motioned to Ajax. "Let's get out of here. If necessary we'll come back after they ID the guy, if they can."

Ajax shrugged. "Whatever you say."

Ted nodded at the woman. She gave him a faint smile, the sunlight glinting off a small blue-white diamond in her front tooth. He closed his eyes against the sight of it. Why anyone would want to wear something like that was beyond him. He'd seen this once too many times before. He opened his eyes, gave a shudder then turned, and made his way off the deck. He made straight for the car, opened the door, took off his coat and climbed in. He leaned forward and pressed his forehead against the steering wheel. He'd made it. His first time back on the scene, and he'd gotten through it. Some sweat, a few shakes, a rapid heartbeat. Nothing he couldn't handle. Thank the good Lord this didn't appear to be another murder. The body might even be that of one of those homeless guys who hung around the beach. Could have had an attack of some kind. On the other hand, Earl's idea of some new drug was possible. Whatever, it was nothing like his partner's death or the string of other Brownstone murder cases he worked on. He let out a long sigh of relief, and felt his heartbeat slow. What he wanted now was to get back to the department, pour a cup of coffee, and eat half a dozen lemon bars.

Ajax opened the passenger door and got in. "You move mighty fast and graceful for a big guy, you know that?"

Ted shot him a sideways glance and started the engine. "Graceful! Christ! That's a hell of a thing to say."

"What, you want I should call you clumsy? I just meant you managed to weave your way around the patrolmen, the gawkers, the patio furniture, and the cars in the alley, so fast I couldn't keep up with you."

"Yeah, well I had to get out of there." He put the car in gear and drove down the alley, turned at the first street and then onto Balboa Boulevard and headed off the peninsula. They drove in silence for a while.

Ajax rapped his fingers against the ledge of the car window. "Shit, it's hot! Don't these cars have air conditioning?" he said.

"Broken. Seldom need it. The Santa Ana winds don't often get this far down. Open the damn window. The air is just as hot out there, but at least it's moving."

They both rolled down their windows, letting the hot dry wind howl through the car. Ted could smell the brine of sea air, fainter than usual with the wind coming from the East. He took in a deep breath, feeling a renewed sense of relief. He'd been dreading this day for a long time. Dreaded seeing the place where his partner had died. He knew it would come. Now it was here, and he'd come out on the other side, barely scathed.

"Are you getting ready to talk about it?" Ajax asked.

"Talk about what?"

"You know. About what happened to you? The reason they keep giving you new partners. Why you won't let anyone get close to you. That kind of crap. And no one will tell me exactly why."

Ted had to smile. The little tarantula was no dummy. No wonder he'd not been able to shake him off. "Yeah. I'm almost ready. One of these days."

"Good. Let me know, will ya?"

"I'll do that."

"Listen, when we get back, could you spare another of those lemon bars? I'm hungry."

"Get your own damn pastry!"

"Right. Fine. No problem." Ajax rapped his fingers on the window ledge again. Ted wanted to bellow at him to stop, but didn't. After all, they'd just seen a man who'd bled to death. The little tarantula had a right to vent his tension.

"You know what?" Ajax said, his fingers stopping their nervous tattoo. "If Earl's right about there being a new drug on the street, we're gonna see a lot more of this."

Ted grimaced. "Well then, let's hope to hell Earl's wrong."

"Or, what if it's like some new disease? You know, like AIDS, only different. Man! That's a scary thought!" Ajax looked at his hands. "Christ, I touched the guy! His coat, at least. I didn't even think to put on rubber gloves. What if he did have AIDS or, God forbid, something like Ebola?" Ajax closed his eyes and growled, "How stupid!"

"Come on, kid, stop borrowing trouble." Ted tried to sound reassuring. He too looked down at his hands for a moment, trying to remember if he'd touched the man. No, he was sure he hadn't.

"I'm sure it's isolated," Ted said finally. "Just some freak thing. We'll have to wait and see." He heard Ajax sigh. The wind blew a violent gust and the car rocked with it. They started up Pacific Coast Highway toward the department. He could hardly wait to get back. First thing he'd do was scrub his hands. Then he'd stuff himself with lemon bars. He might even let Ajax have one or two more.

He switched his thoughts back to Maddy and the bakery, and her wonderful full breasts and her delicious pastry. He'd worry about the case on the peninsula later.

CHAPTER TWO

A gust of wind racketed around the beachfront home like a wild animal chasing its prey. Old timbers groaned and creaked. Elizabeth and Andy Rosemond sat huddled together on the blue cushions of their wicker sofa in the living room. Neither of them wanted to talk about the body that had been found on their deck.

Andy, at thirty-one, needing a haircut as usual, and looking like a pensive five-year-old with his tall slender frame, large dark eyes, and a fan of dark brown hair falling over his forehead. Elizabeth gave a tense smile because he had on red cotton shorts and a white T-shirt that read:

Earthquakes, fires, and floods.
California has it ALL!

Andy held Elizabeth's hand tightly, the skin around his knuckles pinched white. Elizabeth wanted to open the drapes across the sliding glass door and let in some sunshine and fresh air. She wanted to let out the staleness and tension that had filled the room since the discovery of the body. However, opening the drapes would open the window to the remains of the awful scene. Earlier she'd seen the body. It looked as if it might have washed up on the deck with the morning tide. Only it was a tide of dark red blood instead of seawater. The sight of it had made her legs go rubbery, and she had begun to shake. Andy had taken her inside and stayed with her, holding her hand until the shaking stopped.

The wind gusted again and shook the glass in the sliding door. Elizabeth jumped. At thirty, she still had the fresh look of a much younger woman. She wore no makeup except for lip-gloss and a bit of liner around her smoky gray eyes. Her pale blond hair was swept back in a ponytail. The red shorts she wore matched Andy's, topped by a white halter-top. Even though the weather had turned unseasonably hot with the Santa Ana winds, she shivered. Death did that to you, she realized. It gave you a chill, just the thought of it, as if something damp and cold had reached out and touched you with icy fingers. That's how she'd felt three years ago when they'd first moved into her Aunt Mary's beachfront house. The horrible discovery of a young girl's body on the beach, all tangled in strands of wet seaweed, continued to haunt her. Another shiver rippled through her and she huddled closer to Andy. She'd thought about all the terrible things she had experienced back then. She'd believed none of those things could possibly happen again. Now, death was at her doorstep once more.

"Would you like to go work on your latest painting, Lizzy," Andy said trying to lighten up the situation. "Your work usually helps calm you."

"No, I can't paint after what all happened this morning. I don't see you going to your office to write!" The two were silent for a few minutes.

"Do you suppose they're still out there?" Andy asked. "The police and all those people?"

Elizabeth shrugged and shook her head. "I'm afraid to look."

"I can't believe that guy died right out there on our deck. We didn't hear a thing." Andy said in a rather hoarse voice. Then he looked at Elizabeth. "Is the baby awake yet?" he asked, obviously trying to change the subject.

"You know what?" Elizabeth said frowning. "I think I may have been awake when it happened. Dar got me up. I gave him a bottle, but he cried and seemed fussy at first. Then he wanted to play. I guess he wasn't sleepy, although I sure as hell was." She stifled a yawn. "It's awful to think I may have been sitting upstairs in the rocker by the window, holding Dar, while that man was lying out there bleeding to death."

"There's nothing we could have done. That's what they told us."

"Yes, I know." Elizabeth sighed. "But still-"

Someone rapped on the sliding glass door. "Oh God, I hope it's not one of those policemen again. We've told them everything we know." She got up, went to the door, and pulled aside the drapes. "Oh, good! It's Tyree." She slid the door open for her next-door neighbor. "Can you believe what happened, Tyree?"

"Oh, sweetie," Tyree said. "I got such a fright when I saw the police and the paramedics. I thought something had happened to one of you or the baby. Boo and I were at the lab early this morning and we came home to all this mess."

"Are they still out there?" Andy asked. "It's after ten. Seems like they've been there for hours."

"They've taken the body away," Tyree said. "Most everyone's gone, except for some police. I had to climb over all that yellow crime-scene tape to get here. And the blood!" She waved her hand, as if waving the scene out of her thoughts.

"Of all the houses on the peninsula, why did he have to choose our deck to die on?" Elizabeth said. She knew it was a rather heartless thing to say, but it was how she felt.

"The detective I talked to a few minutes ago said they thought he was planning to rob you. The scary part is he had a gun on him. All they know is he bled to death and so far, they don't know why." Tyree gave Elizabeth a small smile and the diamond in her front tooth winked. "You don't know how relieved I am it wasn't one of you. I thought maybe…well, that maybe something had gone wrong with…." Tyree's smile faded and she gave a deep sigh. "Well, it wasn't and it didn't, thank goodness!"

The thought of someone watching their house, planning to rob them, maybe even kill them, made Elizabeth's heart thud uncomfortably. She frowned. "What do you mean by something might have gone wrong?"

"Look, sweetie, do you have any soda or iced tea? This damn heat and wind is getting to me. It's December, for God's sake!"

"I've got a pitcher of tea in the fridge, I'll pour us some," Elizabeth said. "You want sugar?"

Tyree shook her head no. "Got to save a few calories."

In the kitchen, Elizabeth quickly put together a tray of glasses, an ice bucket and the pitcher of iced tea. With the hot winds blowing, she and Andy had been more thirsty than usual. Of course, part of it was due to BX450, the experimental drug that both of them took better known as Sunshine. Extreme thirst and a headache pestered them soon after they'd begun taking it. The headaches left, but the thirst, although lessened, remained. Fortunately, that proved to be the only negative side effect they'd noticed. The benefits had proved monumental.

She filled a small plate with sugar cookies, arranged it on the tray, and carried it into the living room. "I brought some for all of us," she said, setting the tray on the coffee table.

Tyree poured a glass of tea for herself, and sat down in the padded wicker chair. "You know," she said to Elizabeth, "I really was alarmed this morning. I thought something might have gone wrong with…the drug…with the Sunshine you're taking. Of course I knew better."

"What could go wrong? I mean, all the animal toxicology tests were done," Elizabeth asked. "And so far in the second series of double-blind tests nothing adverse has happened."

"Doctor Foxhoven has been monitoring us right from the start," Andy added. "I think we're getting more care than the people in the double-blind tests, so nothing can really go wrong, can it?"

Tyree shook her head. "Of course not. Only, well, you know the version you and the rest of our little group are taking, is slightly different. It's stronger than what the FDA-approved test is using. In addition, when you're fooling around with a person's genetic structure, you're naturally a little concerned. Even still, we haven't run across anything to worry about." Tyree gave them a reassuring smile. "Boo and I have been taking it much longer than the two of you, so have the Zipper sisters, and the others in our little group. Not one complaint. Besides, you stopped taking it when you were pregnant. Dar couldn't be healthier or brighter. It just gave me a start, is all, seeing the police and the paramedics. I shouldn't be such a worry-wart I guess."

Another shiver slithered down Elizabeth's spine. "That body on our deck brought back a lot of bad memories. All those terrible things that the early version of the drug caused."

"Terrible things sweetheart, but that can never happen again." Tyree took in a long deep breath. "I did get a jolt however, when I ran into that detective who was on the case of…well, you know who. At least this case has nothing to do with that one."

Tyree ran her finger around the moist rim of the glass for a moment. Then she tipped it up and drank the cold tea in several large swallows. "Oh, that's much better. I can't believe how hot it is. She got up and set her glass down on the tray. "Hate to drink and run, but I've got a zillion things to do." She started to leave, and then turned back. "Oh yes, Liz, will you have another one of your paintings done soon? We've sold the last two. Sunshine has turned you into a true genius."

"Already?"

"Yep. Got top price for them too. Wait until you see your next check. My little gallery is booming now that I'm showing your work."

Elizabeth grinned. "I'm just about finished with one. Nevertheless, you're going to have to slow down. It takes time for the oils to dry. I should change to acrylics."

"Oh, people don't care about that. They just want to buy into the newest rage in artists. That is you, my little genius. And you've got Sunshine to thank for it."

Elizabeth nodded. A slight frown creased her forehead. "My art wasn't too good, was it? Before I started taking Sunshine?"

"Hey, sweetie, don't sell yourself short. You had great training and wonderful technical skills. It was only your artistic expression that needed tweaking. Sunshine simply woke up and enhanced your natural talent, the same way it did with Andy's writing. Now you two are raking in the money and you deserve it. You've both worked hard. And just think, once the testing is done on Sunshine II and it's on the market, your portion of the royalties will be enormous. Just like everyone in our Sunshine Group." Tyree went to the sliding door and opened it. A blast of hot wind filled the room. "Ta for now. I've gotta dash. Tons to do. Will we see you two tonight for Bloody Marys as usual?"

"Of course," Elizabeth said.

"It may be too windy to sit on the patio."

"I'd rather not do that anyway. Your patio is too close to ours and after what happened out there, well-" Elizabeth felt another shiver, despite the heat.

"Not to worry. We'll turn our air conditioning on and sit in the living room. Byeeee." Tyree said and slid the glass door closed behind her.

Elizabeth gave a little tight laugh and then said affectionately, "Tyree is in her usual manic state, dashing about." She handed Andy a glass of tea and took one for herself. She watched him as he leaned back into the sofa cushions. He looked more relaxed now. The awful events of the morning had visibly upset him. He'd been in his office just off the back porch, working on his latest novel, when the police arrived. As a rule, nothing took him away from his computer. However, he'd stayed away from it for several hours now. Partly, she thought, to comfort her, but also because the whole thing had upset him more than he liked to admit.

Deadly Urges

"Honey," she said. "If you want to go on back to work I don't mind. I'm better now."

Andy took a long sip of his tea. "Yeah, I suppose I should. Got a deadline you know."

"Andy, you've written six books. Four of them in the last thirty-six months. All of them after you started on Sunshine. I can't believe you still worry about deadlines. I can't believe you actually had an impossible case of writer's block when we first moved here."

"The worst damn case ever." Andy closed his eyes as if trying not to remember those days.

"Well, our daily doses of Sunshine sure fixed that."

Andy chuckled. "That my love, to use a terrible cliché, is the understatement of the year."

Elizabeth rattled the ice in her glass. So many changes had invaded their lives in the past few years. She could hardly believe what Sunshine, the experimental BX450 drug, had done for Andy's success as a writer, and her own sudden plunge into the world of first-class artists, all of it incredible, but a trifle overwhelming. Feeling better, she got up and walked to the sliding glass door, pulled the drapes and slid the door open. The beach, thank God, had emptied. No more curious onlookers. No more police. However, yellow tape, wrapped like a tangled maze around their patio furniture, whipped in the wind. The sand appeared silver-violet in the sunlight, marred only by the scudding shadows of gulls flying overhead. The quick bright gleam of the restless sea caught her eye and her ears filled with the sound of tumbling surf. She took in a deep breath, enjoying the scent of brine and seaweed. How she loved it here. However, it hadn't always been that way. She rubbed the iced-tea glass against her cheek, leaned against the doorframe, closed her eyes and for a few moments, allowed herself to remember.

Elizabeth's Aunt Mary had left the two of them her old beach house when she died. The day they moved in the two of them were flat broke, careers floundering, praying the move would give them a new start. They'd worked so hard for so long, only to have success evade them. They hadn't been greedy. Enough money to pay the steep taxes on the house, and also live comfortably, would have satisfied them.

Tyree had been barefooted the first time Elizabeth met her next-door neighbor, and wearing bright blue warm-ups the same color as

18

her eyes. She'd come padding down the sidewalk that ran along the ocean side of the peninsula, her red hair streaming behind her like licks of flames. Little did she know that meeting Tyree that day would totally change their lives.

"Hello there!" Tyree had said in an excited tone. "I'm Tyree Rattigan and I live in that old Art Deco elephant next door. She was tall, thin and ivory-skinned, with a deep peach bloom to her cheeks. Elizabeth thought her a rather elegant woman, except for the small blue-white diamond embedded in one of her front teeth. It was impossible to tell her age. She rattled on about her husband, Beauregard, who everyone called Boo for short. The two of them were part owners of a small pharmaceutical company that was developing the drug, BX450, that everyone called Sunshine. It wasn't until later that Tyree told them about the testing of Sunshine and asked if they were interested in getting involved in the project. She went on and on about the miraculous results of the drug so far. "It's like turning off a dark cold day in a person's mind, and turning on glorious Sunshine," she swore.

"Almost everyone in the tests to date has had unbelievable improvement in every area of their life," Tyree explained. "Their skills increased remarkably, in other words their creativity, their physical abilities, and even their health. It's going to be a truly remarkable drug once we are able to market it."

The temptations to accept Tyree's offer came swooping at them like some bright plumaged bird, overwhelming them with its splendor. Elizabeth doubted that anyone would have turned it down.

It wasn't until much later that they learned the frightening facts about Barry Brownstone. Brownstone was the man who developed the first version of Sunshine. He was convinced it was a gift from God. When he formulated the first version he recklessly tested it on himself. Up until then, it had only been tried in small animals, not even simians. The animals were then sacrificed and their DNA examined. Whatever he found in their DNA excited him, so he took several dozes of the drug. The results were catastrophic. The early version irreversibly altered his DNA in such a way that he'd turned into a crazed, vicious killer. Elizabeth had come close to being one of his victims. Elizabeth's stomach grabbed painfully at the thought. Only now were the nightmares about her terrifying rape and near murder beginning to ebb.

Deadly Urges

It was because of Tyree's insistence, and her husband Boo's pharmaceutical skills, that the carefully reformatted version of Sunshine was finally made safe. Numerous double blind tests in Mexico and South America had proven it benign. They had seen all the reports. Add to that she and Andy were invited to become members of their special Sunshine group, all of whom lived close to each other on the Newport Beach Peninsula. All of whom had been taking the drug for several years, with no bad effects.

"Safer than aspirin," Tyree told them. "But far more valuable. Sunshine is the most momentous drug to come along this century. The version my husband has been instrumental in reformatting has no noticeable side effects except for thirst. BX450 is pure, and we've had the go-ahead for U.S. testing for quite some time."

Elizabeth had asked for a day or so to think it over. She and Andy agreed that it sounded too good to be true. Tyree had grinned and said "Sure, sweetie. Take your time. However, waiting is putting off all the wonderful things this drug will do for the two of you. Our private version of the drug is a little stronger, and more effective than the one for the national test. After all, we can't have everyone in the world turning into geniuses, now can we. Only the members of the Sunshine group receive the special version."

They finally agreed to join the Sunshine group and take the drug. The promises that Tyree made, were kept. The positive changes in their lives were so numerous, it was impossible to catalogue them. Two of Andy's books zoomed to the top of the best-seller list. Elizabeth's paintings now carried a price tag of a thousand dollars and up. They sold faster than she could paint.

The best of it all, however, had nothing to do with Sunshine. It was Dar, David Arthur Rosemond, the child she'd wanted for so long. She'd stopped taking the drug during her pregnancy just to be safe. He'd been born after an easy two-hour labor, so beautiful, so perfect, that she'd shed tears. Her life had become gloriously rich and full. She couldn't think of another thing she wanted or needed. Except perhaps another child, in a year or two.

Elizabeth stood in the doorway looking out over the beach. Yes, a great deal had happened these past few years, some of it horrendous, some of it amazing. Thanks to Dar, she was learning how to forget most, but not all of the bad parts. She took one more deep breath of warm air then shut the door.

"Lizzy?" Andy said, breaking her reverie. "Honey? You okay?" Elizabeth turned to him and smiled. "I'm fine."

"Your face is pale."

"I was just remembering…how things have turned out and…about Barry." Her body gave another icy shiver. The main thing the death on their doorstep had dredged up was the thought of the serial killer, Barry Brownstone. Only those who were part of the horrifying events that Barry caused could imagine the fear that permeated the people who lived on the far end of the peninsula.

Andy got up and came over to her, slipping his arms around her. "Barry's gone, Lizzy. You are safe."

She nodded and kissed him, savoring the warmth of his mouth, making her feel better. He responded to her kiss, snuggling her close to him. She never failed to be amazed by how Sunshine enhanced their sexual encounters. Just the touch of his fingers aroused erotic imagines. She wanted to go upstairs with him and make love in the big old bed that Aunt Mary had left them. Dar was still taking his morning nap. Maybe they had enough time. The phone rang and she felt herself jump. Her nerves obviously still jangled from the morning's appalling event.

"That's probably my agent. He was going to call today about TV rights for the last book. I'll take it in my office." Andy kissed the tip of her nose. "Sorry. I was kind of hoping-"

"Yeah, me too." She felt a pinch of disappointment. "Well, maybe tonight."

"It's a date." Andy picked up his glass of tea, grabbed several sugar cookies off the plate, and headed out of the room toward his office.

Standing there by herself the old house seemed to fold around her like loving arms. She walked around the living room smiling. Such a comfortable room. When redecorating, she'd kept some of the ambiance Aunt Mary had put into the place. Except for the God-awful Egyptian wallpaper. She'd left the blue and white Persian carpets, and had re-padded the old wicker furniture. It was a large room with an open-beamed ceiling and an elephantine fireplace of old bricks. Most of all she loved Mary's old John Booker Germantown clock that stood at the foot of the stairs. Ticking steadily it sounded like the heartbeat of the house.

The whole house had become so familiar; she couldn't imagine living anywhere else. Beyond the living room was a large dining room, complete with Aunt Mary's Regency table and breakfront. Behind the dining room, the kitchen was a scene from a French country manor with a copper hooded stove, blue and lemon yellow hand-painted tiles, and a brick floor. Just back of the kitchen, a small service porch led to a minuscule back-garden which opened to the alley. The porch also led into Andy's office. He liked being tucked away where he couldn't hear sounds from the beach when he was writing.

Upstairs she'd converted one of the three bedrooms into her studio. The room next to that was Dar's with a ring of clowns and carousel horses she'd painted on the walls. At the end of the upstairs hall, their huge master bedroom stretched across the corner of the house, with a black marble fireplace and windows that looked out over a glorious stretch of beach. Day and night, the rumbling sound of surf seeped through the glass panes. Elizabeth felt certain she would never again be able to sleep without that soothing sound. Despite all that had happened since they moved there, she loved the old house and was grateful to Aunt Mary for leaving it to her.

Elizabeth took a long sip of her iced tea then put the glass down. She picked up a small sugar cookie from the tray. It was about time for Dar to wake up from his morning nap. She'd take a cookie up to him. After she changed him, she would put him in the baby-pack and take their usual walk on the beach. She could go through the alley and down to the point, so she wouldn't have to look at all the yellow tape and blood stains on their deck. Dar loved their walks. He cooed, gurgled, and sometimes squealed with delight if they saw a flock of gulls or sandpipers.

As Elizabeth climbed the stairs, she heard Dar jabbering to himself. Such sweet sounds, she thought, thankful for them. He'd had an unusual bad night, for some reason, He cried and fussed until she finally gave him a warm bottle, which he really was too old to be using. After that, she was able to rock him back to sleep. Andy woke up and offered to rock him, but she told him she was fine. She was glad Andy worked most of the day so she could spend more time with Dar. Once Andy was finished writing for the day, he monopolized the boy until his bedtime. It worked out well since she painted better in the evening. Her head continually overflowed with visions she now easily created on canvas.

When she opened the door to his bedroom, she found Dar standing up in his crib holding on to the rail and bouncing up and down on his chubby legs. He'd started walking at a year, and now at twenty-months, he would have been all over the place if they let him. Andy had spent a lot of time childproofing the house.

"How's my little boy?" she said. "All done with your nap?"

He grinned up at her and squealed. He had a halo of golden curls and dark eyes with a bright ring of turquoise. She handed him the sugar cookie. He took it in his roly-poly hand, examined it, and then took a bite. For his age, he was quite tall and sturdy.

"Ummm," he said. "Good!"

"Yes, Dar, good."

He took another bite and then pushed the cookie toward her. "Mama like," he said.

"Yes, mama likes."

"Ummmm," he said, pulling the cookie back and nibbling on it. He grinned at her and quickly finished the rest of the cookie. She picked him up and carried him into her bedroom where she kept his clothes and other things, since his room was quite small.

"Need to go potty?" she asked.

"No, no potty," he replied.

"In a few minutes?"

"Potty, ina foo mints."

She carried him to the rocking chair by the window. He loved being rocked. She usually opened the window so they could hear the surf and the gulls crying, but the Santa Ana wind outside was too fierce.

"Dar want to go rock-a-bye?" she asked.

"Rock bye," Dar said.

Dar put his tiny fingers on Elizabeth's cheek. She kissed them. "Sweet Dar. Such a handsome boy."

"Love mama," he said.

"And dada?

Dar wrinkled up his nose.

"Well you don't have to make a face," she said, laughing. "Come on, say love dada. I know you can say a lot of words. I hear you when you're in your crib."

"Baad," Dar said.

"No, Daddy isn't bad, Dar." Elizabeth sighed.

"Bad man."

Bad, that was a new word. It seemed to her that every day he tried out new words. When he felt like it he could put two or three of them together. However, he only talked when he felt like it.

Dar frowned. He made a chubby little fist with his right hand, and then extended his index finger. He pointed toward the window.

"You want to go outside? Go walking with mama?"

"Bad."

"What do you mean, Dar? Walking isn't bad?"

Dar pursed his full lips and kept pointing toward the window.

"No, Dar. Nothing bad is out there."

"Baad man," he said clearly. "Dar see."

Elizabeth felt the fuzz all over her body stand on end. What did he say? Dar continued pointing his finger toward the window and the deck where the man had died. He couldn't possible mean that, but considering what had happened out there last night, the idea chilled her nonetheless.

"No, Dar. No bad man."

Dar blinked. He pulled back his hand and looked at her. His face puckered up and turned pink.

"Don't cry, Dar. It's okay. No bad man." She rocked him slowly.

He snuggled close to her, his golden curls tickling her nose. She loved the sweet smell of him, so fresh and new. "Mama," he said.

"Yes, sweetheart, mama." She started to sing his favorite song. "Oh do you know the muffin man the muffin man-"

"Bad bad man," Dar said again. Unmistakable! Somehow, he knew something about what had happened on the deck last night. Something that frightened him.

"Yes, Dar," she whispered to him. "There was a bad man on our deck last night. But you don't need to worry about things like that. Mama and daddy will take care of you." She looked down into his turquoise ringed eyes. The sudden look of comprehension there startled her. A peculiar feeling crept over her. Her skin turned cold and dry, despite the heat, and felt as if it were crinkling. A gust of wind rattled the bedroom window and shook the timbers of the old house.

She snuggled Dar to her and began to rock him again. "Oh do you know the muffin man, the muffin man," she sang. "Who lives in Druery Lane?" Dar cooed along with her. When she finished the

24

song, Dar laughed, and clapped his hands. It appeared he'd forgotten about the "bad man" and no longer pointed toward the window. She let out a sigh of relief.

"Come on Dar. Let's take a walk on the beach. It's windy but really warm."

"Ummmm." he said and grinned, cookie crumbs tumbling from the edge of his pink mouth.

The wind had abated somewhat, although occasional hot gusts whipped bits of sand against Elizabeth's bare legs. She carefully smoothed Dar's tender skin with sun screen, then strapped him into her backpack before heading up the beach toward the jetty. Dar enjoyed watching the sailboats as they came in and out of the channel to Newport Harbor. The beach was deserted except for two young surfers and a lone fisherman.

"See the boat, Dar," she said, pointing at a large skiff that had come about and was tacking its way against the wind.

"Bo-at," Dar said.

"Yes, boat. My goodness, you are picking up a lot of words."

Dar suddenly let out a squeal. "Da."

"Da? You mean dada?"

Another squeal, but this one turned into a high-pitched sound of fright. "No! Dah. Dah," Dar yelled.

"What, Dar? What is it?" She turned around, saw nothing, and reached back to comfort him. "Shhhh. It's okay."

"Dahhh," Dar wailed. From the corner of her eye, she could see his tiny face had gone red and tears were welling from his eyes. He held out his fist in the direction of the breaking surf, but Elizabeth saw nothing.

She slipped off the backpack, lifted him out, and attempted to set him down on the sand so she could look him over. Perhaps something was hurting him, or maybe he'd been stung by a bee. She couldn't imagine what it might be, but he sounded terribly distressed. He refused to be put down, clinging tightly to her, his face growing redder.

Over Dar's screams, she heard a harsh growling sound somewhere off to her right. Before she could turn to see what it was, something charged her. A dark shape, wet sand spraying from it, leapt from the ground. Growling deep within his throat, a huge dog hurdled toward them. Dar screamed again, the way only a baby can. She echoed his scream. The dog's teeth snapped just a fraction of an inch from Elizabeth's face. She caught a burst of its sour breath as she tried to leap away, holding Dar with one arm. Her foot caught in a mound of seaweed and she fell. She twisted her body so as not to land on Dar. The moment she landed, the dog charged again, grabbing her shoe, his teeth slashing through the canvas just a fraction short of her skin. This time Dar sat there in her arms, resting his head against her chest, not making a sound. She gave her foot a violent shake, and the dog backed off, barking, and growling by turns. She tried to scramble backward, but found it impossible with Dar in her arms.

The dog lunged again, snarling, its upper lip curled back from sharp yellow teeth. Elizabeth was certain it would take a chunk out of her leg, but suddenly, the animal faltered, his grip loosened, and he looked up at her. He let out a low growl that turned into a soft howling sound. He turned first one way, then another, as if confused as to where he wanted to go. Finally, he moved toward the surf, stumbled, righted himself, walked a few feet, and dropped to the sand. Frantically trying to get up, he let out a strange keening sound. Then he laid his head on the sand and closed his eyes. His feet and legs quivered for several moments before he fell still. As she watched, blood surged out of the dog's body staining the sand around it a dark maroon. She sat there staring at the bloody animal, her pulse pounding in her throat, her hands shaking.

Finally, she managed to straighten Dar in her arms, inspecting him to make certain he'd not been hurt. She wiped sand from his face, brushing tears along with them. Dar hiccupped and let out a shuddering breath, then broke into a tenuous smile.

"Bad dah," he hiccupped.

Elizabeth hugged him to her, rocked him slightly, keeping her eyes on the quiet mound of dark fur a few feet away. "Yes, Dar. A bad, bad dog."

She sat there for a long time after that, gently rocking Dar, making certain the dog was not going to get up and begin attacking again. Short gasps of hot wind flickered across her face bringing with it a faint scent of brine. By the time she started back toward the house, Dar had fallen asleep. She lifted him gently and carried him in her arms, her golden-haired little angel, thanking God that neither of them had been hurt.

Brady Twigs had watched as the woman made her way down the beach toward the point. He was a lank, mustached man in a red plaid Pendleton shirt that looked as if it had been slept in for several weeks. On his head, he wore a red baseball cap, his short blond curls ballooning out on the sides like miniature sausages. His mustache sprouted from his upper lip in dust broom fringe, darker than his hair, with bristles of gray here and there. He had cultivated a certain look, mid years, not too tidy, perhaps caught in the unemployment tide that had hit California in recent years. He'd sat on the beach in much the same spot, his fishing license pinned to his cap, thermos of coffee at hand, every day for the past twelve months. By now, no one paid him much attention.

That morning he'd set his fishing line without bait as usual, so he wouldn't be disturbed by accidentally hooking some creature from the deep. The folding chair he sat in had a swivel base so he could rotate back and forth, and not appear overly interested in the woman. As was her usual habit, she took a walk with her young son riding in her backpack. The only thing different today was the fact that she took her walk before noon. Most often she walked in the late afternoon, usually just before sundown. Earlier, he'd seen some sort of commotion outside her house. Police. Ambulance. For a while, he'd been afraid something might have happened to her, or the child. However, he'd decided not to draw attention to himself by going to the scene to find out. When she'd emerged for her walk, with the boy riding in the backpack, he'd felt a surge of relief.

He made careful notes of all their activities, including the exact times. His notes were important. He knew they had to be precise to be of any value. He was paid handsomely for his work. He took great pride in the fact that he always did a superior job, and had never been detected. When the stray dog suddenly attacked the woman and child, his first instinct was to run to their aid. He curbed the urge, knowing that it would be hard for him to reach her in time to intervene, and it would make him more noticeable than he desired. If the attack persisted, then he would try to help. He kept his sharp fishing knife at the ready.

His instincts had been right. After a few lunges, the dog backed off, howled as if in pain, and then lay down. He wondered why. He waited patiently while the woman sat there, rocking the boy. He checked his watch. A lot of minutes went by before she finally got to her feet, and began to carry the child home. As she moved toward her house, he took out his notebook and jotted down the incident. Then he got up, reeled in his line, folded his chair, and picked up his bucket and tackle box. He moved on down the beach toward where the dog still lay. As soon as the woman was inside her house, he would check out the dog. It might not be important, but then again it might. In a case such as this, nothing could be overlooked.

CHAPTER THREE

Twenty-month-old Dar Rosemond snuggled into the safety of his crib, his fingers fiddling with the colored cubes strung from rail to rail over his head. Turning and rattling the cubes always made him feel better. Six equal sides. Six colors. He had no idea if they had a function other than soothing him. In fact, he felt they probably didn't. He liked them all the same.

Dar also liked the way everything around him became more and more understandable. Bottles and bowls came filled with something for his stomach. Clean dry clothes came when his were wet. Soft fuzzy things to cuddle, some that played music. He loved music. He never tired of listening and learning those sounds. The two people who held him, played with him, took care of him most of the time, were Mama and Dadda. Sometimes it was the Zippers, two silver haired ladies who looked alike, and then there was Ree, the pretty lady with hair the color of his brightest block. The red one. He knew the names of the all the block colors. His Mama had said them over to him a number of times. He'd learned them the first time she'd done this. Yellow, blue, red, green, orange, and purple.

Mama wasn't as colorful as Ree, but she made him feel so good. Just seeing her face, or feeling her arms around him, gave him a soft, warm sensation. Mama was the best thing in his world. His Dadda was the next best. Dadda made him laugh, joggled him up and down, and made funny noises with his mouth. Dar felt contented. Nothing marred his small world. Nothing, that is, until recently.

He remembered the odd sensation that had awakened him last night when it was dark. It was kind of like the way it felt when Mama covered him with a blanket, only instead of making him warm this sensation covered him with icy cold. So cold that it gave him pinchy feelings. He'd cried, and Mama picked him up to take away the cold. Only this time, her arms hadn't helped. She carried him into her bedroom and sat with him in the rocker, singing his favorite song in his ear. None of it helped. The icy cold feeling turned to something he didn't recognize. Something terrible. Something with hurtful prickles all over it.

The prickling came from outside, below them. Someone there, on the deck below, was sending out awful prickly, pinchy feelings that hurt. He bad, Dar told himself. Someone bad out there. Not Mama or Dadda. Not the Zips or Ree. He began to push away the prickles and the pinchys. He closed his eyes tightly and pushed at the hurtful feelings as hard as he could. Shove. Shove them away. Slowly, the hurt eased. The prickles faded away. Finally, they stopped altogether. Dar stopped crying. Mama was still singing. "Oh, do you know the muffin man, the muffin man." Dar had smiled up at her, so pleased he'd shoved away the awful feeling. Later on the beach, when the dog had sent him the same prickly, pinchy feeling, he'd found it quite easy to push them away.

Good, he told himself. This is good. He didn't have to be afraid of anything. He could push away anything he didn't like.

The hot wind blowing in the car window made Detective Ted Bearbower's skin itch and his eyes feel as if filled with gravel. He cursed the broken air conditioner in the department's car. To add to his discomfort, the grisly find on the peninsula had given him a case of the gray willies that he couldn't shake. By mid-afternoon he'd found his attention wandering so he'd checked out of the division and headed for his favorite bakery, "A Little Bit of Heaven". He still had lemon bars left but he craved some chocolate. Chocolate always made him feel better. Besides, he wanted to see Maddy again.

The wind whipped at him in furious blasts. He felt the car rocking as he drove. Dust, rubbish, and palm fronds skittered down the street in front of him as if alive and late for an appointment. By the time he reached the bakery, he almost wished he hadn't started out in the first place. He hoped something chocolate would soothe his nerves.

Sweet yeast-scented air wrapped around him the minute he opened the bakery door. It was moist and comforting unlike the dry and irritating wind. Maddy Malone greeted him with a huge grin. Her starched white uniform looked spotless, her pale blond hair shimmering in a smooth French roll; a zaftig woman, well rounded and comfortable looking. He thought Maddy to be somewhere in her mid-forties.

"Well, well, twice in one day!" she chirped. "To what do I owe this pleasure?"

Ted grinned back at her. "Chocolate attack!" he announced.

Maddy tilted her head back and laughed with a deep, husky sound. "Good, good," she said, as if a chocolate attack was the best thing that could happen to a person. "When it attacks, just surrender, I say. I'm a chocoholic myself." Maddy leaned over and opened the sliding glass door to the bakery case. "We've got chocolate éclairs, chocolate donuts, chocolate cake, chocolate chip cookies, brownies and chocolate turtle delights."

From where he stood on the other side of the counter Ted saw the white rounded tops of Maddy's full breasts peeking out from the top of her white uniform. He'd never been attracted to a full-figured woman. Not until now. His wife had been as thin as sticks all her life. She'd never taken an interest in food, the way he had. He loved to cook and found nothing more sensual than the scent of spices, oregano, thyme, garlic, simmering in sun-tomato sauce, ready to pour over pasta. When his wife died, he'd taken even more comfort in food, his weight ballooning to a new high. However, when his partner died, he'd lost his appetite completely. It was only in the last few months that he'd gotten it back. For him, his appetite was like a lost friend returning.

The sight of Maddy's breasts spilling over the top of her uniform caused him to suck in his breath audibly. "Ahhh, umm," he stammered trying to regain his composure. "What are…turtle delights?" He knew he should look away, but he didn't want to. The sight of her pale flesh gave him intense pleasure. A pleasure he'd not felt in a long time.

"Oh, they're wonderful!" she said, picking one up with a piece of thin tissue paper. "Here, try one on the house. Dark chocolate, pecans and soft caramel."

Ted took the turtle from her and bit into it. His eyes must have expressed his delight because Maddy gave one of her husky laughs and said, "Would you like some coffee with that?"

Ted nodded, shoving the rest of the piece into his mouth. The comforting taste of the dark chocolate made him smile.

She poured steaming coffee into a paper cup and handed it to him. "Sit down, won't you? Mind if I join you? Not much business this time of the afternoon. Would you like another turtle?"

He nodded again then took his coffee to one of the small, round tables that dotted the front of the bakery. He pulled out one of the chairs, looked at its diminutive size, worried that it wouldn't hold his weight. He sat carefully, hearing the wood groan a complaint.

Maddy brought a plate piled with turtle delights and another cup of coffee. "These are my favorites," she said. "They are my own version. The secret is the cinnamon in the chocolate. It really enhances the taste."

Sitting across the tiny table from her, Ted could smell her perfume, something lemony and familiar. It mingled with the yeasty odor of the bakery. He wished he could spend the day there, inhaling the scents, tasting the food and forget about his job. Forget about the rest of the world. Escape. That's what he wanted to do. Escape from the harsh reality of the outside world and live in the sanctuary of the yeasty bakery and bury his face against Maddy's soft, full breasts.

"You're quiet today," Maddy said, breaking his reverie. "Whatcha thinking about?"

Ted gave a small shrug. "I'm wishing I could just sit here forever, stuffing myself with chocolate, instead of going back to the department."

Maddy grinned. "Well, that's okay with me."

Ted wondered if she meant to encourage him. He wondered if she were as attracted to him as he was to her. On the other hand, maybe she was just being friendly, patronizing a customer who bought a lot of pastries and breads. He picked up the second turtle delight and munched on it. As usual, the chocolate somehow found its way to his central nervous system and tranquilized it.

"Troubles, Detective?" she asked. "You looked pretty tense when you came in."

He hesitated for a moment and then said, "Just the usual stuff. Had a nasty case on the peninsula this morning. Shook me up is all. I'm fine now." As if to countermand that thought, his cell phone went off. "Shit!" he hissed.

"Sorry about that?" he said looking at the phone.

"No problem. I'll just sit here and finish my coffee, if you don't mind."

The number on his phone was his partner's. "Shit," he hissed again. The spell of the bakery dissolved as he took the call.

"Ajax here," the voice said. "Is that you, Teddy Bear?"

Ted cringed, picturing the young man at his desk. Damn hairy little tarantula! Wrecking his time with Maddy and Turtle Delights.

"Yeah, it's Ted," he grumbled. "What's up?"

A momentary silence then Ajax said, "I hate to tell you this, but we've got another one. Sort of."

"Another what?"

"Another odd death on the peninsula."

Ted felt his gut wrench. Not two in one day, in the same area where his partner had died so horribly. Jesus Christ! "Okay," he finally said. "Give me the details. Is it like the one this morning?"

"Not exactly. It isn't a person, it's a…well…it's a dog."

"A what? You're calling me about a dog that died?"

"It's not that he died! It's how he died."

"Ajax, can't this wait until I get back?"

"Captain wants us to investigate right now."

"Okay, so how did he die?"

"He lost all of his blood. It's all over the sand. They've taken him away to test him, but we need to check out the scene."

Ted felt the phone go slippery in his fingers. A nasty bite of adrenaline hit him, making his heart do a crazy dance. "You mean like the guy this morning?"

"Yep. We could have something nasty going around. Something that would also affect a canine!"

"Shit!" Ted hissed.

"You think maybe we've got another serial killer? Although I guess a dog and one human really don't qualify as serial killings."

It couldn't be happening again! Ted assured himself. It was not the same guy with the vampire style MO that killed his partner, and half a dozen others. Ted shook his head to clear it, and tried to slow his racing heartbeat. No, this one was something entirely different.

"Well, great!" he finally said. "This is just what I need! A dead dog!"

"Captain wants us to get our butts in gear and get down there."

Ted let out a long sigh, his shoulders hunched forward. "Okay. So where do I meet you?"

"You got the car, come pick me up. It's not far down the beach from where we were this morning."

"Ahhh, nice! Okay, five minutes," Ted said, and hung up. "Gotta go," he said turning to Maddy.

"You want to take some of the turtles with you?"

"I'd love to but I can't stop now," he said, dashing for the door.

"Listen," Maddy called after him. "I'll make up a nice package for you. Chocolate everything. You sound as if you need it. Pick it up later today, or tonight. No charge. You're a good customer. If the bakery's closed, go around to the back. I live in the little cottage behind here."

Ted felt himself smile, despite his effort not to. "That's a deal I can't refuse. It might be kind of late, though."

"I'm up late." She returned his smile.

Was her smile an invitation to...well, to something else he wondered? "See you later, then," he said, opening the door. A blast of hot Santa Ana wind hit him the moment he did. This time, he didn't mind it so much. Even the thought of a quart of blood from a dog waiting on the peninsula didn't seem so bad. Lovely Maddy of the full luscious breasts had invited him to her place. He had not been with a woman since Silvia died. He'd been faithful to her, and had been a virgin when they married. The idea of making love to Maddy scared him to death while exciting him beyond imagination. He reminded himself that Maddy had offered him chocolate, not a roll in the hay. Despite that, he was well aware that he had an enormous grin on his face as he got back into his car and started toward the department to pick up Ajax.

The police had roped off the area where the dog had died with stakes and yellow tape. A spread of congealed blood lay in the middle of the area like a spill of dark Jell-O.

Kneeling beside the blood, Earl Gras, the medical examiner, shook his head and sighed. "Dog's gone. I'm just checking to see how much blood was lost. Taking samples. Got people coming out to clean up the mess. I wouldn't even be here except for the fact that this fellow here died exactly like the man did this morning. Massive hemorrhaging."

"Any chance it's some kind of disease?" Ted asked.

"There is always a chance."

"How about a poison?" Ajax asked.

"Possible. Lab work on both will take some time.

"This beats everything," Ted said. "First a body that's hemorrhaged all over the place, and now a dog that appears to have died the same way. Was he rabid?"

"No, he was just a stray scavenger dog. The county's Animal Control had been trying to pick him up, but hadn't managed it so far. The vet called and said that he can't see any exterior reason why the canine started bleeding. And the question is why it didn't stop until his body was drained." Earl shook his hand and shrugged.

Ajax frowned. His thick tangle of black eyebrows bunched together like lopsided question marks. "Okay, so we have no idea what happened?

Earl shook his head again. "Nope. Don't yet know who the dog's owner is either. No chip, no collar, no call from someone missing their dog."

Ted turned away from the body. The wind whistled through the alley, bringing with it more litter.

"You okay, Ted?" Ajax asked. "You look kinda pale."

"Deja vu," Ted said.

"Yeah, I know that feeling," Earl sighed.

"So you remember the Barry Brownstone affair?"

"I prefer not to remember it!" Earl said. "However, it's not at all the same, Ted."

"I know. I guess I'm just…just too uncomfortable with this area of the peninsula," he muttered nervously. "Too fucking uncomfortable!"

Ajax gave him a sympathetic look, but didn't say anything.

"Let us know what you find out," Ted said

"You'll know as soon as I know."

Ajax opened his mouth and said something but the wind snatched the sound and blew it away with a rattle and whine.

"Let's get back to the department." Ted snapped.

Ajax gave him a sulky look, but dutifully followed him back to the car.

They drove for some time before Ted finally spoke. "Okay, I'm ready."

Ajax turned to look at him. "Ready? For what?"

"To talk about it."

Ajax took a moment as if trying to make the connection between what they'd just encountered, and what Ted wanted to talk about. Ted waited until he felt him lean back in the car seat, ready to listen.

"You know about Steve Locke, my partner who died. You've heard the stories. Locke was…well, kind of like a brother to me, so

35

the loss was tough. So was the way he died."

"So then, the weirdo vampire guy you mentioned got him?" Ajax asked in a hushed tone. "That was before I joined the force."

"Barry Brownstone was the closest thing to a real vampire you'll ever see. He fucked up a new drug he was testing and the result was that he got a taste for blood and sometimes flesh. Couldn't live without it. The drug managed to wake up some dormant genes, possibly ones that prehistoric man needed to survive. It also heightened his senses and made him incredibly strong."

"Sounds like a nightmare!" Ajax said.

"That is putting it mildly."

"So, how many people did he kill, altogether?"

"We really don't know. A lot. We had five here on the peninsula, plus a number of others in the county with the same M.O. He'd been at it a long time before we got him."

"So, where's he now?"

"Dead."

"Ajax was silent for a moment. "Did you do that job?"

Ted shook his head. "He was electrocuted. A high voltage live wire. I watched."

"Jesus! That must have been something!"

"Funny thing is that shit saved my life. After he'd killed all those people, he got me out of harm's way, before he was fried."

Ajax looked over at him, his eyebrows in their familiar question mark frown. "Why the heck did he do that?"

Ted took in a deep breath and let it out slowly. "I've been trying to figure that out ever since."

"Okay, let me get this straight. This case we just saw, it's pretty much like the old ones by that vampire guy?"

"Yes and no. Victims with their blood missing. However, the killer was drinking all of it. In these two cases all of the blood was drained out on the ground." Ted felt the fuzz on his skin stand on end as he thought about it. "Anyway, it can't be happening again. The guy's dead!"

"A copy-cat maybe?"

"Possible, but not likely. Copy-cats usually show up sooner."

"Maybe someone else has gotten hold of that drug the vampire guy used." Ajax tapped his fingernails on the dashboard of the car.

Ted had worried about that possibility. Supposedly, the drug has been totally reformatted and has FDA approved human testing. In its present form, they guarantee it will be a boon for not only normal people, but also those with retardation, brain damage, and only God knows what. He'd been told that the original form of it had been destroyed. However, you never knew. Smart people could be awfully dumb sometimes.

"So you don't think there's a connection to the other guy, the one who bled all over someone's patio?" Ajax asked. "And the dog? That doesn't make much sense. I mean a dog for God's sake!"

"I don't know, but I have this strange gut feeling that there is something. A correlation of some kind." Ted said. "That Tyree woman I talked to at the scene was part of the Brownstone case.

Ajax gave a puzzled frown. "You said she didn't do anything wrong."

"She now partly owns the pharmaceutical company that made the original version of the drug."

Ajax looked shocked. "Yer kidding!"

"She bought it off of Brownstone's estate and her husband completely reformulated the drug. He'd worked on it originally, and knew it wasn't ready to use. Tyree's problem was that she knew something was radically wrong with Brownstone because of the drug, but she had no idea how horrendous the problem was."

Ajax continued tapping his fingernails for a while, not talking.

"Another odd thing," Ted said. "The people who live in the house where the blood soaked body was found are members of a private group of people are also testing the reformulated drug. They call it Sunshine."

Ajax gave him a startled look. "Okay, tell me more," he said in a tight tone.

Ted began going over all the details of both the current case and the Brownstone case. The current one was just the opposite of the serial killer's. No blood left, versus blood everywhere. Ajax's tapping began to grind on his nerves. He was just about to say something when it finally stopped.

"Ted," Ajax said, giving him a stingy smile. "Thanks for telling me the details of what happened. I've sort of felt as if I'd gotten the fuzzy end of the lollipop. Now, we're even. I can see why you are-"

"Why I'm what?" Ted grumbled.

"Why you're such a lovable old Teddy Bear." Before Ted could complain about the nickname, Ajax held up his hand. "Listen, why don't we call around and see if we can find out where this ah…well, this vampire kind of guy, Brownstone, is buried?"

Ted's mouth dropped open in surprise. "Now why the fuck would we want to do that?"

"Just to make certain the guy's really dead. Still buried. Even if his MO was not the same as the one used on the bloody body."

Ted felt a spidery chill crawl down his back. Of course, the guy was dead! You didn't take a shot of twenty-three-thousand volts of electricity while standing knee-deep in water and not end up fried like a hush puppy!

Ted thought about how Brownstone had escaped once by taking a dive off the Balboa pier. He'd been battered by storm-lashed waves, taken half a dozen bullets, and kept on going. Took a licking and kept on ticking, just like a Timex. Even so, he couldn't imagine that the guy could possibly have been resurrected after being electrocuted.

Suddenly Ted's stomach lurched painfully. His worst fear had suddenly emerged. What if the drug had adversely affected someone in the drug testing programs, and they had developed a problem similar to what Brownstone had? Maybe the reformulation had missed something, or maybe only certain people with a certain kind of DNA were affected by the deadly side effect. Alex was right. The one thing he knew he had to do was to rule out any possibility that Brownstone was still around, and involved in the latest incident. If he could do that, then maybe he could relax.

Ted slowed the car and pulled over to the curb. He set the hand brake and then leaned over and pulled a Thomas Guide from the glove box.

"What are you doing?" Ajax asked.

"Looking for cemeteries so we can find out where that fucking vampire was buried. If we find it, and there's any question as to whether or not the guy's resting comfortably or not in his coffin, you're going to have the supreme privilege of digging up his grave."

38

CHAPTER FOUR

Dar's cries echoed through the house. Elizabeth looked up from the book she was reading and smiled. "Little tyrant," she muttered. "I'm coming, Dar," she yelled. He really was getting demanding. It was time for his bottle and he knew it. At twenty months, he was getting too old to still have a bottle. However, he enjoyed it so much she didn't have the heart to take it away. She'd cut him down to just one a day. Soon, she'd stop them altogether. He could drink out of a cup just fine.

In the kitchen, Elizabeth heated Dar's bottle of milk in the microwave. He refused to drink it cold. Outside, the capricious Santa Ana wind rattled the kitchen window, howling as it did. Another yowl from Dar played counterpoint to the wind. She grabbed the bottle from the microwave and quickly made her way up the stairs to his room. When she opened the bedroom door, a teary-eyed cherub, clinging to the rail of his crib, greeted her with a grin. He hiccupped then rubbed at a wet eye with his chubby fist.

"Dar, bat-tal," he said, hiccupping again.

"Yes, Dar. But you know you're too big a boy to be drinking from a bottle. Understand?"

"Yes," Dar said. "One ba-tal. Pease. Tank you."

Elizabeth stared at him, startled at his new words and understanding. "Yes, one bottle only, you little genius. And this is it." She handed him the bottle that he quickly put in his mouth, still standing, holding the rail with one hand. He tilted the bottle up and greedily began to drink. Suddenly he let out a high-pitched scream, and then tossed the bottle over the crib rail onto the floor. He screamed again, louder this time and rubbed at his mouth with his fist.

"Dar! What is it? What's wrong?" She reached for him, thinking maybe he'd pinched his fingers in the rail guard. His scream stopped, his rosebud mouth compressed into a straight line, and the blue of his eyes darkened. Just as she touched him, a sudden throbbing pain squeezed at her hands. She let out a yell that made Dar jump. What the hell? A shock? His crib wasn't near an electric socket. She pulled back her hands, feeling the pain subside slowly. Dar's mouth softened, but his eyes locked on hers, the strange darkness lingering.

She stooped down and picked up the bottle. It was then that she realized how hot it was. She squeezed out a few drops on the inside of her wrist. It burned. The bottle had felt warm, but the majority of the milk was hot. She'd forgotten to shake it up.

"Oh, Dar! I'm sorry. I was in such a hurry! I'm sorry, baby. It burned you, didn't it? Here, I'll shake it up, make it cooler. Does your mouth hurt? Let me see." She put her hand out and touched his cheek. It was then that she saw the strange purple blotches on her hand. "What on earth?" She inspected her other hand. It was mottled with purple also. She touched one of the purple spots, about the size of a quarter. It looked like a bruise. They didn't hurt, but the look of them alarmed her. She wasn't prone to bruising and she couldn't imagine how she had gotten them.

She picked up Dar and took him to her bedroom where she sat in the rocking chair by the window. She cradled him in her lap and began to rock. "I'm so sorry, Dar." She kissed his forehead, smelling the baby sweetness of his skin. "I won't let it happen again."

Dar thrust his thumb into his mouth for a few minutes, and sucked on it noisily. Then he stopped and took hold of Elizabeth's hand. He turned it over and looked at the palm where the bruises were. "Ouchy," he said. "Big ouchy."

Elizabeth laughed. "Yes, Dar. Ouchy."

"Kissy," Dar said, giving the palm of her hand a kiss. "Betta now?" He put her hand down and reached for the bottle. "Hot, no mo?"

"It's still too hot, Dar. In a few minutes."

"Zing," he said.

"What?" Elizabeth frowned.

"Mama Zing."

"Oh, sing. You want Mama to sing."

Dar gave a nod and a grin, and then stuck his thumb back in his mouth.

Elizabeth cradled him closer and rocking him, she began to sing. "Oh, do you know the muffin man, the muffin man, who lives on Drury Lane." As she sang, the purple bruises on the palms of her hands began to burn a little, but she made a point of ignoring them.

Victor Bryce glanced out the wide window of his mainland office overlooking Newport Bay. The harbor, dotted with scudding sailboats and churning cabin cruisers, looked like a blue and white piece of a large puzzle. Far to the west, he could see the deep blue of the ocean and the dark hills of Catalina Island. To see the island was an unusual event that happened mainly when strong Santa Ana winds blew away the layers of Southern California smog. The sight of the island warmed him. He'd managed to buy land there, an impossible feat. Priceless land. On the land, he had built a French-country-style home with an endless view of ocean. Just below the home, he'd installed his laboratory. He loved the quiet and seclusion of the island. It was perfect for his kind of business.

The phone call that morning from Brady Twigs, the man he'd posted on the beach to keep a watch on the child, had put into motion some disturbing but necessary actions. The child had shown some rare abilities, ones that Brady had seen for himself. Victor wished Brady had been savvy enough to pick up the dog before the authorities got there. Then he could have had it examined in his lab. He had been waiting for just such events. He prided himself on his vision of things to come. The boy's DNA would be a gold mine, of that he was certain.

Victor caught a reflection of himself in the glass of the window. He noticed a smile on his face. Smiling was something he seldom did. It distracted from the menacing appearance he had carefully groomed. That look gave him power. He knew he'd never be taken for a kindly grandfather although at 55 he was certainly old enough to be one. However, his hair had not yet grayed, staying the same reddish-brown as it had been since he was a boy. Only his face showed the ravages of time. His steely gray eyes had puckered around the edges, as if someone had sewn a gathering stitch around them. Over the years, two long grooves had engraved themselves along each side of his mouth. The mouth itself held no softness, but was instead a hard dark line framed by a halo of deeply etched creases.

Victor prided himself on the fact that his looks evoked respect, if not fear in people. His longish nose with its widely arched nostrils, set against the sharp bones of his cheeks, gave him a slightly regal appearance, as if he'd filtered down from some ancient monarch.

When he smiled, he lost the regal look, as well as the menace, so he seldom did it. He found it easier to profit from his business when he looked imposing.

He turned away from the window, his thoughts returning to the child. He took a manila folder out of his desk drawer and studied it.

The top page read: DAVID ARTHUR ROSEMOND BX450 progeny.

Pregnancy: Normal. Mother abstained from B X450 until full term. The father continued the use of the drug.

Birth: Normal. Well-developed male. Copious amounts of hair at birth. Small strawberry birthmark, ovoid in shape, on right buttock.

Development to six months: Normal. Two teeth erupted, lower front. Appears exceptionally alert. No other unusual developments.

Development to twelve months: Well above average. Forming a number of words. Beginning to walk. Comprehension extremely high.

Development to twenty months: Well above average. Forming short sentences. Retention equivalent of child thirty-six months or older. Intense curiosity. IQ rating a possible 140+. Too young for accurate testing however. No other unusual developments.

Victor tapped his finger against the folder. Today would be the first time they could record any unusual development by the child, with the exception of what he believed was an off-the-scale intelligence quotient. He flipped through the rest of the pages in the folder, mostly medical records, all of them referring to the child's general development.

He closed the folder, thinking about the call he'd received from Brady Twigs. What he'd hoped for seemed to be emerging. It was about time for him to take over so the process could be carefully monitored. If what was happening proved consistent, then the child could be worth several fortunes. It wasn't right that he should be in the hands of parents who understood nothing about the scientific value of the boy. After all, because of the BX450 he belonged to science.

Victor picked up his cell phone and tapped in a number. "It's Victor," he said when someone answered. "It's time to move on the Sunshine project. We not only have what we were expecting, but an exciting bonus." He listened for a moment, then nodded, and said, "Fine. Fine. Just don't fuck it up! I've got millions tied up in this and

I expect a Two-hundred-percent return on my investment money." He closed the cell phone, smiling again. He'd been right to offer the Sunshine group and the Rattigan couple his financial backing. Not only would the drug itself pay off handsomely once it received an okay from the FDA, but the genetic research with the child would be the crowning glory.

Victor reached for the phone and put in another number. "The smile returned to his face as he said, "We're taking the child. We won't brook any interference. Do you understand? He'll be well cared for. If you give any warning, you're out of the loop, and out of the money. This is a courtesy call so you'll know what's going on. We expect you to come to the island once a week to do your job. It's that simple." He listened for a minute. "Good, then we have an understanding. Don't break my trust, unless you've got your burial plot paid for."

Tyree Rattigan had been in the shower, shampooing her thick swirls of red hair, when the house phone rang. Her husband, Boo, had evidently picked it up downstairs, since it stopped after only two rings. She finished her shower and dried off quickly. She emerged at the bottom of the stairs, hair wrapped in a white towel, body clad in a blue terry robe. Her bare feet made sharp little slapping sounds as she walked across the hardwood floor of the hall into the living room. She loved the ambiance of the room— with their collection of rare paintings, the grouping of soft padded furniture around the fireplace, and her ever-present quilting loom which stood beside her favorite chair.

"Who was that, Boo?" she asked.

Boo Rattigan, his lanky form stretched out the sofa, his head bent toward the book in his hand, looked up at her, his forehead pinched into a puzzled frown. "What's that?" His dark eyes held that glazed far-away look she was used to when he became intent on something.

"On the phone, honey-bunch. Who was on the phone?" She went to the small bar at the far end of the room and opened a bottle of Coke. "Boy, this hot dry wind, along with my doses of Sunshine, sure makes me thirsty."

"Oh…yes…that was Doctor Foxhoven." Boo blinked and shook his head. "He and his wife can't make the Sunshine meeting tonight."

He bent over the book again, flipping the page. His longish black hair fell over his eyes and he brushed it away. Tyree thought he looked tired. Faint blue circles bordered his eyes, and the skin on his cheeks seemed too tightly drawn across his bones. He'd been working too many hours at the lab. He spent too much time researching, continually trying to improve the formula for both forms of Sunshine. She knew there wasn't anything she could do to get him to back off. The drug was his life. Perfection his goal. His memory of what happened with Barry Brownstone kept him profoundly concerned.

Sunshine was going to be the greatest miracle drug since antibiotics. By changing and improving a person's genetic structure, it increased the body's immunity, raised the brain's cognitive abilities, enhanced inborn abilities, and would soon change the world, as they knew it. She felt a tiny shudder, as if someone had run a fingernail down her spine. The thought was awesome indeed.

Tyree pulled a small tray of ice out of the bar's refrigerator and filled a glass with cubes. "That's unusual. It's the first time the Foxhoven's have missed a Sunshine meeting in the last three years."

"Yeah, I think so. So I guess we can forgive them."

Tyree laughed. "I suppose so." She poured the Coke into the glass, took a long drink of the dark liquid, and then sighed. "Oh, that's nice!" She took another swallow. "Did they say what they were up to?"

"Some kind of meeting with our money people," Boo said.

Tyree frowned. "How many money people are there?"

Boo shrugged and closed the book. "I dunno. Foxhoven keeps track of all that stuff. Although to begin with, I thought it was all coming from him."

"Any chance of their pulling out?" she asked.

"Are you kidding? With the results, we're getting! They're going to make a fortune, and they know it."

Tyree smiled again. "Right. No one turns their back on that kind of money." Tyree thought she saw an odd twitch to the corners of Boo's eyes. Just a fleeting one, then it was gone. Odd.

"Right," Boo said, sitting upright on the sofa. "I wonder what's on the news." He yawned then picked up the television remote and clicked on the set. "Would you prefer CNN or Orange County News?"

"Orange County. I'm tired of all that international stuff," Tyree said, planting herself down on one end of the sofa.

The TV showed a pair of shaggy sheep dogs going through trials. Rags and Mop were their names. After that, a picture of a fire in Laguna Beach. Then it shifted to a shot of the Fun Zone not far from them on the peninsula.

"A gruesome find in Newport Beach," the news commentator said. "The body of a homeless man was found in an alley behind the Balboa Fun Zone. In the shadow of the brightly colored Ferris wheel, not far from a merry-go-round where the laughter of children is often heard, a man was attacked, his throat cut. Police have no suspect in the case, but are investigating a number of leads. Unnamed sources claim that this case closely resembles the serial killings in Newport Beach a few years back."

The news went to commercial as Boo reached over and clicked off the TV. He looked at Tyree, his face appearing more drawn than usual. "Good Christ!" he said. "The news is getting more and more depressing."

Tyree shook her head. "It's just a coincidence, darlyn. It has to be. We all know that killer is dead."

"I hope so," Boo said, his voice thick. "I don't think any of us can cope with anything like that again." With that, he got up and walked to the stairs. "It can't be starting all over again, can it?" Without waiting for an answer, he disappeared up the stairs.

Andy hoisted Dar onto his shoulders and gave Elizabeth a wave. Dar waved, too. "Tell Mama good-by, Dar."

"Bye," Dar said. "Dar walk."

Elizabeth waved to the two of them. "Have a good walk, you two. Are you sure you don't want to put him in the backpack? It's easier."

"No, we're not going that far. The wind's really up."

"Be careful," Elizabeth said. She watched as the two of them went out the back door, across the tiny yard, and through the gate. With a sigh, she turned and made her way upstairs to her studio. It was time for her to get some painting done. Now that her painting came easily, and the paintings sold quickly for high sums, they held

45

her interest only during the creative part. Once she knew exactly what she would paint, the colors she would use, and the technique, she lost interest. The painting process itself became mechanical. Once she'd felt great joy in her work. However, that was back when she couldn't interest a gallery. It's strange, she realized, success should bring a sense of achievement, not futility. Perhaps when it came too fast and with such impact, it didn't give the same satisfaction. She wondered if Andy felt the same way about his writing since he'd recovered from his terrible case of writer's block, thanks to Sunshine. Maybe his work had also turned routine and boring also. Still, Sunshine had changed their lives for the better in a thousand ways. She shouldn't complain.

Even if the process of their work had become lackluster, the rest of their lives certainly sparkled—new cars, more clothes than they could wear—a redecorated house, gala neighborhood parties. Lately Andy had taken to buying her jewelry. A gold and sapphire pin, a bracelet with tiny blue-white diamonds, and a lovely antique gold locket with a picture of Dar inside—all of which now sat, rarely used, in her jewelry box. Too much success so fast. It overwhelmed her.

She rummaged through her box of oil paints looking for some cad red. Damn, was she out? She hadn't gone out for more paints in a while. Possibly, she had some in her bedroom in the old chest where she kept extra supplies. Her studio was small, with little storage and what there was she'd filled to overflowing with new brushes, sketch pads and everything she needed to enhance her artwork. She wiped her hands on a rag and went to her bedroom.

Sure enough, she found three tubes of cad red in the old chest. She took out one and closed the chest, glancing out the window toward the beach. she saw Andy and Dar. Andy had taken off his shoes and Dar's, and they were jumping small waves. She could faintly hear Dar's high-pitched laughter and screams of delight as the cold water hit his legs. Elizabeth grinned and moved closer to the window, leaning on the sill. The hot wind ruffled her hair and made her think of summer when the beach would fill with people. She didn't mind that. It was only three months out of the year. After that, although people still came to the beach, the crowds were small. Then the beach belonged to her, and the few other residents who lived nearby. Even if her work was boring, the reward of being able to keep Aunt Mary's beach home was worth it. It was a heavenly place to live.

A large flock of gulls, their wings gleaming silver in the late afternoon light, suddenly swooped low across the beach. They must have startled Dar. She heard his scream change from joy to fear. He looked up as the flock passed only a few feet above their heads. His tiny hands flailed about as if he were trying to keep them away. Suddenly, several of the birds closed their wings and dropped, plummeting to the sand a few yards from Dar and Andy. Elizabeth blinked. What on Earth? She squinted, trying to see exactly what had happened. The birds lay on the beach; wings flapping for a moment, then lay still. Down the beach, she saw several more of the birds drop to the sand.

Below her, she watched as Andy picked Dar up and hurried with him across the sand toward the house. Had someone shot the birds? She hadn't heard anything. How could they possibly have shot and hit so many so fast? She turned quickly and raced downstairs. Whatever had happened would certainly have frightened Dar. She was glad that Andy had the presence of mind to bring him back to the safety of the house.

Andy pushed open the sliding glass door and bounded into the living room, Dar once more on his shoulders. "Lizzy! The damnedest thing just happened!"

Elizabeth reached for Dar, cradled him in her arms, and rocked him. "I know. I saw it from upstairs."

Dar patted her cheek with his chubby hand. "Bird, Mama! Bad birds." He pointed upward with his finger. "Dar soot birds!"

"Andy, what happened?"

Andy sat down on the sofa and looked out toward the beach. "I don't know. A large flock of seagulls came swooping down low over our heads and scared Dar. Then suddenly they began dropping out of the sky. Strangest thing I ever saw!"

"I thought maybe someone shot them," Elizabeth said.

"I didn't hear anything. Nothing! If someone had been shooting, there would have been a lot more noise." Andy shook his head, frowning. "I don't think they were shot. They were all bloody after they hit the sand. I mean bloody all over!"

"Oh my god!" Elizabeth snugged Dar closer to her. "You didn't get too close to them, did you?"

47

"Bad birds. Dar soot!" Dar frowned.

"No, darling, you didn't shoot the birds," Elizabeth assured him

"Soot birds!" Dar said pointing upward.

"I'd better call the lifeguard station and have them check things out," Andy said.

"Good idea." Elizabeth walked to the sliding door with Dar and looked out at the rumbling surf.

Andy got up and went into the kitchen to phone.

Dar patted Elizabeth's cheek again. "Bad birds, Mama. Scare Dar. "

"They wouldn't hurt you sweetheart. They just fly low sometimes." Elizabeth gave a short laugh. "Probably look to see if you had any food."

Dar stuck out his lower lip and pouted. "Scare Dar!"

"I know, sweetheart." Elizabeth assured him. Andy had been letting him watch TV in the evenings until he fell asleep. He'd been feeling more and more afraid of some things lately. Maybe too much TV was having a bad effect on him.

She set Dar down and said, "Go open your toy box, Dar. Find something to play with." Dar gave her a lopsided grin and toddled over to the blue and white toy box they kept for him beside the fireplace. He opened the lid and busied himself with finding just the right toy. Elizabeth sat down on the sofa. Outside, it was slowly getting dark. She really should try to get some painting done, but she certainly didn't feel like it. It had been a long, strange day, what with the body on the patio, then the vicious dog on the beach that died, the strange bruises on her hands, and now the damn birds. She leaned back against the sofa and sighed. A strong gust of wind vibrated the timbers of the house, sounding like the clacking of old bones. She wished the wind would ease. She hated the static electricity it caused. That might also be why Dar was more sensitive than usual. Through the window she could see silver sprays of sand as the wind kicked it up here and there.

"They're on it already," Andy said coming back into the living room. "One of the lifeguards saw the birds falling. They said the poor things are dead. Just like that. At first he said they looked almost as if they had been crushed. Blood all over the sand. Can you imagine?"

"But what would...I mean, they haven't been shot or anything?"

"Not that they could tell at first look. But they are having a bird doc…or vet or whatever, investigate the cause."

"Push," Dar said from where he sat on the floor playing with a pile of plastic blocks. "Dar push birds. Dar push 'em."

Elizabeth felt a nagging sensation in the pit of her stomach. The beginning of anxiety? Fear? Whatever it was seemed to be just lying there waiting. Waiting for just the right moment to emerge. She couldn't put her finger on the reason for it. Odd things happened, certainly, but not so odd that it should cause her that kind of alarm. She looked at the palms of her hands. The bruises had turned the color of old blackberries and they still burned. She was about to show them to Andy, when she changed her mind. She put her hands in her lap, palms down.

"It seems to me," she finally said, "that an awful lot of things have died on that beach today!"

Andy nodded in agreement. "Depressing, isn't it? Well, at least we go to Tyree's tonight for our Sunshine meeting and our usual Bloody Marys. That should cheer us up."

"Oh!" Elizabeth said, listening to their old grandfather clock chime. "With everything going on, I almost forgot about that. I'd better see about feeding Dar and getting him in his pajamas."

"I need to phone my agent. He hasn't called yet. Then do a bit of work." Andy looked over at Dar playing peacefully with his blocks. Then he turned and made his way to his office.

Elizabeth sat on the sofa watching Dar stacking brightly colored plastic blocks. His dexterity was remarkable. He could look at a picture on the block box and build most any of the things he saw there. Even Doctor Foxhoven had agreed that he was extremely advanced for his age. She watched as Dar linked one plastic block with another, building what looked to her like a castle. She heard him humming as he worked. It sounded a lot like "The Muffin Man," the song she always sang to him. She thought how small and vulnerable he looked sitting cross-legged on the floor, his head bent forward, his lips pursed intently. Having a child was far more of a responsibility than she'd expected it would be. Once they were born, your life changed—forever. You were responsible for them. She'd brought this life into the world and knew she would fight to the death to protect it.

Dar let out a squeal and clapped his hands together. "Mama!" he trilled. "Ook! Dar do dis!"

"Oh, very nice, Dar," she said. "You made a castle!"

49

Dar frowned at her. "No. Dar make house."

"Looks like a castle to me," she teased.

Dar's frown deepened. He looked down at his creation, his chubby hands resting on his knees. He said something Elizabeth couldn't understand. Baby jargon, she surmised. Jabbering away, he appeared to be scolding something. She laughed softly. He looked so adorable, his mop of gold curls reflecting the last rays of sunlight through the window.

At first, she didn't realize what it was, the odd crackling sound. It seemed as if something was being torn or crushed. Alarmed, she jumped to her feet. The sound came from where Dar sat. She rushed to him and picked him up. Then it happened. The castle of blocks suddenly burst into a thousand pieces, sharp shards of colored plastic shooting out like tiny missiles. Pieces of it stung her legs. "See!" Dar said, pointing at the flying pieces of plastic. "Bad blocks."

With a sound like a tiny moan of pain, Elizabeth grasped Dar tightly and rushed from the room. As she did, she felt tiny rivulets of blood streaming down her legs from where the shards had hit her.

CHAPTER FIVE

Elizabeth thanked God that none of the shards had struck Dar's eyes. She shivered again, just thinking about how easily he might have been blinded. She picked him up and rushed him to the kitchen. Over the sink, she carefully washed his cuts, making sure he'd not been seriously hurt. Dar sat stoically through it all and when she finally took him upstairs and put him in his nightclothes he said, "Dar got ouchy, Mama." His blue eyes looked up at her, blinking, questioning, and obviously wanting an explanation as to why he'd been hurt. "Yes, Dar," she whispered softly. "You got an ouchy." With that, she cursed the company that made the plastic blocks.

After that, Dar played quietly in his playpen while she and Andy dressed for the Sunshine meeting. Elizabeth couldn't shake off the thought that something was terribly wrong. Her mind kept examining pieces of other incidents that had happened recently, as if they were jagged bits of a puzzle. As she dressed, she'd tried to explain her concern to Andy, but he only frowned at her, shaking his head. Just coincidence, he assured her. But she knew it wasn't. Even still, she really didn't want to fit the pieces together, terrified of the picture they would form. Elizabeth took in a deep breath and tried to dispel her concern.

Elizabeth and Andy arrived at Tyree's on time, flowing in with the rest of the guests, all of them Sunshine users, and most all of them residents of nearby peninsula homes. Andy held a sleepy Dar. It was past eight, and past Dar's bedtime. Elizabeth hoped he would go right off to sleep the moment they put him into the port-a-crib that was set up in the corner of Tyree's living room. However, the little cuts on his hands and face made him fretful.

As usual, Tyree and Boo's living room overflowed with bowls of flowers. Roses, carnations, orchids, baby's breath, and gardenias. In white iron cages, tiny finches and gold-winged canaries jumped and sang. Candlelight flickered throughout the room, and a spicy scent of incense mingled with the sweet heaviness of carnations.

Elizabeth shook her head in amazement. Tyree always went to such expense and effort for their monthly Sunshine meetings. She'd obviously spent a fortune. The Rattigan's had plenty of money. They had no children and Tyree's only work was at her small art gallery in Laguna Beach where she had several employees. She only spent one or two days a week there. Tyree, being their Sunshine guru so to speak, held many of their Sunshine meetings in her home, and Elizabeth had to admit she did a bang-up job of it.

Elizabeth followed Andy and watched as he tucked Dar into the port-a-crib. Dar's eyes closed the moment Andy pulled the pale blue blanket over him. Relieved, Elizabeth hoped he would sleep until they got him up to go home. Elizabeth reached over and brushed back the gold curls from Dar's forehead. Several small cuts, tiny lines of angry red, crisscrossed his skin there. Again, she thanked God that he'd not been seriously hurt.

Shrugging off her concerns, Elizabeth turned her attention to the group that was gathered. Tonight was Sunshine night, and it was meant to be a party. Little finger sandwiches, ice-cold Bloody Marys laced with Sunshine, gossip, laughter, and a sharing of accomplishments by each of the members, all of who were fortunate enough to be taking the strong version of BX-450, better known as Sunshine.

Tyree had turned on the air-conditioning and Elizabeth blessed the cool, moist, gardenia-scented air that flooded the large living room. The hot wind grated at her nerves and made her cranky. The static electricity the wind generated was no doubt the cause of it. It might also have been responsible for the plastic blocks exploding. And possibly the birds on the beach. Santa Ana winds had, for centuries, been blamed for all sorts of things. She pushed the specter of what really might have caused the events out of her mind as she sat in one of Tyree and Boo's comfortable recliners. Andy plopped down on the beige carpet next to her. He was a floor sitter when a room was as crowed as the Sunshine meetings always were.

Looking around, Elizabeth noted that everyone was there. Everyone, that is, but Doctor Foxhoven and his wife Ann. However, the doctor was often late because of his family practice. Out of the corner of her eye, Elizabeth saw a sudden flash of fire-drenched red hair and emerald silk. She looked up to see Tyree standing over her.

"Would you like your Bloody Mary, sweetie?" Tyree asked

Elizabeth saw the blue-white diamond in Tyree's front tooth flash. "I'd Love it," Elizabeth said, her voice husky, reflecting the stress of the day.

"How about you, Andy?"

Andy grinned and nodded. Taking their dose of BX-450 in a Bloody Mary had become a tradition at the Sunshine meetings.

"What's wrong, sweetie," Tyree asked Elizabeth. "You look upset. Still fretting about the body they found on your deck this morning?"

"No. Well, yes, but besides that, it's just been one of those days."

"The Mary will fix you up." Tyree turned on her heel and in a flash of emerald and red, was gone.

Elizabeth closed her eyes for a few moments, attempting to let her tension drain away, but found instead that she grew more and more aggravated. She heard Andy get up and wander off, hearing his voice talking with Boo somewhere on the other side of the room. Over the room noises, she heard the sound of the sea outside. She could picture the swell of the surf, its white phosphorescence rising like a breath of mist from the dark water.

"Hello, dear heart," someone said. "I see your precious little bundle is asleep."

Elizabeth opened her eyes to see one of her neighbors, Mabel Zipper, pull a chair over beside her recliner. Mabel's twin, Sarah, sat in the overstuffed chair to Elizabeth's left. "Hello Mabel, Sarah. You two look spiffy tonight."

Mabel wore a long red caftan with strands of luminous pearls looped around her neck, while Sarah had on a black velvet pants suit set off by an old-fashioned gold pocket watch on a gold chain. Elizabeth adored the twin Zipper sisters. They had to be in their late seventies but were still spry and "full of piss and ginger" as everyone said. Softly plump, with precisely waved silver hair, pointy noses, watery blue eyes and thin pink mouths, the two of them went everywhere— the movies, plays, shopping malls, even jazz concerts. One could hardly go anywhere in the South County without running into the two of them. It was difficult to believe they both had been very slow at one time. Retarded was a word Elizabeth didn't like. Then Tyree started them on Sunshine and the change had been remarkable. They were no Einsteins now, but were certainly bright enough. Elizabeth always felt a sense of awe when she looked at them. The miracle of Sunshine continually amazed her.

Mabel was the twin who always called you "dear heart," and made wonderful origami figures out of any piece of paper she found lying around. Sarah was the shy one, often parroting Mabel instead of speaking her own mind. Then again, she would fool you at times, letting out a torrent of thoughts that must have been bottled up for some time. Elizabeth watched the two of them blossom at her compliment of how nice they looked.

"Why, thank you," Mabel said, touching her fingers to her silver hair. "We both splurged at the hairdressers today."

"Hairdressers," Sarah echoed.

"We missed all the commotion at your place Elizabeth. My heavens! What a terrible thing."

"Really terrible," Sarah said.

"Believe me, you didn't miss a thing," Elizabeth said. "It's just as well you were away."

"My," Mabel said. "I do wish little Dar was awake. I would so love to hold him."

"Oh, I would, too," Sarah, said.

"Well, if he wakes up, he's all yours. He does love you two, you know." Elizabeth scratched at the back of her leg, wondering for a minute why it was smarting and itching. Then she remembered the plastic shards that had cut her. They were larger than the ones that had cut Dar but even still, the cuts had not needed stitches. She'd put butterfly bandages on three of them. The others were small and had stopped bleeding quickly.

Andy came back carrying the two Bloody Marys that Tyree had made for them. Elizabeth smiled up at him, grateful for the rich red liquid that held her daily dose of Sunshine, as well as some nerve-settling alcohol.

"What's up, Lizzy?" Andy said as he handed her the drink. "You look as if you're in a righteous funk. Still worrying about that thing with the blocks?"

Elizabeth nodded, took a long sip of the Bloody Mary and then said, "Plus the seagull incident, and the-" She paused, wondering if she should tell him about the bruises on her hands. An odd foreboding slithered through her mind. No, she would wait until they were home. She would keep the frightening possibilities at bay as long as possible.

"And? What? Something else?" Andy looked up at her, his dark eyes questioning.

"Let's talk about it later," Elizabeth said. "Right now, it's party time. I'm going to eat a ton of finger sandwiches and gulp down several more Bloody Marys, without the Sunshine of course. I really need to unwind. Moreover, so do you, after all the hours you've put in with your writing today. How's the latest book coming? You sure haven't talked much about it lately."

Andy shrugged. "Yes, well it's too dang easy. The plot pops into my head full blown, and all I have to do is type it in to the computer. Sometimes I wish…."

Son of a gun! Elizabeth realized he had the same problem she did! Too routine. The thrill was gone. Maybe creative endeavors were meant to be painful, like giving birth to a child, so you could experience an exquisite sensation when you were finished and the pain stopped.

She took a long sip of the cold Mary and then said "Isn't it remarkable though, Andy? Only a few years ago we would have given everything we had to be able to work so easily. But now, we're…well, maybe a little bored with it."

Andy's eyes narrowed and he tilted his head to one side. "You too? Lizzy, I had no idea. I never thought you'd feel lackluster about your painting? You've always had such passion."

Elizabeth took another sip of her Mary, savoring the tang of Tabasco. "Well, I expect we'll both get our passion back one of these days. Things have just happened too fast."

The room suddenly became hushed and Elizabeth looked up to see that Tyree had started the meeting. Tyree rang a tiny glass bell, a ritual she'd started long before Andy and she had joined the group. The delicate sound always reminded Elizabeth of those little glass wind chimes she'd seen in Chinese restaurants.

"It's time to share what we are doing, and how Sunshine is effecting us," Tyree said to the group. "I believe we have several interesting stories tonight."

A long, familiar wail suddenly echoed around the room. Elizabeth sucked in her breath. Dar was awake. Those darn cuts. She started to get up and go to him, but Mabel Zipper put her hand up and motioned her to sit down.

Tyree raised her voice a little and went on with the meeting.

"I'll get the little darling," Mable whispered to Elizabeth. "You just sit and relax dear heart. Mothers need a break now and then." With that, Mabel got up and wound her way through the seated crowd to where Dar was now standing up in the port-a-crib. Elizabeth could see his distressed little face, fresh tears gleaming on his plump cheeks. Perhaps she should have given him some liquid Tylenol for the pain. Even though the cuts weren't deep, they were obviously giving him a bad time.

Mabel lifted Dar from the crib and carried him back to her chair. He sat on her lap, a grin on his face, despite the tears. He hiccupped once, rubbed at his wet cheeks and then looked up at Mabel. "Zip," he said, using his name for both the Zipper sisters. "Pretty." He fingered the strands of pearls around her neck.

"They are pretty, aren't they?" Mabel smiled, still whispering so as not to spoil the Sunshine meeting.

Dar pouted slightly. "Dar got ouchy," he said pointing a stubby finger at his forehead.

"Ohh," Mabel sympathized. "I'll kiss it and make it better." She leaned down and gave him a gentle kiss. "Now, it's all better."

Dar frowned. "No. Hurt." Then his face suddenly brightened. "Dar have dat," he said pointing over at Sarah. "Tick-tock."

The two sisters looked at each other, puzzled.

"Dar wan tick tock," he repeated. "Zip has tick-tock."

Sarah suddenly laughed. "He means the watch I'm wearing around my neck. A tick-tock.

You bright thing, you. My goodness, before we know it you'll be able to tell time."

Dar grinned again. "Peas, Dar have." He reached out in Sarah's direction and made a grabbing motion with his fingers. "Dar want tick-tock."

"Oh, dear," Sarah said. "I'm afraid not, Dar. This was my mothers. I can't let you play with it."

Dar's smile turned into another pout. "Want," he said firmly.

Elizabeth shook her finger at him. "No, Dar. Sarah said no."

Dar glanced at her then back at Sarah and the watch. "Dar say peas."

Sarah shook her head. "I know you did. And that's a good boy. But even still, I can't let you play with the watch. It's easily broken."

"Dar no break," he said, a glint of new tears in his eyes.

"Dar, we said no, and that's it." Elizabeth reached out to take him from Mabel, but he pulled back. "I think maybe we'd better go home," she said. "Dar is cranky. He had an accident this afternoon and was cut."

Dar lifted his head and stared at Sarah and the watch. His face turned oddly white, as if someone had drained all the blood from it. Out of some dark corner of Elizabeth's mind, a warning rose like an anguished whisper. The whisper grew. Grew with the roaring sound of the surf outside. Suddenly, a strange glow surrounded Dar, like a soft green aura. It undulated, as if breathing in the gardenia scent of the room.

Elizabeth shook her head, trying to discharge the fear that overwhelmed her. She tried to call out Dar's name, but couldn't. As she watched, Dar, shrouded by pulsing green light, lifted his hand and reached toward the watch.

"Come," he said. "Dar want!"

A crackling sound filled the air.

"Dar! No!" Elizabeth shouted. But the warning came too late. The gold chain holding Sarah's watch convulsed violently. Sarah screamed and Elizabeth watched in horror as a thin white slash appeared on the side of the elderly woman's neck. Red blood quickly seeped through the torn white flesh. It pooled in the dark hollows of Sarah's shoulder. Sarah's hand went to her neck. The blood trickled between her fingers. She held them up and stared at them.

"Oh my God," Elizabeth whispered. She wrenched Dar from Mabel's lap, but not before she saw that in his hand, he now held Sarah's gleaming gold pocket watch, its chain neatly cut in half.

CHAPTER SIX

Ted Bearbower sat in his car in front of Maddy's bakery and looked at his watch. The damn thing had stopped again. He thumped it with his thumb, hoping to jump-start it, but the wretched thing just peered back at him as if questioning what he wanted.

"Double shit," he mumbled to himself. "Here we go again!" As a kid, his mother had told him he had too much magnetism in his body, that's why watches didn't work for him. He'd gone through dozens of them, all of them stopping after he'd worn them for a month or so. Then, right after the terrible serial killings and the death of the killer, his watch had run backwards for a number of weeks. Then oddly enough, it proceeded to work normally until now. He looked at the Seiko on his wrist, its second-hand motionless. Well, things were back to their usual off kilter state, he told himself.

Even though his watch said seven, he realized it was much later than that. When he'd left the department, the clock on the wall had said twenty minutes to ten. He'd driven straight from there to Maddy's bakery so he figured it must be close to eleven. The bakery closed at six. He wondered if it was too late for him to be calling on Maddy, even though she'd invited him and told him she'd be up late. He sat in the car staring out the window and thumping his watch with his thumb. As he watched, the wind outside tumbled bits of silvery paper along the sidewalk in front of the bakery. It reminded Ted of confetti on New Year's Eve. Should he go in, or not?

He'd not dated anyone since Silvia had died. The thought of getting to know another woman as intimately as he'd known Silvia, frightened him. Part of him trembled at the thought, while another part longed for the softness of a woman, even if it turned out to be just a causal relationship. Someone to talk to away from the police department. Someone to listen. Someone to feed him not only pastry, but also comfort and understanding. He needed a sanctuary.

He pulled the keys out of the ignition and opened the car door. Maddy had said she lived in a house back of the bakery. He could see lights coming from that direction. The wind helped him close the car door with a resounding bang that startled him. He slipped the keys into his pocket and began walking toward the lights. As he got closer, he could see a small cottage with a large wooden porch. The porch light was on, illuminating a wicker swing and two wicker chairs. A heart-shaped flower wreath hung on the front door, a symbol of welcome that lingered from Victorian days.

Maddy answered the door wearing a loose shift of pale green and peach silk. Her blond hair, free of the French roll she always wore in the bakery, framed her face in soft waves. She wore glossy peach lipstick that matched the color in her shift. And she smelled wonderful! A deep autumn scent drifted through the doorway reminding Ted of sweet spicy cider, crisp red apples, and cinnamon rolls.

"Well, I was hoping you'd make it," she said, opening the door wider and beckoning him inside. "I've put together a lovely assortment of chocolate goodies for you."

To Ted's surprise, she took his hand and led him into a small but comfortable living room. A vase filled with amber, gold and cream-colored chrysanthemums decorated the opening of a large brick fireplace. Two plump sofas covered in the same shades of peach and green that Maddy wore flanked the fireplace. Ted looked around at the unusual pictures on the walls. Photos of carousel horses, Mardi Gras posters, impish pencil drawings of people making love, and signed Disney cartoon gels. Silvia would have called the room eclectic. Whatever the style, Ted loved it. He felt at ease immediately.

Maddy gave a deep-throated laugh. "Kind of a hodgepodge, isn't it? The room, I mean. I enjoy it though."

"I like it too," Ted said, smiling.

"Well then, don't just stand there, plunk yourself down on the sofa. How about some iced coffee?" She let go of his hand but the warmth of her fingers lingered on his.

Ted lowered himself into the soft cushioned sofa, felt it wrap around him like gentle hugging arms. He had the odd sensation that he might never be able to extract himself from its cushy depth, and the even odder feeling that he didn't care.

Maddy turned to leave, and then turned back. "Slip your shoes off, get comfortable. You've had a tough day, haven't you?"

Ted nodded. "One of the worst. That explains my appetite for so much chocolate."

"Poor baby," she said then with a whisper of silk, she left the room.

Ted looked around, wondering why such an odd assortment of decor would make him feel so at home. It wasn't at all like the condo he and Sylvia had shared. The condo still overflowed with all the antique treasures he and Sylvia had gathered during their many years of marriage. Items he couldn't bear to part with. Maddy's home was a mix of charming old and starkly modern. A sense of whimsy hummed from every corner. For a moment, Ted felt a pang of guilt. His reasons for being here were entirely selfish. He'd come for sanctuary, but what had he brought for Maddy? What could he bring, but himself with his need for comfort? He shook his head. Well, she'd soon discover that for herself. He'd let fate take a hand and not worry about it. As he'd seen on the beach this afternoon and on the beach that morning, life was just too damn short not to be selfish occasionally.

"Here we go," Maddy said, wafting back into the room on a trail of Autumn scent. "Plenty of ice, some Ghirardelli chocolate mixed into the coffee, and a little tray of snacks. I bet you haven't eaten a decent meal all day."

Ted chuckled. She'd guessed right. The only things he'd eaten that day were the lemon pastries. He'd meant to have a late lunch with Ajax, but after the investigation of the dead man in the alley, neither of them had been too hungry. "Thanks," he said. "That's kind of you."

She set things down on the coffee table and handed him a tall crystal glass filled with dark iced coffee. "Take some of the cashew and chicken sandwiches. They go nicely with the coffee. Sorry I got so dainty and cut off the crusts. A habit of mine from my tearoom days. Makes them a bit small for you, doesn't it?"

Ted picked up one of the little sandwiches in his large bear-like hands and grinned. "They look delicious, though," he said. He took a bite and savored the sweet spiciness of the chicken salad. It took him only two bites to devour the half sandwich, and he hesitated to reach for another.

"Don't be silly," she said, as if reading his mind. "Eat them all. I had my dinner earlier."

Maddy had made four sandwiches, just about the right amount for his appetite. It was unusual, but pleasant to be with someone who not only understood his hunger, but apparently, shared it. Since Sylvia had been bone thin and really didn't enjoy eating, she never understands why he did. He reached for another sandwich, pleased that there were enough to satisfy him.

They chatted pleasantly while he ate. He drained his glass and Maddy poured him more from the pitcher she'd brought. She helped herself to a glass of the iced coffee and settled into the sofa next to him. He gave her an abridged version of his life, and she sketched a number of incidents from hers. Until a year ago, she'd owned a small tea room in Brea. It took an enormous amount of time and didn't allow her to make the pastries she loved. Therefore, she'd sold the place and opened the bakery. She set up the recipes, hired a baker to do part of the baking and a sales clerk to help.

"I'd love to quit, and just bake for myself," she said, looking a bit wistful. "But when my husband died, due to some damn mix-up his retirement money was canceled so I don't have much to live on. I need some sort of extra income, to pay for health insurance and all. My kids have offered to help out, but they have enough on their hands, with my grandchildren and all. They don't need millstone Maddy around their necks. Do you have children?" she asked.

"No. Sylvia couldn't have any, and we just never got around to adopting."

Maddy nodded. "Kids are great. I'd be glad to share mine with you." She gave a throaty laugh. "The grandkids too, the little hellions."

Ted put down his glass and wiped his hands on one of the peach and green napkins that Maddy had provided. "That was wonderful. I really appreciate the meal."

"You have to take care of yourself. Especially when you're under stress, as I imagine you are a lot in your job." Maddy smiled for a moment, and then her smile faded. "Just listen to me! I'm sorry. I didn't mean to mother you like that. It's just my nature, I guess. I like looking after people."

Ted reached out and touched her hand. "Don't apologize. Sometimes I need a lot of looking after, and I don't mind at all." A sudden panic hit him. It had been so darn long since he'd been with a woman; he had no idea what to do next. Should he put his arm around her? Try to kiss her? Or should he put that off until another time? He was completely in the dark about what people did these days. How fast to move, and what was considered okay and what wasn't. And was her friendship just that? Or was he reading the signals right? Signals that meant she wanted more than just friendship? The room suddenly seemed way too warm, with no air. He had the urge to bolt and run for the door.

Maddy looked down at his hand on hers, and then up at him, a soft smile on her lips. "Ted, I'd like very much if you would kiss me. However, if you have no interest in doing that, I'll understand. I know I'm not a prize, figure-wise. I'm not young. But I'm not over the hill yet, at least I don't think I am."

Ted laughed out loud, relief spilling from him like water in a brook. He put his hand against her cheek and lifted her head slightly. "Maddy, I'd love to kiss you. And I love your figure. In fact, it's been driving me crazy. I'm the one who should be apologizing for my weight."

"I adore well-upholstered men," she said, her laughter matching his.

Ted's mouth closed on hers, and he tasted autumn, sweet, spicy, and delicious. Her tongue gently teased his lips and he opened his mouth to it, let it explore the inside of his mouth. Desire rose in him, something he'd almost forgotten could happen. He felt sixteen again, wondering if he could control himself. Jesus! He should have done this a long time ago! Why had he waited so damn long?

"We'd be more comfortable in the bedroom, don't you think?" Maddy asked, breaking their kiss. "Or am I pushing things too fast?"

Ted thanked God for her directness. Without it, he would have remained a stuttering, pawing, awkward teenager. "Lead the way," he said, taking her hand.

The bedroom matched the living room in decor. A king-size white iron bed, made up with peach satin sheets, dominated the room. The carpet, a pale green, felt as thick as lamb's wool under his shoes. He'd not taken off his shoes, as Maddy had suggested earlier. Now he was sorry that he hadn't. How could he go about undressing in front of someone he barely knew, without feeling and looking totally ridiculous? Of course, he'd talked to her every morning for the past few months, but that didn't help at that moment. Had it been this difficult years ago, when he'd first met Sylvia? He couldn't remember.

Maddy came to the rescue again. "Let me," she said, slipping off his jacket and unbuttoning his shirt. "I've wanted to do this since the first morning you walked into the bakery." It only took her a minute to remove the rest of his clothes.

Ted felt himself smile. A woman lusting after him. He liked that. He knew that despite his age and weight, women often gave him a second look. But outside of that, he'd never considered anything more. Until now.

The satin sheets felt slick and cool against his warm body. Maddy turned off the lights and he heard a whisper of silk as she slipped off her shift and got into bed beside him. The wind rattled against the side of the house, moaning as it did. He reached out and touched her, his hands moving slowly over her body, exploring. He couldn't help compare her wonderfully soft, full body to Sylvia's. He'd adored his late wife, found her sexually attractive, but he'd never felt the burgeoning desire as strongly as he did now. Sylvia's body had always been cool, dry, and sleek, while Maddy's was warm and moist with delightful hills and valley's to explore.

With a sudden moment of alarm, he pulled back from her slightly.

"What? What is it?" she asked.

"I just thought about it. I mean, what about…you know…protection."

Maddy let out one of her husky laughs. "I can't get pregnant, my love."

"No, I mean protection against—"

"Oh, AIDS, things like that? Well, since I haven't been intimate with a man for the past six years, I don't think it's a problem. Besides, I had blood tests awhile back." She laughed softly. "When I first met you. What about you?"

He reached for her again, his fingertips skimming the surface of her warm skin. "I guess we're both safe then. It's been years for me too." His alarm faded, replaced by a renewed surge of desire. "And I get a physical yearly."

"I love your hands," she whispered. "Like soft paws, but so gentle."

He moved his body next to hers, wrapped his arms around her and kissed her. This was the real world, he thought. This is life. This is celebration. The appalling realities of his work were only shadows. He pushed the shadows into a deep recess of his mind.

Slowly he moved his hands over Maddy's full breasts, and then down across her soft belly and in-between her thighs. He slipped his fingers inside her and heard her moan. She arched her back pressed herself against his hand. The warm moist feel of her rose his desire to an almost unbearable level.

"Oh, God, Maddy! I don't think I can wait—"

"That's okay, love. Don't worry about it. Go ahead. Then we'll sit in bed and sip iced coffee and eat chocolate éclairs." She paused and gave another of her throaty laughs. "Then, later, we'll do it again! Slow and easy."

CHAPTER SEVEN

The morning dawned stiflingly hot. Searing wind blew relentlessly across the wooden deck outside Elizabeth's sliding glass door. Over the wail of wind, the air was filled with the sound of surf and the spicy scent of dried seaweed. The Santa Ana wind, blowing in off the desert, unlike the cooling sea breezes Elizabeth and Andy were accustomed to, brought no freshness. It quickly sucked up any trace of night dew and left only a shining lick of tidewater.

Dar had finally gone to sleep sometime before midnight after a tearful interlude that had given Dar a bad case of hiccups. After that, Elizabeth found it impossible to lie down, much less sleep. Andy sat up with her in the living room, asking why she had become so upset over the incident. Tyree had accompanied them home and stayed the night, assuring Elizabeth that Sarah Zipper had not been seriously injured.

"It was only a slight cut," Tyree repeated. "Superficial. The blood made it look worse."

"But what…why?" Elizabeth gestured helplessly and sunk down into the cushions of the wicker sofa. "I just don't understand what happened. What did Dar do? How did he do it?"

"Maybe the chain was weak," Tyree offered.

"No, Sarah said it was 18K gold, and was extremely strong and well made."

"Well, evidently something was wrong with it."

"It was Dar! He did something…strange."

"Don't worry, we'll find out. Dr. Foxhoven is on his way here to check out Dar…and you. He'll get to the bottom of this. Don't fret," Tyree assured her again, as she had been doing most of the night.

Tyree walked to the sliding glass door and looked out. "Foxhoven should be here any minute. He said he'd come by before his hospital rounds. I think he was going to stop at the Zipper's first and check out the cut on Sarah's neck."

Andy, who had been sitting in the rocker beside the fireplace, suddenly got up. "Well, I didn't see it. I didn't see anything. Dar got hold of the watch Sarah was wearing on the chain around her neck and pulled too hard, is all. That's what cut her neck. For the life of me, I can't see what you are so upset about."

"Andy! For God's sake! That's not what happened," Elizabeth cried. "You were at the other end of the room, talking with Boo. Dar reached out for the watch, but he didn't reach it. He couldn't. He was too far away from Sarah, sitting on Mabel's lap. I was sitting in-between them. The next thing I knew, the watch was in Dar's hand. Everything kind of...well, glowed. Greenish. As if some sort of energy clicked on. Like electricity maybe. I don't know." Elizabeth rubbed at her face and shook her head.

Andy sighed. "I know that's what you think you saw. Nevertheless, you know as well as I do, that's impossible. It's a shame that Dar pulled so hard he injured Sarah. I hope she understands it was an accident. Dar didn't realize it would hurt her."

Elizabeth glared at him. "But Sarah had a nasty cut on her neck. How did he get it off of her?"

"He pulled too hard, but then lifted it up over her head." Andy insisted.

"What about the birds, Andy? What about the blocks exploding? And . . ." Elizabeth paused, realizing that she should tell him about the bruises on her hands. However, her suspicions about the man who had died on the deck seemed too far-fetched. Dar couldn't possibly have done that. The bruises however, were something else. "Andy, something more happened."

Tyree turned to her. "More? What, for God's sake?"

Elizabeth looked away from Andy, checking out the palms of her hands. She could still see a purple-blue tinge of the bruising there. "I accidentally gave Dar his bottle too hot. It burned him and he screamed. Almost immediately, pain shot through my hands. When I looked, large bruises were welling up on my palms."

"But Lizzy," Andy argued. "Dar couldn't have caused them. How would he do that? You probably burned them on the bottle."

"No, Andy! They were bruises, not burns. Look!" She held up her hands. "You can still see them."

Tyree took her hands in hers and looked at them, frowning. "Yes, they're bruises all right."

Andy gave Elizabeth's hands a cursory look. He shook his head. "I think the two of you are somewhat hysterical. A little baby can't possible do the kind of things you're trying to say he did." He shook his head again and gave Elizabeth a wistful smile. "Lizzy, I'm sure the doctor will convince you that you're needlessly upset. Look, I really have to get some work done. Would you two mind if I went into my office until Foxhoven gets here?"

Elizabeth looked up at him. His chocolate brown eyes were warm despite his words. She realized that he understood her concern, if not the reason for it. "Sure, Andy. Go ahead. We'll let you know when he gets here." Maybe he's right, Elizabeth thought. The truth of it was that none of it made sense. Maybe she was a bit hysterical. So many odd things happening would push anyone off-center.

After Andy left the room, Tyree sat down in the rocker across from Elizabeth. The wind let out a yowl and rattled the windowpane, causing Elizabeth to jump, and then laugh dryly at her skittishness.

"Easy, sweetie," Tyree said. It's not all that bad."

"Tyree, you must have some idea of what's going on. Tell me what you think. Any ideas you may have."

Tyree looked thoughtful for a moment. She leaned back in the rocking chair and set it into motion with her foot. "Well, the only thing I can think of right now is that Dar may have some psychokinetic abilities."

Elizabeth frowned. "Some what?"

"It's better known as PK. The ability to move things with one's mind."

"But…I didn't think there was such a thing. That it was just a hoax. Like that Russian guy who supposedly bent spoons with his mind."

Tyree stopped moving the rocker and leaned forward. "Some are hoaxes of course. Stage magic. Some are the real."

"I don't really understand."

Listen, sweetie, I have a friend, a woman who buys a lot of paintings from my gallery. Her name is Terri Mann. Doctor Mann, actually. She has a Ph.D. in parapsychology. She works with things like that. Made a lifelong study."

Elizabeth thought about it. Could that explain what had been happening? If it was something like PK, then how come Dar had it? No one in the family had ever mentioned anything like that. On the other hand, was it caused by the Sunshine? After all, she'd stopped it during her pregnancy and while she was nursing. However, she'd been taking it, and so had Andy, the night Dar was conceived. If so, what else might be wrong with Dar?

Troubling thoughts kept tumbling through her mind. She still had horrible nightmares about the night Barry Brownstone had raped, and almost killed her. The terrible fear that he might have been Dar's father had plagued her until Foxhoven ran a DNA test and assured her that Andy was definitely Dar's father.

"Lizzy," Tyree said strongly. "Are you still with us?"

Elizabeth realized she had been ignoring what Tyree was saying. She sucked in a deep breath and let it out, trying to expel all the worrisome thoughts. She couldn't let them overwhelm her.

"Sorry, "she said. "I just can't get my mind around any of this."

"After Foxhoven looks at Dar, I could call Terri if you like," Tyree assured her. "She's pretty much retired now. However, I'm sure she'd be interested in something like this. Never knew her to turn down a good mystery that involves PK."

"Well, okay, if you think it might help. Maybe she could better explain all this stuff to me. Actually, I should look it up online," Elizabeth said. "I always thought it was like the poltergeist thing. You know, where things fly around the room."

"Right. Sometimes it is like that."

"But that's not what happened with Dar. If it is him causing it, then it's different. The birds. They just fell out of the sky. Dead! Dar kept saying he shot them. And the blocks. They exploded! The shards cut both of us. And what about the bruises? That would mean he could...oh, God, I don't even want to think about it. Maybe we're all wrong about this. Maybe Andy is right."

"Maybe, maybe not. However, right now we don't know, so let's not borrow trouble, okay? Let's wait until we find out more." Tyree gave her a soft smile, the diamond in her front tooth gleaming blue-white.

"Yes, of course. Are you sure that Sarah is okay? I keep worrying about her."

"I'm sure. She was a bit startled. All she could say was boys would be boys. The poor dear really had no idea about what happened."

Elizabeth sighed. "She's not the only one."

Dar lay in his crib looking up at the colored blocks. It was time for his mama to get him up and feed him, but she hadn't come yet. He wondered if she was still upset with him. He'd done something that made her cry, but he didn't know why. All he'd done was to take the watch from one of the Zips and look at it. His mama told him he'd given Sarah a bad ouchy. He hadn't meant to do that. He knew how bad an ouchy could hurt. Maybe no one would come to get him up. Maybe what he'd done was so awful they would just leave him there. The thought of nothing to eat made him start to cry. Then he remembered how he'd had those terrible hiccups when he'd cried after everyone had scolded him about taking the watch. He sucked in his breath and made an effort not to cry. He probably could climb out of his crib and go downstairs, but he knew he couldn't reach any place where they kept his food.

He tried to think of something else, and started inspecting the blocks overhead, one at a time. As far as he could see, the things inside them were identical. Not the square outside part, but rather the squiggly stuff inside them. Kinda like chains of things strung together, a bit like the strings of colored beads he played with. Only there were so many chains inside the blocks he couldn't possible count them. He didn't even know the numbers it would take to do that. He realized that not only did the blocks have this kind of insides, but so did everything around him. Only the block insides were different from the crib insides, and those were different from the blanket insides.

He closed his eyes, weary from thinking about all of it. He didn't understand yet, what these chain things meant. What he did know was that with not too much effort, he could rearrange them. When he did this, odd things happened. Like his plastic blocks. He'd gotten angry and decided to stir up the chains of stuff inside them. Only his stirring had made them fly apart and hurt him and his mama. He would have to be careful, he realized. He didn't want to hurt himself or mama again.

He felt a pleasant drowsiness and decided to sleep some more. He wasn't all that hungry. Maybe when he woke up again, his mama would be there. Maybe she wouldn't be cross with him anymore. Maybe she would tell him about the chains inside of things, the way she told him about other things, so he would know what to do with them. He had to learn the right way to do things. With that thought in his mind, he drifted off to sleep. His dreams were filled with bright colors and someone singing "Oh do you know the muffin man, the muffin man."

Andy sat in his office at the back of the house, thankful for once that the room was always cool. In the winter, it was chilly in there, but now, with hot desert winds blowing, he enjoyed the cool quietness of the place. His desk was an old one that he and Elizabeth had bought at a garage sale for $25. Its large oak frame was chipped and faded, but Andy loved it. When they'd finally begun making a great deal of money, he refused to replace it. Actually, he hadn't replaced anything in his office. He still had their old sofa from their apartment days. If he got tired of writing, he could stretch out and snooze, or read some research material. The stuffing was spilling out in several places, but he loved the familiar comfort of it.

He tried to concentrate on his writing which, since taking Sunshine, came easily and quickly. And yet, after the events of yesterday and last night, he found he wasn't able to put down so much as a word. He remembered the terrible yearlong block he'd had before moving to the beach house and hoped to God that he wasn't getting it back. The reason for his concern right then was not what everyone believed Dar had done. Instead, it was with their jumping to such ridiculous conclusions. Certainly, some bizarre things had happened. However, all of it was coincidence, that good old long arm that he tried to keep out of his novels. Coincidence in fiction was frowned on, but in real life, it happened all the time.

Andy made a mental list of the things that had occurred. Nothing was actually the same. Nothing was connected. How could Lizzy and Tyree believe that his son was in some way responsible for all those things? He shook his head. Women! The eternal mothers, fretting over their children. His son was unusually bright, physically advanced, and so beautiful it made his heart twinge whenever he looked at him.

He leaned back in the desk chair and stretched. He'd be glad when Doctor Foxhoven got there to check Dar over. The doctor would put to rest these notions. A man of science, he would convince Lizzy that the only thing wrong with their son was the fact that he was no doubt on the edge of genius.

Feeling better, he got up, went to the sofa, and stretched out.

None of them had gotten any sleep last night. He would take a nap until Foxhoven arrived. After that, he was certain his writer's block would vanish and he could get a chapter or two done before dinner.

Victor Bryce leaned back against the coaming padding of the cockpit, enjoying the spray of saltwater as his yacht, The_Cybele, balanced itself against the wind-whipped surface of the sea. Victor had never been seasick, and the rougher it got, the more he enjoyed it. With its cathedral hull, The Cybele road the high swells like the goddess she was named after. A wave broke over the proud bow, but The Cybele, undaunted, forged ahead as if determined to reach Catalina Island in record time. Victor knew that Travis, his skipper of long standing, was the best to be had, although expensive. Victor, himself, loved cruising, but hated taking the controls. With Travis at the console, he could relax and enjoy the spirit of the sea.

Sounding like the plaintive bleating of a sheep, Victor's cell phone rang. "Victor here," he shouted over the roar of the wind and sea. "What? Wait a minute; let me put the scrambler on so no one can intercept this. Okay."

"It's Twigs. I've just had word that something more is happening with the Rosemond child."

"Tell me."

"Something about a transposition or transportation. Big words." Twigs' voice held a tinge of poutiness, as if he thought he had been left out of something. "I wasn't in a good position to hear all the chatter that was going on, so I don't know exactly what they were talking about."

"I do. It's even bigger than we had hoped for. We need the child now. Tell the others that I want it to happen today. I'm almost to Catalina. I'll send you The Green Latrine as soon as we get there. I don't want The Cybele or the chopper involved in this. The Latrine hasn't been registered to anyone in years. No way to trace it back to me. I'll make sure everything is ready at the laboratory, while you see that the child is brought here safely. We just want_the child to disappear. Make it look like a kidnapping. You know, the way kids vanish at a mall. He's a handsome child. It's the kind of thing that might happen to that kind of kid."

Twigs was silent at the other end of the phone. Victor could picture him mulling over everything. "You Roger me, Twigs?" Still no answer. "Don't we pay you enough, Twigs?"

"Not enough for kidnapping. They can give you the death penalty for that can't they?"

"Not any more. Look, Twigs, you don't have to be part of it. You just get the others to take care of it. Will that make you happy?"

Twigs scraped his throat. "Yeah. That would be okay. You won't be sore?"

"Of course not. Just as long as it gets done, I don't care how. You'll take care of getting it setup won't you?"

"Yeah, sure. I can do that."

"Good man."

"You're not sore though, are you?"

"Hey, you're my information man. I need you." Victor felt The Cybele shudder as it mounted a huge swell. "Gotta go, our connection isn't too good."

"Okay," Twigs said, and hung up.

Victor clicked off his cell phone and laid it down on the deck beside him. He nodded with satisfaction. By night, he would have the child. Then they could start their study. He didn't know exactly what they were on to, but if his suspicions were correct, he knew it would be big. If Sunshine was the cause of it, and if it could be controlled, the possibilities were so enormous he didn't dare contemplate them.

He reached into his jacket pocket, pulled out a tiny digital recorder, and clicked it on. "Note," he said into the recorder. "Consider getting rid of Twigs when the job's completed." He smiled. The world was a rich place if you just had the eyes to see the treasures, and the guts to seize them.

CHAPTER EIGHT

Doctor Foxhoven arrived at eight a.m. wearing a pale blue shirt and a silk suit the color of summer clouds. It matched his hair.

Tyree excused herself. "I've got to go shower. Be back later." With that, she let herself out the sliding door and Elizabeth could hear the slapping sounds her sandals made as she ran next door.

Elizabeth showed Foxhoven upstairs to Dar's room. "Is Sarah okay?" she asked as they climbed the stairs.

"Yes, I just looked at her and she's fine. We put some disinfectant on the cuts. They'll heal nicely."

Elizabeth opened the door to Dar's room. Dar was asleep on his stomach, but stirred the moment they entered the room.

"Mama?" he said, and then yawned.

"Yes, it's Mama, and Doctor Fox."

"Dar no shot!"

"No, Dar, you aren't going to have a shot. Doctor Fox just wants to check you over and talk to you about what happened to Sarah and the watch last night."

Dar sat up in his crib and scrubbed at his eyes with his fists. "Dar give Sarah bad ouchy." He pulled himself up and stood at the crib rail peering at the two of them.

"Can you tell me how you did that?" Foxhoven asked.

"Dar want tick-tock."

"Yes, I know that, but how did you get it? You didn't reach out with your hand and take it, did you Dar?" Foxhoven smiled at Dar, obviously trying to avoid frightening him.

Dar shook his head. "Dar wiggle."

Elizabeth looked at Foxhoven then back to Dar. "Wiggle?"

"Dar made inside wiggle." Dar sat back down in the crib, as if he were tired of talking about the subject. He yawned again. "Hungry mama."

"Yes, Dar. You can have breakfast in a minute. But first, we need to know just how you make things wiggle."

Dar frowned and shook his head.

Foxhoven reached out, picked Dar up, and held him in his arms.

"Let's go downstairs and have breakfast, and you can tell us about it. Okay?"

Dar's face brightened. "Otay. Dar want Fruit Oops."

"What's that?" Foxhoven asked.

"His favorite cereal, Fruit Loops," Elizabeth said.

"Okay," Foxhoven agreed. "Fruit Loops it is."

Downstairs, Elizabeth realized that Andy was still working in his office, but thought better of calling him. She'd let the doctor see Dar first.

"I'll fix Dar some cereal. Why don't you put him in his high chair? You can talk with him while he eats." Elizabeth felt a growing sensation of anxiety. What could Foxhoven learn by talking with Dar? How could a child so young explain how he did such bizarre things? Fear crawled down the back of her neck like a dozen whiskered dust mites. She shuddered.

"Good idea," Foxhoven said. "In fact, why don't you just sit down here in the living room, and I'll take Dar into the kitchen and fix the cereal. I may be able to get more from him if we're alone. He may be afraid you are angry with him."

"Well...." Elizabeth hesitated. "Maybe it's a good idea. I was upset with him last night. He knows that." Elizabeth touched Dar's cheek with the tips of her fingers. "I'm sorry, Dar. I know you didn't realize what you were doing."

Dar giggled. "Fruit oops."

"Sure thing. Let's go. Doctor Fox will fix it for you."

"They're in the cupboard by the stove," she said.

Dar giggled again and waved a chubby hand at Elizabeth. "Byeee," he said.

Elizabeth waved back, trying to muster a smile she didn't feel. As soon as they left the room, she heard a sharp rapping on the sliding glass door. When she opened it she found Tyree standing there. She'd changed into a cotton shift the color of vanilla ice cream. Her streams of long red hair were loose and framed her face like licks of flame.

"Oh, I'm glad you're back. I feel so...I don't know, so nervous about what the doctor will say." Elizabeth said. "He's in the kitchen with Dar, trying to see if he can find out more about what happened."

"I called that friend of mine. Dr. Terri Mann. The one who deals with these types of things." Tyree's eyes glittered like blue marbles.

"I hope it's okay with you, sweetie, but I made an appointment for her to come here and see Dar. Maybe she can make you feel better about this whole thing."

"Oh," Elizabeth said, slightly taken aback. Good old Tyree can't resist being her usual mother hen self. Well, she was probably right. This doctor, what's her name? Terri Mann could probably be more help than Foxhoven. After all, how many medical doctors have patients who can do what Dar has done? "When?" she finally asked Tyree.

"Tomorrow, if that's all right. Around ten in the morning. She was fascinated by what I told her. You probably couldn't keep her away with a shotgun." Tyree handed Elizabeth a slip of paper. "Here's her name and phone number, in case the time's not convenient."

"Ten tomorrow should work out just fine."

"Okay, then. I guess I'd better get on home and fix Boo something to eat. We're all off schedule after last night. You get some rest, sweetie. You look tired."

"I will after we get some answers about Dar. Can't you stay? For a little while at least?"

Tyree gave her a gentle smile, the diamond in her front tooth making a tiny rainbow in the subdued light of the living room. "I'll be back. I just want to take care of Boo. He's seems to be a bit, well, distracted I think you'd say. About all this. Says he's fine, but then you know men." She patted Elizabeth's hand. "Just give me a ring when Foxhoven leaves." Then, tossing plumes of red hair, she disappeared through the open sliding glass door.

It seemed to Elizabeth that Foxhoven had been in the kitchen with Dar for an awfully long time. She fought off the temptation to peek in and see what was going on and instead, settling herself on the wicker sofa, she stared out the sliding glass door at the beach. She felt herself grow small, and nervous. Her fingers laced together looked like white rose petals. Outside, the wind had subsided slightly. Only a few people walked the beach, drifting by like lonely flowers in a stream. Perhaps after Foxhoven left, she'd take Dar for a walk on the beach. He loved it so. In addition, it would be a good chance for her to talk to him about everything that had happened. She had to convince him that he had to control whatever it was. However maybe it was transient. Maybe they'd wake up tomorrow and Dar would be back to normal. Maybe it was just the trauma of yesterday's grisly find on their deck. Dar hadn't seen the body, but with everyone rushing around, police everywhere, people in and out of the house, Dar was bound to feel the tension. Maybe that's what caused him to be able to do those things. The thought made her feel somewhat better. They would all get some sleep, and things would right themselves tomorrow. Nevertheless, if she slept, she knew her dreams would be the color of blood, the way it looked where it had soaked into the wooden deck outside the sliding door.

The ticking of the old Germantown Grandfather clock in the corner of the living room grew louder. What was taking them so damn long? She shifted herself, then shifted again, trying to get her bones stacked comfortably, but her spine began to ache as she sat there. She'd give them five more minutes, and then she'd go and check things out.

Less than a minute later, Foxhoven came out of the kitchen, holding Dar. He set him down by his toy box, came over, and sat across from Elizabeth. "I don't think there's anything to worry about. The boy does seem to have what they sometimes call psychokinetic abilities, but with work, I believe we can help him control them. Otherwise, as far as I can tell, Dar's a healthy little rascal."

"Do you think it was caused by Sunshine?"

"You stopped it during your pregnancy, didn't you?"

"Yes, as soon as I knew. But I was taking it when I conceived, and for a few weeks after until I found out I was pregnant." Elizabeth shook her head. "Oh, God! What if I've done something to harm Dar?"

"No! No, don't trouble yourself. I don't think you took it long enough. And even if it was caused by Sunshine, it's possible it can be a good thing for the child. Once he learns to control it, that is." He leaned forward and tapped his fingers against the top of the large coffee table. "I would like to do some tests though. Nothing difficult. An EEG perhaps."

"A what?"

"Electroencephalogram. A test that measures brain waves. I'd bet we'll find that the boy has some unusual ones. I'd also like to see if he has a…that is, to see if we can measure any source of extra energy he might have. I read somewhere that people who claim to have healing hands there is some sort of measurable electrical energy that emanates from them. Something like that could explain what's happening with Dar."

Elizabeth looked over at Dar who was pushing a small teddy bear around in a toy pickup truck. Nothing bad was wrong with Dar, she told herself. He was so perfect. She wouldn't let herself even consider anything else. She'd take Foxhoven at his word.

"Call my office, please, and they'll schedule the test." Foxhoven got up and gave her a fleeting smile.

"Yes, well, okay. I'll do that."

Foxhoven walked over to where Dar was playing. "Bye," he said.

"You go home?" Dar asked.

"Yep. Doctor Fox has to see some other little children."

"Feed 'em Fruit loops?"

Foxhoven laughed. "Well, maybe." He turned to Elizabeth. "I'd better get going I'm running late. Don't get up."

After Foxhoven left, Elizabeth sat there for a long time watching Dar play. The feeling of uneasiness crept back, making her heart flutter timidly in her chest, like tiny bird's wing.

The hot winds abated to a light breeze by afternoon. Elizabeth felt it was a good time to take Dar for a walk on the beach, as long as there were not too many seagulls. Andy agreed. After that, he would probably nap. She decided to go barefoot, as she walked in the sand better that way. She helped Dar remove his shoes. They both wiggled their toes and Dar let out a giggle. Andy lifted him into the backpack Elizabeth had strapped on, and buckled him in.

"Don't go far, you two. If the winds come back, you'll get stung by blowing sand." Andy gave Dar a kiss on the forehead, and then hugged Elizabeth. "You feeling better, Lizzy?"

Elizabeth gave him a wan smile. "Yes, a bit. Maybe when this Dr. Mann friend of Tyree's comes tomorrow, she'll be able to explain more about all this."

Andy chewed on the edge of his lip for a moment, "Well, if she can help you feel better," he finally said. "Then I'm all for it."

Outside, the sky had turned a brilliant cloudless blue. A faint odor of salt and seaweed hung in the air now that the wind wasn't blowing so hard. Small ocean waves lapped gently against the sand. Elizabeth looked around warily for any flocks of birds. The thought of what had happened yesterday turned her stomach to jelly. She purposely set a strong stride, hoping to out-walk her apprehension.

The sand under her feet was strewn with shards of ecru seashells.

"Dar," she said as they walked down the beach toward the jetty. "I want you to listen to mama."

"Otay," Dar said.

"You know the things Doctor Fox asked you about. The things that you can do, like shoot the birds, or make your blocks go bang. What you have to learn is that you can't just do these things whenever you wish. You can hurt people."

"Bad hurt?" Dar asked.

"Yes, bad hurt. You must stop doing them."

Dar was silent for a while. Finally, he said, "I try."

"No Dar, you can't just try. You have to. I don't want anyone or anything else to be hurt."

"Dar hurt bad things? Like bad doggy? Bad man?"

His words sliced at Elizabeth. She stopped and slipped off the backpack, setting Dar on the sand. "Dar! Did you...do something to that dog? Was that you? And the-" Oh, dear God! Not the man! Dar couldn't possibly have done that. "Dar, the man was sick. You didn't do it." She could accept the birds, the blocks, and what happened to Sarah, but the dog had died, and so had the man. She just couldn't believe Dar had anything to do with their deaths.

"Man bad, mama. Got gun. Bad."

Elizabeth sat down in the sand, her legs giving out on her. "How, Dar. What made you do it?"

"Pinch...." Dar waved his hand in the air as if he could explain what he meant by that. "Give Dar pinchys."

"You felt something, like pinchys? Where?"

Dar pointed to his tummy and then to his chest. "Hurt! So Dar pushed and made bad man's insides wiggle." Dar put his finger in the air and wiggled it. His chubby face sobered and the color drained from it. "Dar do bad thing?" His lower lip trembled.

She looked down at him in fascinated horror. "Oh, Dar!" She pulled him to her and hugged him. "I don't know. I don't know what to do!"

Dar pulled back from her and studied her face. "Don't cry, mama. Dar be good. Otay?"

Elizabeth felt her hands tremble as she picked him up. "Okay." Her early hopes that all this would be gone tomorrow, eroded like a sand castle invaded by the sea.

"We see da bots?" He pointed at the jetty where a patchwork of sails dotted the blue sea.

"Yes, Dar. We'll see the boats, if you promise me you'll be good and not…well, that you won't make anything else…wiggle."

"Dar pro-mice," Dar said giving a tiny laugh, like a birdsong, that made Elizabeth's heart hurt.

Detective Ted Bearbower sat at his desk, leaning back in the chair, his shoes off and his feet propped on the edge of a slightly open desk drawer. He'd just finished reading the medical report on the man they'd found dead on the redwood deck, near the end of the peninsula. He blanched and reread the report.

Subject died of massive hemorrhage due to a total collapse and sudden deterioration of capillaries, veins, and arteries. Smooth tissue areas appeared to have jellied in places and become porous in others. No causes for such aberrations were found. Preliminary blood tests show no bacteria or virus present. Drugs were also negative; however, more sophisticated testing could possibly turn up something in this area.

Ted shook his head. "Good God!" he said aloud. "I've never heard of anything like this before."

Ajax glanced over at him from his desk. "Problem?"

Ted let out a growl low in his throat. "Our corpse turned out to be a pulpy mess."

"Oh yeah?"

"Coroner says the soft tissue had jellied in places."

"Jesus! Maybe it's Ebola! Christ, that bug's deadly! And contagious!"

Ted looked at Ajax's even featured face and dark sincere eyes and frowned. The eyes had gone enormously wide. "I don't think so. No mention of that here."

"They'd have to send samples to the CDC in Atlanta to check it out. Takes time. Christ, what if we've been exposed to it. It's about eight-five-percent fatal!"

"Well, AIDS, so far, is one-hundred-percent fatal, and we're around that one every day." Ted handed Ajax the medical report. "Take a look."

"Yeah, but AIDS can be treated for years! You can get a cocktail of drugs to fight it. And it isn't nearly as contagious as Ebola. In addition, the big E kills you in a week or less. If we touched the guy on the deck, we could be infected. Keyrist! I've had a headache all morning. That's how Ebola starts." Ajax's neck muscles went as taunt as violin wires.

Ted gave a sharp laugh. "Ajax, you little tarantula, you're getting neurotic. You watch too much TV. I'm sure if the coroner suspected something like that, he'd have warned us. Warned everyone for that matter!"

Ajax looked at the paper in his hand. "It says here they don't have any idea what caused him to die. They're going to do further tests. Probably sending stuff to the CDC. I told you." He tossed the paper back on Ted's desk.

"So, don't borrow trouble." Ted pulled open his desk drawer. "Here, have some aspirin for that headache."

Ajax took the bottle from him. "Thanks, I really need these." He poured out three of the white tablets, tossed them into his mouth and chewed them. "Nasty tasting things."

"Have you ever considered taking them with water?"

Ajax shrugged. "Okay, so we don't know yet about the first guy. How about the body we found down by the Fun Zone?"

Ted shook his head. "No report yet, but we should have it soon. Actually, that case bothers me more than the first one. The first guy probably died from some natural causes. But the second one is obviously a homicide. Someone drained all of his blood, or most of it, from the look of it." Ted felt himself shudder at the thought. He definitely wasn't up to coping with something so similar to those past serial killings.

Ted's phone rang and he picked it up. "Bearbower," he growled.

"Teddy Bear, its Stewart in the coroner's office. I have something for you on the Fun Zone case."

Ted winced again at his familiar nickname. "We were just talking about that one. Shoot."

"Well, the report isn't typed up yet, but I thought you would want to know. We found something...unusual."

Ted leaned forward in his chair. "Like what?"

"You remember those cases a year or so back? The Barry Brownstone cases. Sort of Vamipirish. Well, this one has some of the same earmarks. But even more surprising is the fact that in the small amount of blood left, we found an enormous amount of natural endorphins. Natural ones, not synthetic."

A cold chill swept over Ted. He heard the faint purring whisper of his breath as he absorbed the information. In the serial cases, all of the victims had large amounts of endorphins. The killer used a substance that souped up the body's natural endorphin level to where the victims were totally passive and unable to defend themselves.

"Teddy Bear? You still there?"

"Yeah," Ted said. "I'm here. But I don't like what you're saying. I mean, I watched that guy go to hell; he can't be back!"

"That's why I wanted you to know about this. Sorry."

"Thanks anyway." Ted hung up the phone and looked over at Ajax. "Same M.O.," he said. "Our new killer has the exact M.O. as the Brownstone serial killer."

"Hey, we checked out the cemeteries," Alex said. "Couldn't find the guy. Besides, didn't someone tell you they thought the guy had been cremated? Had the ashes sprinkled at sea because the guy loved to surf? Something like that." Ajax's face muscles relaxed as the conversation shifted away from the mention of the virus.

"Yeah, right. But come to think of it, I never did see the body after that night in the alley, where the guy was electrocuted. Never saw a doctor's death certificate either. He didn't have much family left around here, but a whole bunch of people showed up to claim the remains."

"You don't really think that the-."

"What? That the serial killer guy is still alive?" Ted shook his head. "That's impossible! If you'd seen it, you'd know." A sudden flashback hit Ted. For a second he could clearly see the dark storm-flooded alley where he'd perched on top of a shed and watched 22,000 volts of electricity fry Barry Brownstone. Smoke curled out the man's ears. His eyeballs boiled. Almost popped out of his head. No, he had to be dead! Ted squeezed his eyes closed to disperse the grisly image.

"Let's check with whatever family he has. Find out who sprinkled his ashes around."

"Just to find out if somehow the guy was resurrected?" Ted sighed. "Okay, if it will make you feel better."

Ajax looked off into space for a moment. "You know what though? It really doesn't matter, does it?"

"What doesn't matter?"

"If it's the same guy or…."

"Or what?"

"Or a copy-cat!"

Ted thought about it. A new cat or an old cat, all that counted was that someone was killing people again. He gave a short, bitter laugh. "I'm gonna retire," he said. "Go live in that cabin I bought in Julian where it's peaceful."

"Hey, not yet, I'm just getting used to you as a partner."

Ted swiveled his chair around and looked out the window beside the desk. Palm fronds blown down by the winds littered the grounds around the police station. He wondered how long the damn winds would hang around. Sometimes they stayed for a week or more, abating just enough to fool you into thinking they'd stopped. Then they would start up again, even fiercer. He could see a fog bank hanging off Catalina Island. Even though the wind was lighter now, it was still strong enough to keep the fog away from the mainland. One good thing about the winds, they made the city looked so bright and colorful. Cleared the air. Chased away the smog. However, even though Newport Beach was an attractive city on the surface, the underbelly was slowly becoming just as ugly as that of any other city.

Ted closed his eyes again, feeling them hot and tired against the lids. He sighed. Maybe he'd go by Maddy's again tonight. He'd called her twice already today and she had urged him to stop by after work. He didn't care if they made love or not. He just wanted her soft comfort. In addition, he could sure use some of her brownies right about now.

Ajax thumped his fingers against his desk in an odd, disjointed rhythm. "I ask you Ted," he said to the beat of his drumming. "Where else but here could you have the thrill of fleeing from the Ebola virus, and tracking down a vampire?"

Elizabeth reached the end of the peninsula, letting Dar walk with her down the long stretch of broken cement chunks that made up the jetty. Only a few people sat on the benches overlooking the bay or walked along the sandy paths. On the water, numerous sailors had taken the break in the heavy winds to sprout their boat's sails. Dar yelped with joy as he pointed out each one. Cabin cruisers were also gliding through the bay. Two were moored just below the jetty, their owners dangling fishing lines in the dark water. Elizabeth took in a deep breath. The sight of Newport bay meeting the ocean never failed to thrill her.

"Look," Dar squealed, pointing at a rocky shelf on the jetty. "Seal, mama! See seal!"

Elizabeth squinted against the late afternoon sun. Sure enough, a large harbor seal lay sunning itself on the rock. "Oh, yes, Dar, isn't it wonderful?"

"Dar like. I pet it?"

"No, Dar. Seals don't like to be petted. We can just look at him."

"Otay. Dar look."

"Would you like to walk a little further out on the jetty? It looks safe. No big waves and the wind is down."

"Walk," Dar chirped.

She took his hand and carefully led him down the cracked and jumbled chunks of concrete that were hard to call a path. She regretted not having brought her shoes along because the jetty was wet and slippery under her bare feet. The ocean rolled noisily in along one side of the jetty, while the water from the bay lapped against the other. Elizabeth took in another deep breath letting the cool sea air soothe her. The seal suddenly barked and she laughed along with Dar.

"Seal honk, Mama." Dar grinned up at her.

"Yes, it sure did."

Elizabeth took a long step from one piece of broken concrete to another, and then felt her foot slip almost as if someone had pushed it. She flung her free arm out to balance herself while still holding Dar's hand. But found it useless. Her footing was lost. She let out a yell as she went down, praying she wouldn't knock Dar over the edge of the jetty. Out of nowhere, two strong hands suddenly grabbed her by the shoulders and stopped her fall.

"Oh, thank you," she said breathlessly, and turned to see who had rescued her. As she did, she felt an odd stinging in her right arm, as if some venomous insect had bitten her. "Ouch! What the hell? What...was....?" She had a terrifying sensation as if someone had knocked the breath out of her. A dull red pulse thundered in her ears.

She heard a man's voice say, "Get them in the boat, fast!"

Where was Dar? She couldn't see him anywhere. Then her head began to spin like a silent gyroscope. She looked up at the wind-washed blue sky and watched it turn to velvet black.

CHAPTER NINE

"Dar!" Elizabeth yelled. Her tongue felt like it was stuffed with sand. "Where are you?" No answer! She tried to open her eyes, but couldn't. Her right arm ached fiercely but she didn't understand why. She attempted to sit up so she could find out what caused the pain, but discovered she couldn't move. She lay flat on her back, the ground moving uncomfortably beneath her.

She'd slipped on the jetty path! That's what had happened. Knocked her out. Maybe broke her arm. Damn, she knew better than to go barefooted. And Dar! Where was he! Had he fallen with her? She called his name again, but this time her voice only crackled like the croak of an aging frog.

She stopped struggling and tried to sort things out. Something else had happened that she couldn't remember. She could feel her heartbeat in her ears, racing like an engine. The ground under her lurched in one direction, then another. An odd slapping sound rose above that of her heartbeat, a familiar sound but she couldn't think what it was.

Her whole mouth tasted like wet newspapers. At last, she managed to open her eyes. Sunlight blinded her for a minute. She blinked and tried to focus her vision. With tremendous effort, she got herself to a sitting position, the pain in her arm slowly easing. The movement made her nauseous. She lay back again, breathing slowly, trying to calm the queasiness. More sounds invaded her ears. Someone talking. A dull rumbling. Creaking sounds. She lifted her head and felt it spin. Okay, she told herself. Don't panic. Nothing else hurt but her arm, so she probably wasn't badly injured. If only she could see well enough to find Dar.

"Dar, baby, where are you?" she cried. "Mama's here." She managed to sit up again, blinking her eyes trying to focus against the sunlight. Suddenly, she recognized the slapping sounds. Waves hitting the jetty? No, not exactly, but something like that.

Oh God, what if Dar's fallen into the bay? She felt the space around her, hoping to find him. "Dar! Please! Where are you?" she managed, her voice still hoarse. "Does someone have my child? Dar!"

A dark shadow hovered above her. "Your boy is just fine," a deep voice said. "Lay back and rest. He's resting too. He's not injured." She heard footsteps moving away from her.

A warm spill of relief washed over her. Dar was okay. He hadn't fallen into the sea. She blinked her eyes again, hard, and they finally began to focus. She sat sprawled on an odd-looking wooden floor. Where had that come from? No wood on the jetty. Everything kept undulating. Shaking her head, she tried to quell the dizziness. Then she realized she wasn't dizzy, the floor was actually moving. Suddenly she realized where she was...on a boat! The sound she heard was the sea lapping against the side of the boat.

She turned and looked over the railing. The boat was moving rapidly through the water and as she looked around, she saw nothing but ocean. The racing engine that was her heart went into overdrive. She tried to get to her feet, but her legs wobbled too much. She sat back down.

"Dar? Where are you?" she called. As far as she could see, he was nowhere in the cockpit where she sat.

"He's safe below," said a voice somewhere above her. She looked up against the sun and saw a man standing on the fly bridge. At first, he was only a dark silhouette.

"Let me see him," she demanded. "Where are we? Why are we here? What happened?"

The man began to descend the latter to the cockpit. "You took a bad fall off the jetty into the ocean. We picked you up. Your son also."

Elizabeth looked at her clothing. None of it was wet. "I don't understand. Where are you taking me?"

"You've been...out of it for a while. We're heading for our mooring. There was no place to put you ashore by the jetty. We thought you should have medical treatment."

As the man came closer, she could see him better. He had a dark, mahogany-tanned face, square and rough looking, with black eyes and a thatch of coarse black hair. At first, she thought he was coming toward her, but then he veered and went to a storage box at the stern of the boat and took something out. She couldn't see what it was.

Slowly, Elizabeth got to her feet, gripping the deck with her toes, trying to keep her balance. She made it to a bench seat without falling and sat down heavily. Her body felt ten times its normal weight.

Something was wrong with all this. She knew she hadn't fallen into the ocean. Her hair would have stayed sticky from the seawater. She looked in the direction the boat was heading and saw a faint outline of land. But it wasn't the mainland. It was Catalina Island. They were in the middle of the San Pedro Channel! Why was this man lying to her? None of it made sense.

She rose from the bench, and with concentrated effort got her wobbly legs in sync with the movements of the boat. Then she carefully made her way toward the cabin door. She had to find Dar. She slid the cabin door open and looked in. It took a moment for her eyes to adjust to the dim light. Directly below her were ladder-like steps. Gradually she began to make out a small galley and beyond that, several bunks. Dar lay on the one farthest from her. From what she could see, he was asleep.

"Dar?" she called huskily. "Dar, sweetheart, it's Mama." He didn't stir and Elizabeth felt a stab of alarm. "Dar!" she called louder and began to climb down the steps.

When she reached him, she saw his tiny chest move up and down. Thank God! He was breathing! She picked him up and held him in her arms, embracing the warmth of his body. "Dar," she whispered in his ear. "Wake up, sweetheart." She felt him stir slightly. "Come on, Dar. Open your eyes for Mama."

His eyelids flickered, opened for a second, and then closed. "Dar seep, Mama."

"Okay. Dar sleep." She carried him through the galley and made her way up the ladder to the cockpit. With the weakness in her legs still slowing her, she wasn't sure she could make it to the bench with him, but she did. She sat down, still cradling him in her arms.

The wind rose suddenly, bringing with it a heavy smell of brine. The Santa Ana winds had kicked in again, blowing salt foam across the stern. The water turned from gentle swells to rugged whitecaps, and the lurch of the boat became rougher. Now that she had Dar in her arms, she felt better. But what now! What the hell was going on here? Could it be true that they were taking her to medical care? And why to Catalina? She decided to just sit and wait. There wasn't much more she could do in the middle of the ocean.

Andy sat in his office looking at the stack of manuscript pages he'd completed in the last two hours. He felt better about his writing now. The writer's block he'd felt moving in on him seemed to have edged away. He wanted Lizzy to read his latest work to assure him that it was as good as usual. With so many books behind him, he was often unable to tell anything about the quality. The fact that they sold well should have convinced him of their worthiness, but he still troubled about it. What if the effects of Sunshine eventually wore off? What if his body and brain became immune to it? He gave a little bark of a laugh. What the hell was he worrying about? After all, some people had been taking Sunshine for more years than he had, with no sign of anything like that. Anyway, he and Lizzy had made a great deal of money already, enough to retire on early.

He looked at his watch. Almost four p.m. He frowned. Lizzy and Dar had been gone for close to two hours. Lizzy never took Dar out for that long. She usually restricted their walks on the beach to a half-hour or less. He pushed back the manuscript, got up, and made his way into the living room. He opened the sliding glass door and walked out onto the deck. The wind hit him and tore at his cotton shirt. Christ! He'd warned Lizzy that the wind might come up again. Dar shouldn't be out in all this blowing sand. It stung Andy on the side of his cheek and he winced. Well, maybe they'd stopped off at Tyree's and had gotten to talking. Those two often forgot the time when they got together. He went back into the house and dialed Tyree's number. When she didn't answer, he hung up and tried the Zipper sisters. No answer there either. Obviously, Lizzy hadn't stopped at either of the houses. Now where in the hell had the two of them gone?

He decided to walk down the beach to the jetty and see if he could spot them. They might have gone to the Fun Zone, he realized. Dar adored the merry-go-round. But with this wind up again, they should have started home by now. Only a few hardy souls walked the beach in the hot wind. Andy found the jetty deserted. He turned and made his way back to where he could cut through the beachfront homes, and headed for the Balboa Fun Zone.

The Zone turned out to be almost as deserted as the end of the peninsula. Most of the rides had shut down due to the wind. Tour boats tied to the dock slammed roughly against the pilings. Only the video arcades did any business. Several teen-agers in ragged Levis shoved quarters into the flashing machines. However, Lizzy and Dar were nowhere in sight.

It would be dark in another hour. What was Lizzy thinking of, staying out so late with Dar? A sense of unease nagged at him. He remembered the incident with the birds and wondered if something like that had happened again. He didn't want to believe his son was responsible, but despite his fighting off the thought, somewhere in the back of his mind he had to admit it seemed the only explanation. He turned and headed home. No other place where they could have gone came to mind. Well, he supposed they'd call if there was a problem. His uneasiness grew as he battled the blistering wind toward home.

Through the window beside his desk, Ted watched the daylight fade. It would be a glorious sunset. When desert winds blew all the smog and junk out to sea, the debris made for brilliantly colorful sunsets. Much like the debris from a volcanic eruption. Beauty from ugliness. Nature's balance, he thought.

"Hey, Ted!" Ajax said. "Don't you think we could cut out of here now?" He scratched at the five-o'clock shadow on his face. "I've got to get home. Jenny is making cold lobster salad for dinner and I'm a dead man if I'm not there. She's taking gourmet cooking classes."

Ted laughed. "I think I'll go home with you. Sounds good."

"Not at the price of lobster, you won't!" Ajax got up and put his jacket over his arm. "But I'll think about you when I eat it."

"Thanks a lot," Ted said. "You're a real buddy."

"Are you leaving now?"

"Not just yet. I'm trying to ferret out some things about these new cases. I'd like to talk with the coroner. Maybe they left out some little things that might help. Little things often turn the trick."

"Yeah, well okay. See ya tomorrow." Ajax gave him a mock salute then turned and walked away. Ted heard Ajax's rubber soled shoes squeaking like a tiny mouse fading away into the distance.

Ted sat alone in the detective's room. The night-shift people were in the coffee room. He liked the quiet. It gave him a chance to think. He went over each of the cases in his mind. So far, it seemed that the dead man on the deck of the house on the peninsula had died of odd, but natural causes. Yet something about the description on the medical report caused him to wonder. He had to agree with Ajax that it did sound alarmingly like the Ebola virus. However, it had already been ruled out. No outbreak of it had been reported anywhere in the U.S. to date. Except in animals. Simians. Besides, that outbreak had been quelled, the monkey house thoroughly sterilized. He couldn't offhand remember where that had happened. No. It wasn't Ebola. Nevertheless, what in heaven's name could cause a person's blood vessels and capillaries to disintegrate? To have it happen so suddenly, so completely. He wasn't sure he really wanted to know. He opened the folder for that case and perused it. Then he closed it and shook his head.

He opened the folder for the second case, the man they'd found near the Fun Zone. So far, no finalized medical report. He felt alarmed by the fact that Stewart in the coroner's office had called to tell him about the enormous amount of endorphins found in the man's blood. Ted looked at his own scribbled notes from the scene.

> The victim's throat has been cut with
> what appears to be a slightly blunt object.
> The edges are ragged. No sign of blood
> anywhere. Assailant had scrupulously
> cleaned up.

Ted leaned back in his chair and tried to relax. At least this wasn't like the M.O. in the serial killings. In those cases, the victim's throats had been cut with an extremely sharp blade. From each victim, the killer had taken one or more bites of flesh. If this was the work of a copycat, the person wasn't getting it right, something copycats usually took pride in. Yet, if it were the same person, then it wasn't right either. He frowned. Christ! The puzzle pieces refused to go together. He wasn't sure which he preferred, the copycat or the real thing. Both ideas made him shudder.

Restless, he closed the folder, and opened the first one again. The M.E. had noted the effect of whatever it was that killed the victim, but not the cause. He picked up the phone and dialed the coroner's office. It rang several times before someone answered.

"Dr. Kimijuju," the voice said.

"Oh, I thought Stewart would answer," Ted said apologetically.

"Gone home. It's Bearbower, right? What can I do for you?"

"The case of the man found on the peninsula. I was wondering if there was any more information than what was in the preliminary report."

"Is puzzling," Kimijuju said. "Very puzzling. I am not seeing any case like this before."

"Yeah, me either."

"It's as if someone has taken all of the man's molecules and put them in a blender. Just whipped up everything. Made holes in everything. He body is much like a sieve. His blood volume dropped fast. Died in minutes. Everything leaked out from everywhere. Nowhere else am I ever seeing such a thing."

Ted heard the man sigh, and pictured the doctor shaking his head. Kimijuju, a tall, reedy man in his fifties who always wore round gold-rimmed glasses and spoke with a slight East Indian accent, had worked on the Brownstone serial killer case with him, as well as a case ten years before called the Blackbird murders. The man was sharp. He never missed a thing in an autopsy. If this guy felt puzzled over the manner of death, it had to be an enigma.

"Are you going to call it natural causes?" Ted asked.

A long pause followed and Ted wondered if they had been cut off. Then he heard the doctor sigh again.

"Not necessarily. I know of no disease that would cause this. But then, I also know of no external thing that would do this. We will wait until the other tests come back. If they are showing nothing, then we will investigate outside causes."

Ted thought about it. "What possible outside element could churn a man up like that?"

"I am not knowing this yet. Perhaps some form of radiation. Maybe he was working around a strong electro-magnetic field. Or possibly near strong lasers. These things can affect a human adversely. Then again it could have been some experimental drug. We should know soon. "

Ted considered what Kimijuju had said. "He appears to have been a hard case criminal with a long record. Even if he had been exposed to something like you mentioned, how come it happened so suddenly? He was working the job, wanting to rob the Rosemonds. He was probably just standing on their deck. Even some form of radiation would show symptoms long before death, wouldn't it? Could it have been something he came in contact with while standing there?"

"Yes, that is what I am thinking, but it would seem impossible to encounter such a thing at the place where he was found. I'm sorry I am not yet having more answers for you detective."

"Yes. Well, thank you. I appreciate your time."

"Is no problem. If you have further question, call me." Dr. Kimijuju hung up.

Outside forces! The thought rambled through his head. He should to try and track the movements of the man before he ended up on the deck of the Rosemond family on the peninsula. He should interview the couple again and see if they noticed anything they hadn't mentioned. Any strange noise. Anything that might have led to the man's death. He should also talk with the redhead who lived next door. What was her name? Rattigan. Tyree. A strange one, that. Still, she usually seemed cooperative. After all, she was the one who fingered the serial killer. He should be grateful for that.

He made a note on his desk pad to call and set up appointments with both the Rosemonds and the Rattans tomorrow. For now, he was through. He considered going to Maddy's right away, but decided against it. He heard his stomach rumble. What he needed was a big meal first. Perhaps a pile of good old fried chicken with mashed potatoes and coleslaw. Maybe have a beer with it. After that, perhaps he'd have Maddy for dessert.

As she sat clutching Dar, Elizabeth felt the swells under the boat rise, causing it to pitch and sway uncomfortably. When the boat rose to the top of a swell, mounds of cinnamon-colored kelp rushed by the railing. The taste of salt invaded Elizabeth's mouth. Dar was awake, somewhat, although still slack-eyed and blinking at the strange surroundings. She felt a twinge in her right arm and began exploring the reasons why it hurt. Something had stung her, right after she'd started to fall. Not an insect, something else. A needle! Yes, that's what it had to be. That's why she'd been_unconscious. They had injected her with something. But why? What could they want from her? Granted, she and Andy had some money, but did they have enough to warrant kidnapping? And Dar, had they injected him? That would explain his sleepiness. Why in God's name would anyone do that to them?

She looked up at the boat's bridge and saw a second man she'd not seen before. This one stood a lot shorter than the first, and was completely bald. A squat, trollish man, he had an ugly mouth and huge eyes. The two men talked quietly together. Elizabeth couldn't make out what they were saying. The slap of the sea against the boat's hull and the rumbling of the engine drowned out their words.

"Hey!" she yelled up at them. "One of you come down here and explain what's going on. Why are we headed toward Catalina?"

The two men looked at her, then went back to talking, completely ignoring her. Dar sat up in her lap and looked around brighter-eyed now. He rubbed at his mouth with a fist and then yawned.

"On bot, Mama?"

"Yes, Dar, a boat." She ran her fingers through his golden curls and found them damp with salt spray.

"Where go?"

"I don't know. We seem to be heading toward an island. Do you know what an island is?"

Dar frowned then said. "No."

"Well," Elizabeth said, hoping to keep his attention so he wouldn't be upset by what had happened. She pointed toward the dark form of Catalina and realized her hand was shaking. "See, that's an island there."

Dar frowned again, and then looked up at the ships bridge, at the two men. "Who dey?"

"I don't know. We were both…well, kind of asleep. When I woke up, we were here with them." Elizabeth wasn't certain how to explain it.

"Bad men," Dar said, his frown darkening. "Give Dar ouchy."

"It's okay, Dar. I don't think they'll hurt us." She wasn't at all sure about that but didn't want to frighten him unnecessarily.

"No," Dar said, his face glum. "Bad men. Give Dar prickles."

A jab of alarm struck Elizabeth. "Dar, remember your promise! No more…ah…wiggles."

Dar looked at her, then back at the men and shook his head.

She turned his face toward her so that he had to look at her. "You promised me, Dar. No more! No matter what!"

Dar let out a soft sigh and finally nodded. "Otay," he said quietly, his eyes still shifting to keep a watch on the two men.

Elizabeth pulled his head down on her shoulder and rocked him.

"You want me to sing you a song?"

"No," he said. "Dar got prickles."

"They'll go away. Just let them go away." She began to hum softly and at the same time tried to quell her rising fear. The bow of the boat rose up, riding a huge swell, then nosed down, leaving Elizabeth's stomach at the top of the swell. Dar let out a squeal. She looked down at him to see if the squeal came from fear or fun. He had a half smile on his face and she realized he'd enjoyed the roller-coaster action. The boat rode another swell, then another and Elizabeth felt her stomach spasm. Salt spray hit her, soaking her shirt. Oh, God! Don't let me get seasick. Or Dar! How much further to Catalina, she wondered. She couldn't tell from the dark shadow of the island how far away they were. Shortly afterward, Dar's squeals turned to tiny moans.

"Are you okay?" she asked.

"No bot," Dar said. "Ups too big."

"Sweetheart, we can't get off until we get to the island. There's water all around us." She hugged him closer, trying to keep the salt spray from soaking him.

The squat, troll-like man began climbing down the ladder to the cockpit. Dar sat forward in her lap like a guard dog. She saw his eyes squint and he pursed his mouth forward. "Dar," she warned softly.

Dar didn't move. He just sat there looking at the man as he approached. When he reached them, he kneeled down in front of Dar.

"Well, well. I see you're awake, little man. Would you like to come up on the bridge and steer the boat?" Flashing sunlight gleamed off the man's baldhead as the boat moved up and down. "Come on, you can drive if you want." He reached out for Dar.

"No!" Dar shouted, pulling back from him. "You bad man." He put his arms around Elizabeth's neck and held on tightly.

"Hey there, I'm not going to hurt you. I just thought you'd like to be the captain of the boat for a while. We'll be in Catalina soon. Not much time left."

Dar glowered at him. The man smiled which twisted his ugly mouth into a grimace. Then, suddenly, he reached out and grabbed Dar, wrenching him away from Elizabeth. She let out a scream but the wind scooped it out of her mouth and blew it away. Dar began to yell and kick. The man carried him to the ladder and took him up to the fly-bridge.

"I've got the boy," he yelled to the other man. "Put the engine on auto and take care of the woman."

Elizabeth stood up and gripped the railing. She had to go after Dar, but she could barely stand, much less navigate. No time to develop sea legs. She dropped down on all fours and began to crawl toward the ladder. Before she reached it, the tall man was standing in front of her. She sat back on her haunches and glared up at him.

"What in the hell do you think you're doing? What is all this?" she yelled.

The man looked at her dispassionately then grabbed her wrist and yanked her to her feet. With little effort, he pulled her toward the side railing, picked her up, and held her over his head. She let out a scream! Dear God! He was going to throw her overboard! She had so little strength she found herself unable to struggle. She could swim, but not far enough to reach dry land! They were going to kill her! And maybe Dar. But why? For a moment she was too stunned to be afraid. Below she saw the foam-laced sea swelling toward her.

"Lambis, you dumb Greek!" the troll man yelled. "Weight her down! We don't want her washing ashore tonight."

The Greek lowered her, held both wrists firmly in one of his massive hands, opened the storage box, and lifted out a white snake of rope.

Oh my God, Elizabeth realized, this is really happening! Severe tremblings shook her but they were carried off by waves of wind. He roughly bound her hands and feet so tightly she could feel her circulation slow. He reached back into the storage box and took out what appeared to be a weight belt, the kind divers wore. He fastened it around her waist then started to pick her up again.

"Wait!" she screamed. "Please! Wait! Tell me why! What about my son?"

"We don't need you," the Greek said, his voice deep and rumbling. "Just the kid."

"Dar? But why? What for? Is someone paying you?" She'd heard of things like that. People wanted blue-eyed, blond children. She felt herself begin to cry. "We can pay you more money!" she cried. "Andy and I have money. We'll pay whatever you want."

The Greek shook his head. "No," he said, lifting her again. "They don't want you around. They don't want any interference."

"Who?" she cried. "Who's paying you?" Struggling frantically, she tried to free herself, but it was useless. She thought about falling into the sea with her hands and feet tied and with the weights tied round her waist. How long could she hold her breath? How long before she had to inhale water. She couldn't believe she was actually going to die.

"Dar!" she yelled. "It's okay to wiggle!" She looked up to see the other man holding Dar. Dar gave the man a strange look. With a yelp, he dropped Dar as if he were boiling hot.

"Mama!" Dar screamed. "Bad men! Hurt Mama!" He couldn't get to his feet because of the motion of the ship, so he quickly crawled toward the ladder. The man made no attempt to go after him.

"Dar, please, wiggle!" she yelled.

Reaching the ladder, Dar began to climb down but his chubby little legs failed him and he lost his grip, and fell, hitting the deck with what must have been a painful thump.

"Mama say no wiggle!" He cried, sitting up and looking over at her.

Elizabeth could hear a sob in the Dar's voice. She'd told him no, and he wanted to mind her. Now she'd confused him by telling him it was okay. Please, God, she said quietly, let him help me.

The Greek, obviously enjoying the peculiar conversation, laughed huskily. She could feel his hands grip her more firmly and then move her out over the side of the boat. Dark waves, like hungry animals rumbled below her.

Dar crawled to the Greek and began flailing his chubby little arms at him. Then he stopped his struggle and looked up at the Greek. The Greek peered down at him, a puzzled look on his face. Slowly, he lowered Elizabeth toward the deck and gave his head a shake. When he tried to lift Elizabeth again, he stumbled and dropped her. She hit the edge of the railing and, for a moment, she was certain she would roll over into the water. The boat lurched, tilting her even more precariously, then lurched back, throwing her onto the deck of the cockpit.

She squirmed around so she could see what was happening. The Greek stood a few feet from her, grasping his arms around his middle, moaning.

Please, untie me. I can help," Elizabeth said. "Please!"

The man bent over her, glaring at her. "What the hell is happening?"

"Just untie me and I may be able to stop it."

To her surprise, the man reached down and jerked the ropes on her loose. Then he began to stagger. It was too late for him, Elizabeth realized. As she watched, the man began to bleed. First from his nose came a thread of scarlet. Then a rush of blood welled up in his ears and spilled down the sides of his neck. The Greek rubbed his ears with his fingers and looked at the blood that had come from them.

"What?" he growled. "What's happening? I'm…bleeding like a stuck pig!"

"Dar," Elizabeth whispered and looked away. The boat moaned in her ears, like someone in pain. She should stop him now, but if she did, the man would probably still be able kill her. She had no choice but to let Dar do whatever he could do.

She listened to the moaning of the boat for a moment, and then finally looked back at the Greek. Blood now ran from his eyes and mouth, and oozed out of the pores of his skin. Dear sweet Jesus! Her baby son could kill people! Just like that! Without even touching them. She had no idea how, or what was actually happening inside the Greek. But she knew it was deadly. She lowered her head against the boat's deck and closed her eyes in dark horror. She did not want to see what might happen next

CHAPTER TEN

Andy sat on the living room sofa staring at his watch. Ten minutes to five. He felt a growing sense of panic. Something had to be wrong. The sun was almost down, and still no sign of Lizzy or Dar. He wanted to call the police, but realized they would not take him seriously at this point. He picked up the phone and dialed Tyree's number. To his relief, this time she answered.

"Hello," Tyree said.

"Tyree, its Andy. I'm worried. Lizzy took Dar for a walk over three hours ago, and they aren't home yet. It's not like Lizzy. She would call if she was going to be this late. Her phone's not on."

Tyree was silent for a moment, and then said, "Right. Well, maybe they stopped to eat or something."

"Lizzy wouldn't do that! Not without telling me, or calling me. They were just going to walk to the jetty and back."

"Okay, listen sweetie, doesn't panic. Boo and I will come over and see what we can do. I'm sure there's an explanation."

"Tyree?" Andy said. "I haven't wanted to admit this, but what if...I mean, all this about Dar, and the things everyone thinks he can do. Like what happened with Sarah last night. What if...."

"If he'd done anything...whatever it was...in public, I'm sure you would have heard about it by now," Tyree assured him. "Just hang in there. We'll be right over."

Andy hung up the phone and leaned back against the cushioned wicker sofa. He fingered the blue print that Lizzy had used to cover the cushions. A seashell pattern. It seemed such a short time ago when he and Lizzy had been penniless, moving here to her Aunt Mary's old house, with little hope for the future. They had such hunger then, for money, for success, for personal fulfillment. Now, thanks to Sunshine they had all of that. Yet, now, none of it seemed important. If anything had happened to Dar and Lizzy...well, he couldn't imagine life without them.

A rap on the sliding glass door startled him. Tyree slid the door open without waiting for him to get up. "It's just me," Tyree said. "Boo had a phone call, so I came over by myself. Any word yet?"

"No," Andy said, shaking his head. "Nothing. I walked the beach earlier, and checked out the Fun Zone. No trace of them."

"Okay," Tyree said sitting beside Andy. She reached for the phone. "Then maybe we should start by calling the lifeguard station, to see if anything might have happened on the beach."

Andy sat forward. "That's a good idea. And we can check the hospitals, and then see if the police have any record of an accident or anything."

When Tyree began dialing, Andy got up and paced across the Persian rug in front of the sofa. For once, he felt glad that Tyree was the take-charge type. She could mother hen you to death at times but now he found the trait comforting. He walked to the sliding glass door and peered out, hoping that he would see Lizzy with Dar snoozing in the backpack heading toward the house. However, the wind was up strong. The sand blew in slivery waves, and the only person he could see on the beach was a lone fisherman sitting in a folding chair, his fishing pole pegged in a holder. That fellow must be the consummate fisherman, Andy thought. He'd seen him out there every day for God knows how long. Wind, rain, fog, nothing kept him away.

He turned back to Tyree who was dialing again, and listened, not really hearing the words, just picking up the sound and rhythm of her voice. He purposely tuned her out. If the news was bad, he didn't want to hear. Finally, Tyree hung up the phone and looked up at him.

"Sorry, sweetie, but so far, nothing. I still need to check with the police though."

He nodded. "Okay. Listen, I think I'll go fix us some coffee. I could use a caffeine boost."

"Could you make that iced coffee?" Tyree asked.

"Sounds good," Andy agreed. Better than hot coffee, he thought, with the weather still so hot. In the kitchen it only took him a few minutes to fill tall glasses with ice, and pour in some cold coffee left from breakfast. He added sugar and milk to both of them and carried them back to the living room. The ice in the glasses played music as he walked.

Tyree, the phone still to her ear, raised her hand, as if signaling him she was on to something. "Yes," she said into the phone. "Okay. That would be fine. Thank you." She put the phone down, and then motioned to Andy to sit beside her.

He handed her one of the glasses and sat down, a terrible weariness tugging at him. "What?" he asked. "Was that the police? Did they...?"

"No, nothing. However, they had me talk with that detective who came out this morning. Bearbower, I think it is. Since they found the body on your deck, they wondered if it had a connection to Lizzy and Dar's...well, our not knowing where they are."

"Is Bearbower going to do anything?"

"Normally he wouldn't, but since we got to know him during the Brownstone case, he said he would help. He's coming out here in a few minutes. He says he'll put out a bulletin to the squad cars to be on the lookout for them. That should help."

Andy sighed. "You know, we're going to feel pretty foolish if all of a sudden the two of them walk in that door." He looked out the sliding glass door. The wind blew all alone on the beach now except for a few hearty sea birds. Even the lone fisherman had left. A half sun now crouched low on the horizon like a great orange cat, its glow staining the ocean the color of hot coals.

"God, I wish they would walk in right now. I'm as worried as you are. As you said, it isn't like Liz not to call."

Andy felt the hairs on his arms tingle. "You really don't think they're connected, do you?"

"What?"

"The body on the deck and...." He paused, feeling as if someone had sucked the breath out of him. "Lizzy and Dar being so late?"

Tyree reached out and took his hand. "No, of course not. The police are just checking things out. If it wasn't for the body this morning, and Bearbower, they probably would make us wait twenty-four hours before looking into it." She gave his hand a squeeze then sat back and sipped at her iced coffee.

Andy did the same, savoring the slightly bitter taste of the strong coffee. As he swallowed, he felt the chill of it snake all the way down to his stomach, cooling him. It was past Dar's suppertime, he reminded himself. He'd be so hungry by now. The sense of panic rose in him. Maybe he should take the car and go out looking again. Tyree could stay here in case they came back.

"Andy, are you okay? All the color's drained out of your face." She reached over and brushed his too long hair off his forehead. "Come on, don't fret. I'm sure they're okay. Lizzy will have a hilarious story to tell when she gets back. Wait and see."

"I can't just sit here. I've got to look for them." The phone rang, making Andy jump, his bones vibrating inside his skin. Before he could reach it, Tyree answered it.

"Rosemond residence, Tyree speaking." Tyree frowned slightly, looked up at Andy and frowned more, making a deep furrow in her forehead. "Yes. Yes we are. Are you certain?"

Andy closed his eyes. Oh, God! Bad news. He knew it was bad news. A car had hit them. Or worse! He opened his eyes and looked quizzically at Tyree. She put up her hand, signaling for him to wait. It seemed like forever that Tyree listened to whoever it was on the other end of the line.

"Okay. Yes," she finally said. "I'll do that. Thank you. We appreciate it." Tyree put the phone down and was silent for a moment.

Every nerve in Andy's body felt raw. "What? What's happened?"

"Well," Tyree began. "That was the Balboa Lifeguard Station calling back. After I spoke with them, someone called in about something they'd seen earlier that had been bothering them."

"What? They saw them! Saw Lizzy and Dar? Where?"

Tyree raised her hand again. "Just listen. This person, a woman, said she was walking her dog at the Peninsula point. She saw a woman with a young child walking out on the jetty. From her description, it appeared that the woman became ill suddenly. The woman collapsed and two men caught her. The part that bothered the caller was that instead of going for help, they put her and the child on board a boat that had been moored near the jetty. She tried to see the name of it, but couldn't. Then the boat started up and headed for open sea, instead of into the bay."

Andy jumped to his feet. "It was Lizzy. It had to be. But why would they take them to sea? Why not call paramedics? Get them to Hoag Hospital fast? What was wrong with them? Getting ill like that! Oh, Christ Tyree! What can we do? Is the Coast Guard going to look for the boat?"

"Yes. But it won't be easy to find. Not a couple of hours later."

"A chopper then. Call the police and get a chopper to look for them."

Tyree got up and stood beside him. "The detective will be here any time now. Just take it easy. We'll find them."

Andy moved to the sliding glass door and looked out at the sunset. The orange had changed to a metallic purple, the color of fresh bruises. He could hear the thunder of surf over the wail of the wind. The sea looked rough. Huge swells waved translucent scarves of white foam lace. What if Lizzy and Dar were still out there somewhere on that troubled ocean? He knew the small craft warnings would be up in this weather. No one in their right mind would take a boat out in that. Especially so late in the day. But someone had, and he sure as hell was going to find out who and why.

≈ ≈

The man who had been holding Elizabeth sat on the deck, blood streaming from his eyes, nose, mouth, and ears. It was close to dark, but Elizabeth could still see the blood, and smell its metallic stench. Her stomach spasmed and she struggled not to get sick. The boat was riding giant swells, which didn't help. The troll-man on the bridge stared down at the Greek, his speech obviously snatched from him by the sight of so much blood.

"It's you, kid! It has to be you!" the man yelled down at them. "They told me you could do things. To be careful. But, I never figured on anything like this! What the hell did you do to him?"

Dar looked sullen. "Bad. Dar wiggled."

"Ah, shit! Look at him. I think he's dying!" the man cried out.

With the sea so rough, Dar went down on his hands and knees and started crawling toward the ladder. Elizabeth tried to sit up, but she found herself slipping in the Greek's blood. Dar didn't look at her, but kept his eyes on the troll-man on the fly-bridge.

"Dar! Listen to Mama. That's enough. Now come here to Mama." Elizabeth's voice grew stronger as she called to him. She managed to get a purchase on the slippery deck and pulled herself to a sitting position. When she looked over at the Greek, he was slumped on the deck. She wondered if he was breathing. If they could call the Coast Guard, maybe they could get him to help.

Dar turned around and began crawling toward Elizabeth. When he was finally next to her, she looked up at the man on the bridge. "This man needs help. Do you have a cell phone or a boat to shore radio? Can you call the Coast Guard?"

The man didn't answer. He was only a shadowy figure, moving

102

slowly about the bridge. She tried to make out what he was doing, but found it impossible. The red glow of the sunset, so brilliant just a short while ago, had burned out, as if someone had turned off a light switch, leaving the horizon swathed in streaks of deep purple.

"Dar bad boy," Dar said to her.

"It's okay, Dar. The man would have thrown me overboard."

"Dar need Mama." Dar put out his chubby hand and touched the side of her face.

"Listen, Dar, we've got to figure out a way to get back home. These men are crazy." Elizabeth spoke more to herself, than to Dar. To plan aloud made her feel as if she really could do something about the situation.

Dar sat on the deck next to Elizabeth who put her arms around him. He looked down at the pools of blood around them. "Dar go home now, otay."

Elizabeth held him closer. "Yes, Dar. Mama wants to go home, too. Maybe now the other man will let us. Maybe he'll call the Coast Guard."

"Fat chance, lady," the troll-man growled, his voice much closer to her than she expected. She looked up to see he had come down the ladder and was standing just a few feet from them. "I hadn't bargained on something like this. I'm not paid enough."

"Who paid you…to do this?" she asked. "And why? What do they want with us…with Dar? He's just a baby."

"Bad man," Dar said pointing at the man.

"I see now why they want this kid. They're going to study him, find out how he does these things. Probably plan to make a fortune fooling around with his DNA."

Elizabeth squinted against the growing darkness. She wondered what this man would do next. If he threatened them, she was certain he'd end up like the Greek. She could see he held something in both hands but she couldn't make out what. A huge swell lifted the boat then dropped it sharply. Seawater poured over the bow and sluiced down the foredeck toward them. Salt spray, like flying buckshot, hit their faces. Dar put his hands over his eyes and let out a small cry.

"It's okay, Dar. It won't hurt you. Just pretend you're walking in the waves with Daddy." She wiped his face with her fingers.

"Daddy come get us?" Dar asked.

"Maybe he will," she said, trying to sound reassuring.

Deadly Urges

The troll-man moved toward them and then squatted down in front of Dar. Dar pressed himself against Elizabeth. She wrapped her arms around him and as tight as she could.

"Okay, little man. I'm not going to hurt you or your Mama. I promise."

Dar blinked at him, his small mouth pinched together. He slowly shook his head then said. "Man give Dar pinchys!"

"Now, now, I just want to...." Suddenly, the man went rigid. He let out a gasp. "No! Now don't.... I...."

His right arm flailed about and Elizabeth saw something shiny in his hand. A syringe! He was going to inject Dar with something. He wanted to put him out, so he would be helpless. But Dar had sensed that, and stopped him. The syringe flew out of the man's hand and tumbled across the deck. Then Elizabeth looked at his other hand. It held a small, silvery gun. Even in the darkness, she could see its polished metal. With all of her strength, she held Dar and swung him around, away from the path of the bullet, leaving herself exposed. But the shot never came. She looked back to see that the man had been pushed about five feet away from them. He struggled to his feet, searching the deck for the gun. Then it began, the same way as it had with the Greek. Blood seeped from his nose and ears. The man stumbled to the railing and leaned against it.

"Stop it!" the man screamed. "You're the goddamned kid from hell! I'll find that gun and blow you into a million pieces! I swear!" He looked at the deck, spotted the gun, and started to move toward it. But Dar had turned back and now looked at him with his eyes gone dark and that odd, greenish aura around him that Elizabeth had seen the night before at Tyree's. The man slammed back hard against the railing.

"Dar," she commanded. "It's time to stop. It's okay now. You've wounded him. Stop! We can get to the controls. Call the Coast Guard. They'll find us."

But the man started screaming and Elizabeth felt her bones go icy cold. "Dar! Please! Listen to Mama! Stop. Now!"

Dar turned and looked at her. He blinked and she saw tears welling in his eyes. "Don't know how!"

"Try, Dar. Try!" She made a supreme effort and got to her feet, her legs less wobbly than before. She lifted Dar to his feet and put her hands on his shoulders. "Come on, try!"

Dar looked back at the man and gave his head a shake. "Wiggle too much," he said.

The troll-man stopped screaming as a stream of blood flowed out of his mouth. His eyes seeped blood, as did his skin. The boat hit another high swell, and Elizabeth gripped Dar even tighter. On the other side of the swell, the boat nose-dived steeply. As it hit flat water, the sea roared over the bow, reaching higher than the fly bridge, and came cascading down on the cockpit. It hit Elizabeth and Dar with a roar, slamming them down on the deck, and rolling them against the transom. As the water drained away, Dar came up coughing, and Elizabeth felt as if she'd swallowed a gallon of salt water.

As the boat leveled, Elizabeth looked around. The deck was washed clean of both blood and men. "Sweet Jesus!" she whispered. "They're gone!" She could see no trace of them. She got to her feet and admonished Dar to stay where he was. She looked over the railing at the florescent wake of the boat. Nothing. Nothing at all but a lacy veil of dark red foam, trailing away from them. She slid down beside Dar and pulled him to her. It was as if the two men had never existed.

"Bad men gone," Dar said, looking up at her. "Dar do dat, Mama?" he asked.

Elizabeth hugged him close. "No, Dar," she assured him. "The ocean did it. We'll talk about it later. Right now, before we hit another one of those swells, we have to call for help."

Dar leaned his head against her and yawned. "Dar tired." He popped his thumb into his mouth and closed his eyes.

Elizabeth looked at him, at his wet mop of gold curls, at the way his long pale eyelashes rested against his cheeks, at his rosebud mouth sucking away on his thumb, and she began to sob.

Ted Bearbower lifted his hand to rap on the glass of the sliding door, and then hesitated. He had an uncomfortable feeling of deja vu. He really didn't want to investigate this. Didn't want to get involved in anything at all with these people on the Peninsula. His plans for a huge chicken dinner and then some time with Maddy had all gone down the drain. He felt irritable as hell, and twice as resentful. Nevertheless, it was his job, and he always did his job, no matter what. Maybe he should be less conscientious. But he knew it wasn't his nature. He rapped sharply on the glass and then stood back. The lights were on inside the house, and he could see into the living room. He felt as if he were invading their privacy. He supposed people who lived on the edge of the ocean were used to having their windows uncovered most of the time. If he lived there, he imagined he would do the same, so he could see the open sea whenever he wished.

Ted watched someone get up from the sofa and come toward the door. The door slid open and a tall, slender man inspected him with dark serious eyes.

"Detective Bearbower?" the man asked.

"Yes. Newport Beach Police. We've met before Mr. Rosemond." Ted put out his hand and the man shook it.

"Just Andy. Come on in. Have you…heard anything at all?"

"No. We haven't heard anything except the report from the Lifeguard station. They said they had notified you also."

"Yes, they did." Andy motioned for him to sit down.

Ted looked around for something that would bear his behemoth size. He chose the smaller of the two wicker sofas. Seated on the other sofa was the red-haired woman. Tyree. He nodded at her and she returned the nod, then he sat down, hearing the wicker sofa give out a complaint.

"We have to do something," Andy said, his serious eyes looking somewhat wild now. He plopped himself down on the sofa beside Tyree. "We can't just sit here and wait, for crying out loud! Can't we get a police helicopter out there looking for them?"

"If they're very far out to sea, it's out of our jurisdiction. We already have them searching the whole channel. Not much to see at night however. Even with their searchlights."

"Well, there must be something we can do!"

"Andy, I need to ask you a few questions. Then we'll put something more into action. But I need information first."

Andy looked toward the sliding glass door which had turned into a mirror with the darkness behind it. Ted could see the young man's narrow, somber face distorted in the ripple of the glass. He looked away.

"First," Ted said. "Do you have any idea why someone might have taken your wife and child?"

"No. No reason for something so…terrible."

"You're positive?"

Tyree leaned forward, the blue of her eyes as bright as polished turquoise. "Detective, Elizabeth is a quiet, normal young woman. Why would anyone want to kidnap her?"

"If she wasn't kidnapped, is it possible she went willingly?" He looked at Andy. "Have you two had any problems lately?"

Andy shook his head firmly. "Nothing more than the usual married people squabbles."

Ted took out his notepad and pen. "What about money. Do you have enough to make someone greedy?"

"We're quite well off, but not what you'd call rich." Andy squirmed around on the sofa as if he were extremely uncomfortable.

Ted sighed. Nothing much here. They really didn't have any idea of why she and the boy were missing. "Okay, so where are we? What we know is that it's possible someone saw your wife and child being taken aboard a boat that was moored by the jetty. According to the observer, they appeared to be ill. Has either one of them been sick lately? Anything unusual happened to them the last day or two?" Ted saw the two of them exchange odd glances. Now what was that all about, he wondered? Then it suddenly dawned on him that a dead man had been found on their deck that morning. Damn, he should have remembered that immediately. Fatigue was taking its toll.

Ted felt a little self-conscious. "I guess you could say that man on your deck was a rather unusual happening, wouldn't you?"

Andy's expression changed to one of shock. "Oh God! You don't mean that could have something to do with this. With Elizabeth and Dar disappearing? I mean, we didn't know this guy. They told us he meant to rob us. How could he be connected?"

Ted was silent for a moment, and then said, "I have no idea. However, we have to look at everything." Right now, all he wanted was to take the report, check with the men in the field, and go home. Exhaustion gnawed at his bones. He would make himself a quick cheese sandwich and head for bed. He could look at this more clearly in the morning. However, he hoped that the woman and child would show up before then. Unharmed.

The phone rang, and all three of them jumped. Andy picked up the phone. "Yes!" he said anxiously. "Yes it is. What? Where?" Andy's sober expression turned to a wide smile. "Yes, he's here. I'll let you talk to him." He handed the phone to Ted and put his hands over his face. "They found them," he cried. "They're okay."

"Where?" Tyree jumped to her feet. "Can we go to them?"

Ted shushed them loudly and put the phone to his ear. "Bearbower here."

"Ted . . . it's Ajax. They've found the woman and the boy. On Catalina Island."

"Where? Oh, for Christ's sake! Are they okay?"

"Shook up, I guess, not too coherent. Soaked, bruised. But yeah, pretty much okay," Ajax said.

"Are they're bringing them to the mainland, or should we go there?"

"Better find a chopper. The doctor there thinks it's wise if Mr. Rosemond comes for them."

"Okay, fine we'll take a department chopper. I'll get someone to okay it. Arrange that for us, will you? Thanks." He hung up and looked at the two of them. "Great news," he said. "Your wife and son are on Catalina Island. In Avalon."

"Catalina!" Tyree exclaimed. "How in the hell did they get there?"

"We don't have all the facts yet. But we'll know shortly."

"But she...they're both really okay, aren't they?" Andy asked.

"As far as I know. Suffering from some exposure is all."

"We'll go get them now, right?" Andy said.

Ted let out a moan. "Yes, we'll go get them. I'm going out on a limb, but I know how this has been for you. They're being checked out by a doctor over there. They should be ready to leave by the time we get there. Since the boy's so young, it's probably best if his father is there to come back with him."

"You'll go with us?"

"Yes, but I'm afraid there won't be room for...Mrs. Rattigan."

Tyree smiled; the diamond in her front tooth gleamed. "I have to be getting home anyway. Boo will be missing me by now. Oh, I'm so damn relieved I'll just duck out. See you when you get back, Andy. I'll get Mabel and Sarah Zipper, and we'll fix the three of you something nourishing to eat." Tyree walked to the sliding door, opened it, and then turned back for a moment. She grinned and waved then disappeared into the darkness.

After Tyree left, Andy asked. "What's happened to them? Do they know?"

Ted felt his eyes narrow. "Not completely. Seems Elizabeth's story is rather discombobulated." He put his hand on Andy's shoulder. "But that may be just from the trauma. Later, when she's rested, we'll sort it out. In the meantime, you and I can chat."

"Chat?" Andy said as they walked out the door together. "What about?"

"About what you haven't told me."

Andy's face flushed a deep pink and tiny beads of sweat broke out on his upper lip. Ah, Ted said to himself. Dig around in the sand long enough and you're bound to come up with something. "Come on," he said. "When we're airborne, we'll talk. We've got a chopper waiting."

CHAPTER ELEVEN

Victor Bryce poured a shot of Aquavit into a chilled glass. He carried the cold glass to his favorite chair, a recliner covered in pale blue suede. The chair not only reclined, but also rocked and swiveled, something that gave him great comfort. The chair stood directly in front of the living room window of his French-Country style home. From there, he could view Avalon Harbor, great expanses of Dark Ocean, and the mist-clouded cliffs of Catalina's northern reach.

He slowly rocked as he sipped the Norwegian vodka, feeling the liqueur's warmth radiate through flesh and bone. He concentrated on adjusting his eyes to the darkness below. The roof of his laboratory was built on a craggy precipice just below the house. He could make out the faint outline of The Cybele, his sixty-foot yacht, as it bobbed in the rough night tide. He looked further out to sea, trying to locate the outline of The Green Latrine. Long overdue, the craft should be docked by now, but he saw no trace of it. His anticipation of seeing the child first-hand was offset by his anxiety for the boat.

He watched as wind whipped up rugged waves. Florescent patches of sea-foam skipped across the waves like pale leaves. Off in the distance, heat lightning prowled the horizon like an animal afire. Not a good night to be at sea. Earlier, his men had called him as they headed out of Newport Harbor. They had the boy and his mother aboard. After that, he'd heard nothing. He'd tried shore-to-ship as well as cellular calls to the Latrine, with no response. The last thing he wanted to do was call the Coast Guard, considering the circumstances.

Below him in the laboratory was the nursery awaiting the Rosemond child and the nurse's quarters. He had gone to great lengths to make certain the child would be comfortable and well looked after. The bill for the full-time nurse skyrocketed every minute. Still, she was essential to his plans and he could certainly afford it. In a few years, the boy would forget his birth parents. He would be Victor's child then. Take his name and be his son. A boy with special abilities. A boy worth a thousand fortunes. He would not be a laboratory specimen. He would be educated and well trained. His billion-dollar boy.

The thought of having a son, after all these years, warmed Victor more than the sips of vodka. His distaste for women, for their squeamishness, for their maudlin response to his ideas for improving the world, and especially for their bleeding heart attitude toward the less fortunate, made them abhorrent to him. He could never imagine himself in physical contact with them. Even as a young child, he had squirmed away from his mother's hugs and kisses. The smell of her perfume repelled him. He knew then he would never have a natural son of his own. Since the day that he'd first heard of the Rosemond child, he had thought of nothing else but getting possession of the boy. The child would not only be his, but in time, he would be the major contributor to his growing fortune, an appropriate role for a son.

He looked toward Avalon Harbor, confettied with ship's lights reflecting off dark water. The tiny town of Avalon, stretching up the small hillside, lay quiet, even at this early hour of the evening. The heavy wind made the two-hour trip by catamaran a nightmare, keeping tourists away. The Casino area sat dark, as did most of the shops along the main street of the town. Even when the town was mostly dark, he loved the misty view from his home. He'd been fortunate to be involved in a business deal a few years back that allowed him to lease land on the island, a virtually impossible feat. He'd built the house and lab over the fierce opposition of most everyone who lived on the island. However, as always, the citizenry soon went back to its everyday concerns and forgot the battle. He completed his building and after that, no one seemed to notice or care.

He finished the last of the vodka and set the glass on the chair-side table. Glancing back at Avalon, he saw the lights of a helicopter as it approached the landing pad. He watched as it hovered for a moment, and then settled onto the ground like a mother bird sheltering its young. Then he went back to searching the dark sea for a sign of the boat he awaited. He heard the antique clock on the living room wall strike eight. The boat should have arrived hours ago. A surge of tiny goose bumps rippled across the skin on his arms—a harbinger of apprehension. Things did not go wrong for Victor Bryce. He did not allow mistakes. Nothing had ever stood in his way of getting what he wanted. Perhaps the Latrine had simply developed engine trouble. On the other hand, the gale winds had probably stopped their headway and made them turn back. But if so, why hadn't they called or radioed him?

He leaned back in the recliner, rocking it slightly. He would wait another half hour. If he'd not seen or heard from the Latrine by then, he would take some sort of action. He would allow nothing to stand in his way of getting the boy. Not even Mother Nature. Outside the window, a huge white moth tapped its wings against the glass. Fascinated, Victor stared at it. Its wings, he thought, looked like snowflakes. He wondered how long it would continue its futile struggle to get to the light.

✺ ✺

Elizabeth sat on an overstuffed sofa in the hospital waiting room, Dar slept in her arms wrapped securely in a lightweight blanket. She looked down at him as he slept, at his cheeks ruddy, and a tangle of golden curls framing his face. His strange, frightening ability had taken the lives of two men, to save hers. How would she ever teach him what was right and what was wrong? How could she help him sort out the difference? The thought of the immense responsibility threatened to overwhelm her. She shoved the thoughts aside. Somehow, she and Andy would manage. She would let nothing harm her child.

The waiting room, occupied by four other people, looked to Elizabeth like the lobby of a hotel. Saffron-colored lamps on plastic-topped tables cast a pale yellow light on everything. Even so, she was thankful to be there, instead of in the emergency room where the walls were chalk-white and the lights so bright they'd made her head ache.

"Excuse me, miss," someone said. "May I ask you a few questions?"

Elizabeth looked up to see a short, sandy-haired young man standing over her. "I've already spoken to two doctors," she said.

"I'm not a doctor. I'm with the Coastguard." He gave her a reassuring smile, showing straight white teeth.

"Oh, I see. Well, I spoke to them also." She shifted Dar in her arms, and then decided to lay him down on the sofa beside her. He stirred slightly, but then thrust his thumb into his mouth and continued to sleep.

"Yes, I'm aware of that. But please, humor me. I just want to go over things once more." The young man sat on a green plastic chair opposite her. The red sweater he wore matched his cheeks. He looked, she decided, too young to even shave.

Elizabeth sighed, weariness pressing on her. "Okay," she said. "But I can't really tell you much."

The young man nodded and then took out a notepad, which made him look like a schoolboy. "First of all, I should tell you that your husband and a Newport Beach policeman just landed at the chopper pad. They'll be here in a few minutes."

Elizabeth sat up abruptly. "Andy! Oh, thank God!" She grinned, despite her fatigue.

"So, before they get here, let me ask…do you have any idea who the two men were who abducted you?"

"No. As I told the others. No idea at all. But you have their boat. Won't that give you a clue as to who they are?"

The man shook his head. "Probably not. If they're into kidnapping, they'll have it registered to someone else. A chain of people maybe. Tough to untangle. Bodies may help."

Elizabeth felt the blood in her face drain. A cold chill wracked her. Bodies! Even though the men had meant her harm, the thought of their agonized death sickened her. "All I know is they were after my son. They were going to throw me overboard before…before the wave hit and washed them away."

"Do you know why they wanted your son?"

Elizabeth hesitated. "Why does anyone kidnap a child?" she finally said.

The young man nodded. "So, after they went overboard, you managed to get to the radio and call for help."

"Yes."

"They found you, and brought you here."

"Yes," Elizabeth's head pounded and exhaustion rolled over her in cold waves. She wished he would stop talking and leave her alone. She'd answered a constant stream of questions for the last few hours. She couldn't tell them anything more. Especially not about Dar's role in the whole thing. With Andy on his way, along with a police officer from the mainland, there were bound to be more questions. She looked down at Dar, envying the way he could sleep through all of this. If she could, she would do the same. Just curl up and sleep. But

113

she had to stay awake, had to plan. Someone wanted her son. Someone who risked a great deal to get him. She was positive it had do with Dar's unusual abilities.

As soon as Andy arrived, they would decide how to get their son out of harm's way. They would leave, move, and go somewhere safe. Maybe she could convince the police to watch the house for the night. Tomorrow the parapsychologist Tyree had called would be there at ten. They would stay to talk with her, to perhaps find out more about Dar's frightening endowment, and what to do about it. After that, they would go. She knew they could no longer live in Newport Beach.

She suddenly realized the young man had been asking her another question, one she didn't hear. "I'm...sorry," she said. "I'm just so tired I can't think straight right now. Can we do this later?"

"Yes, of course. I didn't mean to upset you. This has to be extremely traumatic for you. We're just thankful you're safe."

Elizabeth narrowed her eyes and looked at him. Was it just her fatigue, or did she hear a hint of something odd in his voice? Did he doubt something she said? Was he suspicious that the men's death was caused by more than the ocean? And when they found the bodies, what would they reveal, if anything? She put her hands over her ears to stop the questioning, both his and her own. Her head pounded furiously; an elephant stampeding through it would have hurt less.

"I need some air," she said. "And some aspirin." She rubbed at her forehead. "I should have asked the doctor for some."

The young man smiled his straight-toothed smile and reached into his pocket. "Will Excedrin do?" He held out a small, white tin.

Grateful, she reached for it, took out two tablets, and popped them into her mouth. She spotted a drinking fountain a few yards away banked on a bile green wall. With a quick movement, she tucked the blanket snuggly around Dar, then got up and went to the fountain. She swallowed the Excedrin, drinking as much of the sweet cool water as she could. After so much salty seawater, it tasted wonderful. She checked Dar, then walked to the entrance door and opened it. She stood in the doorway where she could keep an eye on Dar. The night air smelled raw and fresh. It revived her somewhat.

The young man got up from the chair and put his notepad away. "Your husband should be here any minute. They'll probably fly you back in the chopper. I bet this is a night you'll want to tell your grandkids about."

She gave him a curt nod, wishing he'd disappear. Her wish came true. He gave her one more of his straight-toothed smiles, and ducked out the door. The night swallowed him up. She let out a sigh of relief. Then suddenly he was back, his smile gone.

"Oh, yes, I forgot to mention, we did retrieve one of the bodies," he said quietly. "Got hung up on the boat's out-drive. They're getting him ready to ship back to the mainland for an autopsy. I wonder what they'll find." With that, he disappeared again.

Elizabeth closed her eyes, took in a deep breath, and went back into the waiting room. The door shutting behind her, its pneumatic closer hissing like a nest of snakes.

CHAPTER TWELVE

Tyree, wearing a pair of emerald-green silk pajamas, sat on the edge of her bed and vigorously brushed her hair. Boo had gone out suddenly saying he was needed at the lab. She checked the clock on the bedside table. Almost ten p.m. Elizabeth, Andy, and Dar should be home by now. Tyree had helped the Zipper sisters put together some roast beef sandwiches and coleslaw for Andy and Elizabeth's late supper. Elizabeth would probably beg off, never having much of an appetite, but Tyree believed the poor thing should eat after such a terrifying experience. Her energy would surely be depleted.

Tyree gave her wild curls another brush, hearing them crackle with static electricity whipped up by the dry wind. She got up and put the brush away in her dresser, then decided to go down to the living room and wait for Boo. She made her way down the stairs wondering what the heck was up at the lab that would take Boo away so late in the evening. He'd been going there more and more often at night. She'd hoped that once Sunshine had a major money partner Boo's responsibilities would ease. Ever since he'd first started working with the drug, he'd been driven. Certainly, it was a miraculous drug. Without it she would have fallen prey to one of the most dreaded diseases ever. Alzheimer's. Her mother had it, as did her grandmother. Tyree gave a shudder. Her case had been early onset and at forty, she had already felt the loss of memory of how to do simple things, like tying a shoe. Then along came Sunshine and her terrible symptoms had receded. Sunshine had cured her, or so she believed. Even if the disease had only arrested, as Dr. Foxhoven deemed, she was thankful for the reprieve. However, Boo's devotion to Sunshine's development and testing went beyond what she considered normal. A person obsessed was how she saw him. Determined to cure as many of the ills that so many people suffered from as possible. A true crusader. She sighed as she plopped herself down on the living room sofa, picked up the remote and clicked on the TV.

The news came on but only droned in her ears as she thought about what had happened to Elizabeth and Dar. Their abduction couldn't have been random. She was certain it had something to do with Dar's strange and rather frightening abilities. Only she couldn't figure out how the abductors had found out about him so quickly. The only people who supposedly knew were Sunshine people, those at her house last night. She knew Mabel and Sarah wouldn't have said anything to anyone. As for the rest of the group, they'd been busy with their gossip and chatter. She doubted many of them even noticed what happened at the meeting. So who could have passed on the information about Dar's unusual ability?

She changed the TV to a news channel. It showed a parade of some kind in Laguna. Then they displayed a Newport Beach man with his head pierced by a steel rod. More Santa Ana winds were predicted for the rest of the week. She clicked off the TV.

"A slow news day," she muttered, tossing down the remote. She got up and walked to the window that looked out over the beach. She could see the florescent edges of large waves as they rolled in along the sand. Usually the sight of the ocean calmed her. But not tonight. Instead, she felt edgy. It wasn't Elizabeth and Dar's abduction that bothered her so much, or Dar's newfound abilities. Something else plagued her, a concern she'd harbored for some time now. She hadn't broached Elizabeth on the subject. Certainly, Elizabeth and Andy had considered it—or had they? She reached over to the end table and picked up the cordless phone. Before she talked with Andy and Elizabeth, she'd check with Doctor Foxhoven. If her fears were groundless, there was no sense in worrying or upsetting them.

Convinced this was the way to go Tyree dialed Foxhoven's number. It would take her a while to get the information she needed, but the doctor had some contacts that could make things happen. He too would see the need for some answers. Maybe he already had them. As she waited for someone to answer the phone, she silently prayed that her suspicions were unwarranted.

Dar slept through the helicopter ride with his head on Andy's shoulder. Elizabeth, Andy, and Detective Bearbower sat quietly during the trip. Despite the wind, the pilot gracefully set the chopper down on the sand only a few yards from their house. They scrambled out and made a dash for the deck behind their home. Ted gave the pilot a wave. The chopper lifted off, wavered a little in the wind, and disappeared into the dark night sky.

A note taped on the sliding glass door told them that sandwiches and coleslaw were in the refrigerator for a late supper. Andy gave a tight laugh. "Looks like Tyree and the Zipper sisters have been at work again," he said. "I'm glad we gave those three mother hens a key. Detective, are you hungry?" he asked.

Ted Bearbower gave him a sheepish grin and nodded. "I can always eat." He looked at his watch. As usual, it had stopped again. He gave a tired sigh. "My partner is going to pick me up in the alley behind your house. It will be a little while before he gets here. However, we already have two unmarked cars watching your house."

Elizabeth gave him a tight smile and then carried Dar upstairs, thankful to be able to put him in his own crib at last. She pulled the small blanket over him, and brushed the curls off his forehead. His pink mouth turned up in a quiet smile before he rolled over on his side and began sucking his thumb. She snapped on the night light on his dresser and turned off the overhead light. After one last look at him, she left the room, closing the door behind her and made her way downstairs. Her body complained with odd aches and pains all over it. It was from all that tumbling around on the deck of that ship, she told herself. If it got worse, she'd see about taking another dose of Sunshine. Since taking Sunshine, neither she nor Andy had had so much as a headache.

Downstairs, Andy sat talking with Detective Bearbower. Three plates filled with sandwiches sat on the coffee table. Both Andy's and Bearbower's were already half eaten. She wondered how Andy could eat after all that had happened. She yawned then stretched, trying not to let the fatigue catch up with her. She didn't want to sleep; didn't want to let her guard down. Whoever had tried to kidnap Dar might try again. After the detective left, she and Andy would spend the night packing so they could leave tomorrow afternoon, after Doctor Terri Mann's visit. She still had no idea where they would go. But maybe Andy would think of someplace. When they got there and were safe, she could sleep. Only then.

"Lizzy," Andy said, motioning for her to come and sit beside him. "Detective Bearbower says that if we want, they can call in the FBI and have them provide some extra protection."

Elizabeth gave the two of them a frown. "We appreciate it detective," she said. "But are you sure we should make this a federal case?" Elizabeth sat down on the sofa, feeling the weariness settle over her like a warm blanket. She knew she wasn't thinking as rationally as she should. She should go upstairs and take a hot shower, wash her hair, and put on fresh clothes. She felt sticky and salty all over.

"Kidnapping usually is a federal case, by definition. But if nothing else happens, we can probably handle this on the local level. We know two men were involved, and from what you've told me, there's at least one more. Obviously, someone paid them to do it. If we can identify the one body we have, that may lead us somewhere."

Elizabeth thought about it. The more people involved, the bigger the chance others would find out about the frightening things Dar could do. Worse, the things he had already done. She felt torn.

"Well, whatever," she said in a tired voice. "In the meantime, I'm taking no chances." Elizabeth looked at Andy. "Tomorrow we take Dar, and a few of our things, and we go somewhere safe."

Andy frowned. "Where? And for how long?"

"For as long as it takes to feel safe. Maybe for good, Andy. I don't know. Get someone to sell the house. I was hoping you could think of someplace safe."

The detective gave them an odd look. "Can you give me any reason why this happened? Why someone would go to such elaborate plans to get your son? You're well off, but not wealthy."

Elizabeth tried to appear passive although she felt her face flush. "I have no idea. But whatever the reason, I'm not going to give them a second chance. We have Doctor Terri Mann coming tomorrow morning—" She stopped, alarmed, realizing what she'd said. She hoped the detective didn't recognize the doctor's name. Tyree had said she was very well known worldwide. It could be a giveaway about Dar, and that something unusual was going on. "She's a friend of Tyree's next door," she said quickly. "She's just coming to the house to check Dar over. Make sure he isn't too traumatized by everything he's been though." With that, she reached out and took Andy's hand, a signal to him not to blow it. He must have understood because his frown faded and he squeezed her hand.

"Where did you find a doctor like that?" Bearbower asked.

Elizabeth felt herself go rigid. Did he know about her specialty? "Like what, detective?"

"One who makes house calls?"

Relieved, Elizabeth just smiled in return, trying to see from his expression, whether he believed her or not. But he looked away from her toward the sliding glass door, as if listening to the wind as it moaned along the eaves of the house. She heard a muted horn honk several times.

"That's my ride. So I won't bother you more now," Bearbower said. "We have enough for a preliminary report. But before you leave tomorrow, I need to get more information. Unfortunately, two men died in this incident. And wherever you go, I'll need to be able to get in touch with you."

"But I don't want anyone knowing! Not even the police!" Elizabeth felt a jolt of alarm. She knew that telling anyone where they were would be a danger.

"Okay, we'll see about that tomorrow. What would be a good time? In the afternoon? I'll do like the doctor, and make a house call. But for us to do a thorough investigation, you'll have to cooperate to some degree. We'll keep someone posted here until we can let you go." He stood up and picked up the rest of the sandwich left on the plate. "Thanks for the food." He turned to go and then turned back. "The two men from the department are on guard, so you can sleep easy tonight. I'll see you tomorrow afternoon if that's okay." He shook his head, a wry look on his face. "You both look exhausted."

Elizabeth tried not to glower at him. No one was going to tell her she couldn't take her child to safety. Not even the police!

Andy stood up and walked Bearbower through the kitchen to the back alley door where the detective had parked his car.

Another gust of wind rattled the windows, making a sound like the clatter of brittle bones. Elizabeth let out a sigh, closed her eyes, and laid her head back against the sofa. What was happening to their idyllic life? It was crumbling! Disintegrating! What Sunshine had given them, Sunshine might now be taking away. She gave a little laugh and heard it echo around the living room like the cackle of a lunatic. Her son could do terrible things. How would they ever teach him not to use his abilities? What if she and Andy made him angry or upset? Would Dar turn his terrifying energy against them? She suddenly realized something. She had not yet told Andy that Dar had killed the two men on the ship. The thought of it made her heart jump. They had probably deserved it, but taking a life was something that Elizabeth felt only God had the right to do. A surge of hot tears welled in her closed eyes.

"It's not hopeless!" she said aloud, trying to persuade herself.

"What's not hopeless?" Andy said as he came into the living room.

"Oh, I didn't hear you come back." She sat up and brushed at the tears that had begun to slip down her cheeks.

"You're exhausted. Let's get you up to bed."

"No, Andy, we can't sleep. We have to pack. We've got to get Dar away where he's safe."

Andy sat down beside her and touched the side of her cheek with his fingertips. "Honey, he is safe. The police are watching. They'll find out who's behind the kidnappers. This will all blow over and things will be fine."

Elizabeth buried her face in her hands and began to sob. "It won't ever be over, Andy. Nothing will ever be fine again!"

Andy took her in his arms and began to rock her gently. "Yes, it will. I promise."

"But Andy! Dar can kill!"

It took Elizabeth a long time before her sobs ebbed and she was able to tell Andy about what Dar had done. Andy listened, chalk-faced. When she finished, Elizabeth's exhaustion pressed on her like unseen hands. She abandoned the idea of going upstairs and taking a shower. She didn't have the energy. For a long time, they sat huddled together, listening to the eerie sounds the old house made as the gusty Santa Ana winds blasted it.

Ted slept fitfully, tossing about with each rumble of the wind. Bright dreams haunted his sleep. Dreams the color of carnivals. The air-conditioning unit in his condominium stopped functioning suddenly, waking him from the rainbow of nightmares, leaving him drained and sweating, and his head throbbing like a bass drum. He turned the switch on the lamp to check the time, but the light didn't come on. Thinking the light bulb had burned out, he reached over to the other nightstand and tried turning on the other lamp. That one refused to work also. He got up and looked out the window. The whole area was dark.

"Oh, great! Just what I need. A power outage!" he grumbled aloud. The wind had probably blown a transformer somewhere. An eerie memory of a high-voltage wire whipping about in wind and rain, invaded the darkness. An image of another time and place. An image of the night the killer Barry Brownstone died. Shaking it off, he swung his legs over the side of bed and got to his feet, feeling his way across the room to the chest where he kept a flashlight. He'd been regular about checking and replacing the batteries so he was certain the light would work.

He groped through the top drawer, found the flashlight, and switched it on. It cut a crystal-white hole in the darkness. He padded down the hall to the linen closet and found the oil lamp he kept there for just such times. In the kitchen, he carefully lit the lamp and set it in the middle of the kitchen table. Its flickering light illuminated the entire room with an egg-yellow light. He looked at the clock on the oven panel. It had stopped at four-thirty. He wondered how long the power had been out. He set about manually grinding some fresh coffee and brewing it, thankful his stove was gas, not electric. He was also thankful to be awake and out of his ragged dreams.

He had just finished his second cup of coffee when the phone rang. Ashy sunlight had begun to creep through the kitchen shutters as he picked up the receiver. "Bearbower," he said.

"Hey, Ted!" Ajax's voice sounded half-asleep. "Those crazy guys at the coroner's office just called me at home."

Ted heard him yawn. "So?"

"So, they wanted us to know that the guy who was hung up on the boat—the one who's supposed to be involved in the Rosemond kidnapping that he…well, I'm not sure I understand, but they said he died the same way as the guy on the patio!"

Ted's coffee cup banged down on the table. "What? The cause of death was the same. That can't be right! We assumed the guy on the boat drowned. He was swept off the boat according to the Rosemond woman. The guy on their patio wasn't drowned."

"The guy on the boat, no water in the lungs." Ajax said.

Ted heard him yawn again.

"I'm too sleepy to make sense of all this," Ajax said. "They wanted to talk to you, but got the numbers mixed up as usual."

"Okay, I'll get back with them. Shit, that can't be what they meant!"

"Ebola, I told you! That's what it is! It's spreading!" Ajax moaned.

"It's not Ebola, you hypochondriac tarantula! Go get a shot or something and stop worrying."

"Okay, okay. It's not Ebola."

Oh, by the way, is the power out there in Huntington Beach?"

"No. Why?"

"It's out here in Newport. Don't know how widespread it is. I hope it doesn't affect the department. I'm going over there right now," Ted said.

"I'm going back to bed. Didn't sleep too good last night."

"Yeah, me either. I'd rather be up and moving. Don't be too late. We may have a real mystery on our hands, if what the coroner said is true." Ted hung up the phone. He leaned over and blew out the oil lamp. How the hell could the thug on the patio, the dog on the beach, the birds, and the kidnapper on the boat have died from the same thing, he wondered. The Coast Guard was searching for the body of the second man on the boat. If they found it, he wondered if the cause of death would be the same. That all three could die from some unknown cause, suffering the same effects, seemed impossible.

What the hell, maybe Ajax was right, not about Ebola, but that it was some contagious disease. The victims didn't have anything in common. Ted thought about it for a minute. He suddenly jumped to his feet. Of course! The Rosemonds! At least, the Rosemond woman and child. But what the hell did that connection mean? The baby couldn't be involved, but could the woman? If so, in what way? The link was there, but it didn't make any sense. At least not yet.

Ted shook his head. He poured another cup of coffee and took it into the bedroom with him. He was going to talk to the Rosemonds again as soon as possible. He felt certain they knew more about what was going on than they let on. They'd been seriously involved in the serial murders that had taken his partner's life. That fact alone made him suspicious. He had no idea what was happening or why, but he knew damn well he was going to find out. One way or another.

CHAPTER THIRTEEN

Dar lay on his stomach in his crib listening to the sound the waves made as they rolled in along the sand. He could hear them even though Mama had closed and locked his window. He preferred to have the window open so he could smell the crisp scent of the salty water. But Mama was upset. Frightened. He could feel her fear.

Mama was afraid some bad men would try to hurt them again. He would never let that happen. No matter what Mama said. She kept telling him that some of the things he did were wrong, but he didn't know what that meant. He only knew that it upset Mama when he did them. But when she'd said that hurting someone was a bad thing, he understood a little. He didn't like to be hurt either.

Dar turned over on his back, trying to sort everything out. It was bad to hurt people, but was it bad to hurt them if they were going to hurt you? He looked around his bedroom in the early morning light. He had discovered that he could look at things more than one way. He could see just the outside of things if he wanted to. Then, he could kinda shift his eyes and see the inside of things. Everything had layers, like sheets of paper in the books Mama read to him. He liked the outside layer of things best, but for some reason he could not do things to this layer. It was only when he shifted his vision to some of the inside places that he could wiggle them and make them move and change. Some of them were like the long strings of colorful paper his Mama had strung around the patio on his number one birthday. Strings that twisted around each other. So many of them he couldn't begin to count, even when he tried. He just didn't know enough names for numbers.

An odd thought crept into his head. So far, he had not seen Mama or daddy "wiggle" anything. He wondered why. And when Mama was in trouble, when the bad man was going to hurt her, she'd called out to him to help. Why hadn't she done the helping? Why hadn't she wiggled the man's insides, the way he had? He lay there for a few minutes thinking about that. As he did, he inspected the insides of the teddy bears sitting on his dresser. Their inside layers didn't look at all like the insides of people. He wiggled one of them, and saw the bear's furry coat split apart in a number of places.

"Whoops!" he said, using the word Mama used when she dropped things. "Dar put back," he told himself. But he couldn't put the bear back the way it had been, no matter how hard he tried. He could remember a lot of how it had been done, but not all of it. He would have to look at things better before he wiggled them, so he could remember how to put them back if he needed to. He looked at the bear, the expression on its face so sad that Dar thought it might cry.

"Poor Teddy," Dar said. "Dar bad boy." With that, he turned over and began to suck his thumb. Mama would be in soon to get him dressed and feed him. He would have to tell her he was sorry for wiggling the teddy bear so she wouldn't scold him. He closed his eyes and breathed in the scents the air carried, the soft powdery talc Mama patted on him after his bath, the smell like dried flowers that emanated from the old house, and best of all, the sweet whispery odor of Mama, kinda like the taste of his favorite candy.

Elizabeth awoke tangled in Andy's arms, still sitting upright on the living room sofa. Damn! She'd fallen asleep after all, although she certainly didn't feel as if she'd benefited from it. Andy, his head back against the sofa, mouth slightly open, snored softly. She untangled herself and got up, leaving him to sleep. He looked so peaceful she hated to spoil it.

The morning seemed all black and white. Bright sunshine flooded in from the small windows on the northeast side of the living room, leaving other corners of the room in inky shadows. She took in a deep breath and closed her eyes for a moment, hoping foolishly that when she opened them she would find there had been no kidnapping, no strange killings by Dar, none of the awful things of the past two days. Sunlight bubbled and bounced against her eyelids. She blinked her eyes open, knowing nothing had changed. Knowing she would have to face whatever came next.

Doctor Terri Mann would arrive at ten. She checked her watch. It was only eight so she had plenty of time to dress and dress Dar, and feed them all some breakfast. After the doctor left, she would pack some things they would need, and the three of them would go and find a place where they would be safe. She still had no idea where, but that didn't matter. Even if they just got in the car and drove, deciding on where as they went. Getting away from the old house, from the beach, from the breakwater where she and Dar had been kidnapped, would at least give her an illusion of safety. She realized that all of these places were ones she'd fallen in love with. The idea of leaving them behind hurt, but it couldn't be helped. They were symbols now—symbols of danger.

Upstairs in her bathroom, she peered at her face in the mirror. "Dear God!" she growled. "I look bleached!" Her pale face peered back paler than usual, her hair, sticky with salt-water, lacked color. It was as if the whole ordeal had sucked away any trace of pigment. Her hair had taken to clinging to her head as if glued. She took off the brine-stiff clothing she had on, took a long warm shower, and washed her hair. Then she put on fresh jeans and a clean sweatshirt. Her whole body still ached but the clean clothes made her feel better. Best of all, her head felt clearer. She brushed on a trace of blush, added some lipstick and then towel-dried her hair.

Downstairs she found Andy sitting up, staring at the cold fireplace, his hands jammed tightly between his knees. His overly long hair stood at odd angles to his head and his brown eyes blinked rapidly.

"Hey," he said to her. "Did we sleep here all night?"

"I'm afraid so."

Andy lifted his arms and stretched. He continued to stare at the fireplace, his eyes appearing unfocused. He began to pick imaginary lint off his warm-ups. Elizabeth went to the sliding glass door and pulled the drapes open. A uniformed policeman sat on one of their deck chairs, sipping coffee from a thermos cup. He nodded at her, and she nodded back. She could hear the murmur of surf outside. The wind had ebbed to a slight breeze. Early morning joggers kicked up wet sand as they trotted along the water's edge.

"Andy, why don't you go make us some coffee while I get Dar up and dressed? We have that doctor coming, remember?" Elizabeth asked.

Andy frowned for a second then looked up at her. "Oh! Right! My head's so foggy this morning I can hardly think." He let out a tight little laugh

"We've got to get moving, Andy. After the doctor leaves, we have to pack the car so we can get out of here." Elizabeth turned to go upstairs.

126

Dorothy McMillan

"Lizzy, we can't leave until the police say so."

Elizabeth turned back to him. "Andy, someone tried to kill me yesterday, and take Dar. The next time, they might be successful."

Andy got up and walked over to her, trying to smooth down his unruly hair with both hands. "We have police protection, Lizzy. We need to cooperate with the police. We can't just run and hide."

"Andy, they want Dar because he can do unbelievable things. I don't know how they found out, but they did. Now, I don't trust anyone. Not even Tyree and Boo."

"Lizzy, you know they wouldn't harm you or Dar!"

"I don't think so either, but we can't be certain. We just need to get away."

"You want us to have to hide the rest of our lives? That's no way to live." Andy turned away, went to the sliding glass door and looked out

Elizabeth felt herself close to tears. "I don't mean forever. Just until we know it's safe again." Her voice broke and she put her hands over her eyes. "Just for a while, okay?"

Andy was silent for a moment then he turned and went to Elizabeth, putting his arms around her. "Okay, for a while. I just don't want to admit that all this is happening to us. Everything was so-"

"Perfect. I know."

"Dar is remarkable. He learns things so quickly it takes my breath away. I showed him the letters on the computer keyboard, just once, and now he knows them by heart. I can point to any one of them and he tells me the letter. He can spell his name and a lot of other words as well. And numbers, my God! He can count to a hundred, but he gets bored doing it. Not to mention adding and subtracting. The answers just seem to jump into his head, with no calculating. With a mind like that, there's no telling what he can become. If only…."

"If only his mind couldn't do the other things. The frightening things." Elizabeth wiped her eyes with the back of her hand.

"All this may be…well…temporary. Some crazy kind of phase he's going through. Like those reports about kids going through puberty who make things fly around, drawers open, stuff like that. They all outgrow it. Dar may, too."

Elizabeth looked up at him, feeling a slight smile creeping across

127

her lips. "Yes, perhaps it will. That's something maybe the doctor can tell us. She's an expert in this kind of thing from what Tyree has said."

"Great. Okay, I'll go make us coffee. Strong! And you get Dar up." He gave her a hug. "We'll get through this, Lizzy. And things will be okay again."

"Maybe they will," Elizabeth agreed. With that she turned and ran up the stairs, two steps at a time. As she did, she could hear Dar in his room, jabbering away to himself.

Ted sat at his desk going over the folders concerning the two recent deaths on the peninsula. So far, nothing connected the two. For that, he felt thankful. He was impatiently awaiting word from the coroner's office on the other victim, the one they'd found hung up on the out-drive of the kidnapper's boat. He'd been promised a full report by nine a.m. They were working at breakneck speed to get him the information. He would have to send over some of Maddy's pastries as a thank you.

The vision of Maddy wearing peach silk, dallied through his mind. He'd called her this morning and said he hoped he could come by in the evening and she had seemed delighted. She would prepare supper for them as well as dessert. The idea of holding Maddy in his arms again, feeling the warmth and softness of her body, made his groin ache. The last thing he wanted to do was investigate a bunch of murders. He only hoped that whatever the coroner found wouldn't be a stumbling block to his seeing Maddy that night.

He closed the folders and leaned back in his chair. Ajax sat across from him, his gold earring in place as usual, reading the newspaper and drinking a cup of coffee. To Ted, the coffee looked as black and syrupy as crankcase oil. He reached for his own thermos and poured a cup of the brew he'd made at home from fresh ground beans and powdered chocolate. One might have to suffer the indignities of the world, but he could think of no reason why anyone had to do it without the small but important pleasures in life.

A tall, lanky uniformed officer approached Ted's desk. "Umm, sir? Are you Detective Bearbower?" he asked.

Ted gave him a wry look and pointed to the nameplate on his desk. "That doesn't say Joe Blow, does it?"

"Ah, well, no sir. It says Ted Bearbower. So this folder must be for you." The young man handed Ted a manila folder with a heavy sheath of papers inside. "From the coroner's office."

Ted took it and nodded at the man, then immediately opened the folder.

"Is okay?" the young man said.

"What? Oh, Yes! Thanks." Ted waved him away. Rookie cops drove him nuts. At least the timid ones. Thankfully, there weren't many of those. He opened the folder and began to read.

"Jesus Key-rist!" he howled. "I can't believe this!"

Ajax looked over at him, his thick eyebrows pinched together. "You got your shorts in a bunch again, Ted?"

"This report would bunch anyone's shorts!" Ted looked over the report to make certain he'd read it accurately. "Take a look." He handed Ajax the folder. "According to this, the guy we saw on the Rosemont's patio, and the guy who tried to kidnap the Rosemond woman and child, actually did die the same way. Both of them suffered sudden, fast hemorrhaging. Both of them have insides that look like soft pudding. And both of them have severely scrambled brain tissue."

Ajax perused the folder then looked up at Ted. "What in the hell is this? A fucking virus like I suggested? Maybe something they caught from one of the Rosemonds? But if that's the case, why haven't the Rosemonds gotten sick or died?"

"Haven't you've heard of Typhoid Mary?" Ted asked. "The Rosemonds could just be carriers. You were with them once when we first interviewed them, and I was with them a second time last night. Christ, I even ate a meal with them!" Ted felt a touch of apprehension. After all, Ebola victims typically died from massive blood loss.

The idea that there might be an outbreak of something that lethal made the little hairs on the back of his neck stand on end.

"Well," Ted added slowly, trying not to jar Ajax's usual runaway anxiety any more than necessary, "The one thing the victims do have in common is the Rosemonds. Hopefully it doesn't have anything to do with a virus. Coroner didn't say it was."

"So, what else could it be?" Ajax tossed the folder back on Ted's desk. "Voodoo? Is one of them practicing some sort of witchcraft?" He snorted a laugh that sounded a bit like a pig at a trough.

"I don't know yet, but it's time we got busy and found out. If there's a tie between them, then we'll find it. I'm due to see the Rosemonds this afternoon, virus or no virus. If they know something about what happened, I'm betting it will show in their reactions."

"You want me to come along?" Ajax asked.

"No. I need you here trying to identify the transient we found in the alley behind the Fun Zone. I know he doesn't fit the Rosemond case. But damn it, four dead men and one probably floating around somewhere off the coast! What a great week this is turning out to be. I knew I should have retired when I planned to." Ted frowned. "I wonder what in Hades we'll find if the second floater turns up? If we get three deaths out of the four exactly alike, then it's beyond coincidence."

"You know what?" Alex said softly.

"What?" Ted said.

"It really is a strange world, isn't it?"

❦ ❦

Tyree, frustrated by not being able to get a call through to Doctor Foxhoven, decided to go to the source. She realized he was a busy doctor, but the concern she had about Dar prodded her to action. It took her only eight minutes in her Mercedes to reach the suite of professional offices that surrounded Hoag Memorial Hospital. The hospital sat on a hill just above the start of the peninsula. Foxhoven's office was a block higher, with a sweeping view of the harbor and coast. She parked the car and got out, taking in a deep breath of fresh air. The wind, gentle now, brought with it the scent of sage off the desert

From where she stood, she could see all the way to the end of the peninsula. Was that huge old deco house hers? She was certain it was. Its white walls reflected the morning sunlight like opaque glass. She turned to the south, trying to spot the Sunshine laboratory which was located down the coast, nestled into a hillside. But the curve of the coastline made it impossible. On such a lovely day, in such a glorious place, she hated to think about her concerns for Dar and Liz. However, that's what she'd come for. She needed some answers. Answers that would affect all of them, the entire Sunshine group. She had to know.

Tyree gave the doctor's receptionist her name and explained it was

130

urgent that she talk with the doctor as soon as possible. The receptionist, a heavyset woman with bovine eyes and a bright red lipsticked mouth, gave her a cheery grin and hustled off to give the message to Doctor Foxhoven. Less than a minute later, Foxhoven came out to greet her and ushered her into his office.

"I'm sorry, Tyree," Foxhoven said. "I got the messages that you called, but I had some emergency surgery this morning. What's up? Aren't you feeling well?"

Tyree paused a moment before answering. "I'm fine. It's about Dar, and Elizabeth. I want to know…actually I need to know something that you aren't supposed to tell me. Confidential medical records concerning those two."

"Well now, if you'll tell me what it is you need to know, we'll see." Foxhoven leaned back in his leather desk chair, looking relaxed.

"I'm sure you went over this with Elizabeth. It had to concern her also." "For those of us taking the stronger…ah…illegal form of Sunshine, it's important to get some answers. Barry Brownstone raped Elizabeth. Not too long after that she found she was pregnant."

"You're wondering if Barry could be Dar's father, not Andy."

Tyree nodded, glad Foxhoven broached the subject first.

"I can understand that. You wonder if Dar's unusual talents came from Andy, who was taking the stronger Sunshine, or from Barry Brownstone who took the raw form that turned him into such a vicious killer. If Andy is the father then his enhanced abilities could be passed on to Dar." Foxhoven gave her a gentle smile. "You're right, this is confidential information."

"So then you can't tell me if it is possible that Dar is Barry's child?"

Foxhoven shook his head. "Let's just say that in all the DNA tests I've taken on babies in my practice, I never found one that was the progeny of Barry Brownstone."

Tyree felt a great sense of relief. If Barry had fathered Dar, she would be terrified that he too would eventually become the monster that Barry was.

"Do you get my meaning? Foxhoven asked.

Tyree let out a deep sigh. "I can't tell you how relieved I am. Dar is such an adorable child I just couldn't bear the thought of something happening to him, the way it did to Barry.

"Dar is unusually bright," Foxhoven said. He may be difficult to cope with. Elizabeth and Andy had best think about putting him into a special school, or under the care of people who can help and encourage him to use his abilities best."

Tyree shook her head. "Not a chance. Neither one of them would let that child out of their sight!" Tyree looked away from him, staring at the picture of the horse on the wall. A striking roan with long well-formed legs, nice proportions, apparently from prime stock. She looked back at Foxhoven.

"There are days when I wonder if any of us should have started on Sunshine. Are the rewards worth it?" she said.

Foxhoven gave her an odd look. He turned his chair so that he was no longer facing her. "We're a part of medical research, you, and me. Even though we're not part of the overall testing for FDA approval, we are still an important part of Sunshine's research. The things that happen to us may be critical factors in the drug's future."

"Yes," Tyree said. "I suppose you're right."

"In the end, Sunshine will be one of the wonder drugs of the next century. If any of our group suffers from using the drug, we must accept it as a necessary part of the research."

"Well, let's pray that never happens. Barry was more than we needed to cope with." Tyree got up from the chair and started toward the door.

"If you have any more questions, don't hesitate to call," Foxhoven said.

Tyree let herself out of the office, waved at the receptionist who waved back, and went out into the parking lot. The wind had kicked up slightly. From the height of the sun, she thought it must be close to ten. She debated on whether or not she should go down to her small art gallery in Corona del Mar, or back home where she could talk to Elizabeth after Dr. Mann left. Her curiosity about what Dr. Mann would say made it impossible for her not to find out. After all, her partner could take care of the gallery. She did most of the time anyway. As a rule, Tyree bought the paintings and her partner sold them.

With that settled she got back in her car and quickly made her way off the hill and down the peninsula toward home. She felt a lot better than she had earlier. Dar was not Barry's child he was Andy's. The DNA tests proved that. Now all they had to worry about were the unusual things that Dar could do, which in themselves might be far more than they bargained for when they first started taking Sunshine.

CHAPTER FOURTEEN

Ted stood looking down at the body crumpled under the pier pilings. The tide was turning and ripples of sea water had just begun to shift the body around. Sea water was also seeping into Ted's nearly new cordovan wingtips. Four uniformed men were searching the area around the body and two where on the pier checking it out.

"You guys find anything?" he asked one of the uniforms.

"No, sorry. Nothing at all. We are mostly waiting for the medical examiner."

"Sheee-it!" Ted spat, and looked up at Ajax who stood across from him chewing a wad of gum and fingering his gold earring. "Do you know what's happened to this guy?"

"Yeah," Ajax said. "He's dead! That's why they called us."

Ted was silent for a moment. The last thing he needed now was levity. "I mean," he said slowly, his voice oozing a tone of gravity. "Do you see how he was killed? His throat's been ripped out. By someone's teeth!"

Ajax looked startled. He leaned down and inspected the corpse closely. "Yes, I know." Then the realization obviously hit him. "Christ, just like…!"

"Right, just like the Brownstone serial cases."

"You weren't kidding when you called the killer a vampire, were you? This is a first for me. And I hope the last." Ajax turned away. "Maybe that Barry Brownstone guy isn't dead after all."

"Maybe. Or maybe a copycat. The only thing is that Brownstone used a blade, not his teeth. His teeth were for ripping out bites of flesh from the victim."

"Which one do you hope it is?" Ajax said. "Copycat or the real thing?"

Ted turned away from the scene and headed across the sand toward the squad car, feeling his shoes and socks squish saltwater. "I hope," he said over his shoulder. "That it's all a bad dream and I'll wake up soon!"

Ajax caught up with him. "Okay. Now you've got me scared. I'll do more checking around until I get positive proof that this

Brownstone guy is really dead and buried, or cremated. First we pin that down and know for sure he's worm food, and then we can look for the psycho that's doing these new killings. Did forensics turn up anything yet on the guy in the alley?"

"Not yet. It was pretty clean," Ted said. "And like all the Brownstone killings, there was no sign of a struggle."

They reached the car and Ted got in the driver's side, pulling the door shut behind him. He glanced back at the Balboa Pier at the forensics crew as they bagged and dragged the latest victim. Despite the warm weather, a violent chill raked down his spine. It just couldn't be happening again. He leaned his head against the steering wheel as Ajax climbed into the passenger seat.

"Do you know why the victims didn't struggle in the serial cases?" Ajax asked.

"Yes," Ted said, straightening up. "The killer used a drug that numbed the victims. He made a scratch on the victim, and then rubbed in the drug with his fingertip. The stuff was powerful. A thousand times more powerful than anything we've seen on the street."

Ajax whistled. "Where'd it come from?"

Ted put the key in the ignition and started the car. "It was made by the same company that has created BX450, better known as Sunshine. Something that's being developed by a company here in Orange County. I don't know any more than that, except that Brownstone used to own the company, and he tried out the first raw forms of the drugs on himself. The early form of BX450 screwed up his genetics."

Ajax whistled again. "So, it looks as if whoever's doing these new killings is using the same substance Brownstone used to subdue his victims.

Ted sighed. "Looks like it. If so, it's someone who's got access to the same drugs Brownstone used. Once we confirm for certain that Brownstone is dead then we look for our killer among those involved with the pharmaceutical company."

Ajax drummed on the dashboard with his fingers, then stopped and leaned back against the seat as if fatigued. "Shit! Maybe I should have opted out of this job. I could work undercover. Instead I…"

"But instead, you got me!" Ted laughed. "Well, when all this shit is over, I'm definitely planning on retiring to that place I bought in

Julian. My mountain cabin. I should have done it a long time ago."

"Oh, damn! I forgot to tell you. We got word just before we left that the floater washed up. The second guy who washed overboard. The surf plunked his body down on the beach at Little Corona. Scared the bejesus out of some women and kids who were sunbathing there. So that makes how many deaths?"

Ted gave him a sideways look, frowning. "That makes way too many!"

"Sorry to spoil your day."

"Great. Anything else you forgot to tell me?"

"No. Only that at first glance the M.E. thinks the guy died of whatever it was the other guys and the dog, died of. Excessive loss of blood and their insides screwed up."

They reached the end of the peninsula and Ted turned the car down the coast toward the police station. He remembered something suddenly and looked at his watch. It had stopped as usual. The clock in the car didn't work either, at least not when he was in the car. "What time is it?" he asked Ajax.

"Ahhh, close to eleven. Why?"

"I'll drop you off at the station. Get started on the Brownstone thing. I want proof that vampire-like guy is dead. Get the death certificate, eye witnesses, whatever. I'm going to grab a bite to eat and then head back down the peninsula. Got an appointment to talk with the Rosemonds. I'd swear they're covering up something. Three men that they came into contact with them are dead, all from the exact same unknown cause. Kind of makes you feel as if you'd been grabbed by the balls, doesn't it?"

Victor Bryce, sitting in his Newport Beach office, leaned back in his desk chair, facing away from the window, and stared into space. His eyes appeared unfocused and the color that was creeping across his face frightened Brady Twigs. It was an odd mottled purple that made Victor look unearthly, like some creature out of an old alien sci-fi movie. Twigs wondered if the man had run across some problems in his attempt to get what he wanted.

Twigs sat across from him, afraid to break the silence, afraid to broach the subject of failure. Of course, none of it was his fault, but with Victor that didn't matter. He took out his temper on anyone in close proximity. People had a way of disappearing when Victor got angry. Twigs squirmed around in his chair, desperately wanting a cigarette, but knowing it wasn't possible until Victor gave him leave to go. Instead, he took off his baseball cap, finger combed his scraggly hair, and then put the cap back in place.

After a long silence Victor said, "Those men on the Green Latrine had been with me for years."

"Yeah, yeah, I know. It's too bad."

"No one to tell me what went wrong!"

"No sir."

Victor seemed to pull himself together, his eyes focusing once more. He glared at Twigs. "You!" His voice boomed around the large office.

Twigs felt himself pull back and wince. He had no idea what to say.

"You are the one now." Victor pulled open one of drawers on the right side of the desk.

"Me?"

"Yes, you. There's no one else I can trust with such an important job. You understand?" Victor pulled out a large envelope and closed the drawer. He riffled through the contents of the envelope. Twigs tried to see what was in it, but couldn't.

"Well, no sir. I'm not sure what you mean."

"The child! It is now up to you to get the child."

Twigs began to shake his head. He really didn't want any part of it. Nevertheless, he was afraid to tell Victor no again. It was bad enough that he'd refused him the first time. Maybe Victor would blame him for what happened to the boat and his two men. If he hadn't refused to abduct the kid, those two might still be alive. But what if the thing he feared was true, that the child was the cause of their death? Like the birds and the dog on the beach. No, he did not want to go near that child again!

"It appears that hazard pay is in order here." Victor pulled three crisp new thousand-dollar bills out of the envelope. "This is over and above what I agreed to pay you." He pulled out another thousand-dollar bill. "And this is to pay for something that will tranquilize the child."

Twigs leaned forward. "Hey, yeah! That's a good idea. From what I've seen, he's harmless if he's asleep. Maybe that would work. What should I use?"

Victor shrugged. "That's up to the doctor." H reached into his pocket and pulled out a card. "If you see this guy, he'll take care of it for you. Just be certain the child isn't harmed."

Twigs took the card and leaned back. This might not be so bad. If he could put the kid out of it long enough to get him to the lab in Avalon, it could work. After all, three extra grand was nothing to sneeze at. He reached out and touched the bills with his fingers.

"Go head, one of them is yours now. The rest that I owe you will be waiting when you get to Catalina with the child. When you have him, bring him here and you'll find a chopper waiting on the pad atop this building?" With that, Victor turned away from him and looked out the window.

He'd been dismissed, Twigs realized. He could go. It would take some thinking and planning, but he could do what Victor wanted. He felt certain of that. However, it was the last thing he'd do for Victor Bryce. Victor played with dangerous toys. Twigs figured once it was over he'd bank the money and get the hell away from Orange County, and even California. Start a little business."

"Oh, and Twigs...." Victor said, still facing the window. "See to it that I have the child by tomorrow morning."

Twigs slipped the bill into his pocket and got up from the chair. "I'll try," he said.

"No, Twigs, don't try. Do it!"

Twigs rushed from the room. By the time he was outside, he had already lit a cigarette. He hoped to God it would help calm the fandango shakes that were beginning to take hold of him.

꧁ ꧂

Andy was amazed at the way Dr. Terri Mann seemed to connect with Dar. She'd been there about two hours, and Dar had invited her to sit on the floor with him and help build something with his blocks.

"Lizzy, it's great. Look at them," he whispered to Elizabeth. She nodded with a slight smile on her face. The smile made him feel good. She hadn't smiled once that he could remember in the past two days. Seated on the sofa next to her, he slipped his arm around her and gave her an encouraging hug. "It's going to be okay. Wait and see," he whispered.

"Oh," Terri said. "Dar, that's nice. Tell me about what we're building."

Dar looked up at her and screwed up his face, the way he often did when he was thinking. "We build a…bow-at."

"Oh, Dar, you're smarter than I am. And a faster builder."

"Dat's otay. Terri do good." Dar nodded his head vigorously, affirming Terri's status.

"It's a nice boat, isn't it?"

"Terri like?"

"Yes, I do like."

"Dar like too." He added another block to the boat and then inspected their work. He looked down at his chubby legs and frowned. "Dar got ouchy. See." He straightened out his left leg where there were several small but angry-looking cuts.

"Oh, Dar. I bet they hurt. How did that happen? Did you fall down?"

Dar was silent for a moment, still looking down at the cuts on his leg. "No. Dar do…bad ting." With that, he turned and looked over his shoulder at Elizabeth and Andy.

Andy smiled at him. "It's okay, you can tell Terri about what happened," he said.

Dar turned back to Terri and screwed up his face again. "Dar make some of his blocks go bang."

"Oh, my goodness Dar. How did you do that?"

"Wiggled dem."

"I see. Did you mean to do it?"

"Dar mad at dem."

"Does that kind of thing happen when you're mad?"

He nodded yes.

"Can you do it when you're not mad? Wiggle things I mean?"

"Mama says bad. Dar do bad."

"It would be a bad thing if it hurt you, or hurt someone else. But not if you did it to something that didn't matter. Like…well, like one of the pillows on the sofa." Terri looked at Elizabeth for approval who nodded it was okay.

A quiver of apprehension hit Andy. If Dar was responsible for the things that had been happening, as Lizzy believed, wasn't it dangerous to encourage him?

Then again, if he wasn't responsible, maybe this would prove it. For a moment, Andy was tempted to excuse himself and go to his office. He could barricade himself in there until things were right again. He could hide, that's what he could do. Then he looked at his son, so bright, and so loving, and Andy knew he wouldn't run away from the situation, as much as he would like to. Both Dar and Lizzy needed him. He'd find the strength, somehow, to see it through.

Dar squinted at Terri, obviously trying to understand what she had meant.

"What do you think, Dar?" Terri said.

"Dar wiggle pee-low?"

"Yes. If you can wiggle a pillow."

Dar looked at Elizabeth. "No bad, Mama?"

Elizabeth shook her head. "No, Dar. It's not bad, if we tell you to do it."

"Otay," Dar said.

Elizabeth picked up one of the blue feather pillows from the sofa and handed it to Terri.

"If he's able to do this, maybe we'll get a little clue as to how," Terri said.

"Dar do it," he said.

"Yes, I bet you can," Terri said. "And after you do, we'll try and measure the kind of energy you use. That will be a fun game." She turned back to Andy and Elizabeth and lowered her voice so Dar wouldn't hear. "Of course, in most cases, the person can't perform on command. So don't be discouraged if Dar can't do this. We've only just started."

Her words discouraged Andy. How long would all this take? Hours? Days? Months? Years, maybe? He tightened his arm around Lizzy and gave her an encouraging smile. He watched Terry as she placed the pillow a few feet away from him. Then she sat down beside him

"Is this okay, Dar?" she asked.

"Otay. Dar wiggle?"

"Yes." Terri turned to the two of them. "Watch closely. I need your observation too. It's important."

Dar looked at the pillow, his little forehead crinkling.

"You watch the pillow, Lizzy," Andy whispered. "I'll watch Dar." He felt her nod, but she didn't say anything.

Andy heard a soft crackling sound, as if there were a small fire in the hearth. From where he sat, he thought he could see Dar's eyes moving, but he wasn't certain.

Terri must have seen it also because she said, "What do you see, Dar? What is it you're trying to wiggle?"

"Inside," Dar said. "Wiggle inside."

Andy heard Terri give a moan. Then, the air suddenly felt as if it were charged with electricity, an invisible wind surging through the room. Something white erupted and filled the air. A snowstorm was all Andy could think of. Dar had created a snowstorm. But it wasn't snow. It was feathers! From the pillow! The feathers blew high in the air, and then slowly floated down, covering everything in sight. Andy couldn't believe that so many feathers had come out of one small pillow.

When Andy looked at Dar, the boy was covered with feathers from head to toe. Feathers perched on his legs, hands, shoulders, ears, nose, and the top of his head. He turned and looked up at Terri, raising a shower of white down.

"Dar wiggle big," he said sheepishly.

"No," Terri said, reaching for him and hugging him. "Dar wiggle just right."

Andy watched the last of the feathers slowly float to the floor. Then he looked at Elizabeth. "Sweet Jesus!" he said. "What do we do now?"

CHAPTER FIFTEEN

Dr. Terri Mann stood by the sliding glass door, gazing out at the pounding surf. Elizabeth shrugged Andy's arm off her shoulder and got up from the sofa. She hesitated a moment, reluctant. Then, determined to know all the ramifications of Dar's condition, she strode over and stood beside Terri. The Germantown clock struck one p.m. They had been working with Dar for almost three hours. He'd finally fallen asleep on the floor among his playthings. Terri had carried him upstairs to his crib, saying she wanted to see his room. So far, she had remained mum about the tests she'd done. Elizabeth could not restrain herself any longer. She had to know what the doctor thought.

"Are we in a lot of trouble?" she asked.

"You have a breathtaking view," Terri said gazing out at the ocean.

"Yes, we love it." Elizabeth deliberately kept her eyes away from the sweep of blue sea. She needed no distractions. "How bad is it?" she said, her voice hoarse, almost a whisper.

Terri turned to her, her face tight and colorless. "Well, as the old saying goes, there's good news and there's bad news."

"The bad news first, please," Elizabeth said.

"Lizzy," Andy started, and then he shook his head and fell silent.

"Okay." Terri took one more look out the window at the ocean, and then turned away. "Dar's ability far surpasses anything I've seen in a lifetime of study. From what I gather, using what he's able to tell us as criteria, he is somehow able to detect the molecular level of just about anything."

"But how can he do that? He can't see inside something," Elizabeth said. "No one can."

"No, I don't think he actually 'sees' inside something. What I think is going on, is that he has some unusual, to say the least, energy source. The energy seems to be a two-way passage for him. He can import information as well as export physical force. It's strong enough for him to reach out and detect the inner working of not only things, but people. It's also strong enough for him to be able to

142

manipulate what he sees. Wiggle them, as he calls it. Doing so obviously damages the physical structure of whatever he's concentrating on."

Elizabeth frowned and said, "But what about when the object of his attention is at a distance? Like the man on our deck. Can he sense something that far? And what about the prickles or pinchys he says he got—from the dog, and from the men?"

"The fact that he can sense something that may be a threat isn't so unusual. It's a common psychic ability. Even if that threat is coming from some distance. Lots of people have it, although they don't all recognize it. However, to actually be able to do something about that threat is extremely rare. I've never seen it myself, but there are a few obscure papers on the subject. For Dar, at his young age, the pinchys or prickles are his way of sensing danger."

"Okay, put all this together for us," Andy said from where he sat on the sofa.

"Unfortunately, it means your son may possibly be able to destroy just about anything he wants. Something for further study would be discerning just how large an object he could disrupt. However, if anyone angers or frightens him, it's obvious he can easily kill. If something or someone gets in his way, he can wiggle it into a million pieces. We don't yet know the limit of his energy but it appears enormous. The bottom line is he can be extremely dangerous!"

Elizabeth, weak in the knees, went back and sat beside Andy. He took hold of her hand and squeezed it. "What did your test show? The one you used to measure energy?" she asked.

Terri moved to the chair and sat down, looking weary but unruffled. Her silver hair caught the early afternoon sunlight just beginning to flood through the window. "It went off the meter," she said. "I know it's stronger than I could measure, but I have no way of knowing how much stronger."

Both Elizabeth and Andy sat quiet for a moment. Elizabeth tried to digest the information Terri had given them. It seemed far too immense for either of them to assimilate. "Okay then, what's the good news?" she finally asked.

Terri nodded, her face animating somewhat. "Dar seems fairly able to control his actions. It's not something that just spontaneously happens. Of course, he may have a hard time not using it when he's frightened or angry. Nevertheless, he can be taught control. He can learn how to use his, let's call it a gift, for positive reasons. That's the good news."

Andy leaned forward, looking directly at Terri. "Now the hardest question. What caused this? Where did it come from? And why Dar? If we have more children, will it happen again?"

"Oh, Christ, I can't answer those questions! I can only give you suppositions. The drug you explained you're taking is certainly one possibility."

"But I stopped taking Sunshine during my pregnancy," Elizabeth said.

"But you said you were on it when you conceived. Both of you were."

"So both of us could be culprits?" Andy asked.

"Yes. However, I have no idea if that's the cause or not. It could be…well, just a fluke of Mother Nature. She has a weird and dangerous nature at times."

Andy got up from the sofa and began to pace the floor in front of the fireplace. "Some fluke!"

"Would…." Elizabeth stopped, trying to put the entire puzzle together. "Would Dar's 'gift' make him…well, valuable to someone?"

Terri frowned. "You mean the kidnapping? If they knew about what Dar can do, I would guess, yes. Genetic research is making giant leaps. Anyone who could duplicate Dar's abilities in other children would have a tremendous advantage. And if they could control those abilities, well…." Terri shook her head and sighed. "Think of an army of Dars. Think of being able to rule the world. That sounds extremely Orwellian, I know, but it's true."

"So Dar is in danger. If they want him, they won't stop. They'll try again." She turned to Andy. "You see, Andy, we do have to get away from here. Get to someplace where they can't find us."

Terri stood up and looked from one of them to the other. "What if I can find a lab somewhere where Dar could be studied and trained? Someplace safe."

Elizabeth felt her face reflect the horror she felt. "No! Absolutely not! We won't allow him to become a guinea pig. He needs people who love him. He needs Andy and me."

Terri nodded. "Yes, I agree. But where can you go?"

A sudden rapping on the sliding door made Elizabeth jump. When she looked up, she saw Detective Bearbower standing outside on the deck, peering in.

As Ted stood on the deck peering through the sliding glass door, he wondered if the Rosemond woman was to going open the door to him. A fresh wind ruffled the collar of his jacket. She peered back at him for a moment, then put her hand on the door, but didn't slide it open. She waved her other hand at him as if to dismiss him. Ted could see from the expression on her face that she didn't welcome his visit. Excellent, he thought. No better time to question someone than when they were rattled. He motioned to her that he would like to come in.

"Detective," she shouted through the glass. "I'm afraid the doctor is still here, about Dar."

"Good. I'd like to talk with her also. May I Please come in?"

"We're kind of busy."

"I know. But it's absolutely necessary."

With a reluctant tightness to her face, Elizabeth finally slid the door open.

Ted made his way into the room, the toes of his shoes kicking up little eddies of what appeared to be white feathers. He wondered what that was all about.

"Hello, Andy," he said, acknowledging the young man slumped on the sofa. "Elizabeth. I only have a few questions. It won't take long." He turned to Terri. "I'm detective Ted Bearbower, Newport Beach Police. I'm investigating the kidnapping of Elizabeth and her son." He extended his hand.

Terri nodded and shook his hand. "Dr. Terri Mann. I'm just about finished here, Detective."

"Did you find the child well, Doctor?" Ted heard the name Terri Mann echo around in his head. He'd heard it before, but where?

"He seems to be just fine right now." Terri turned to Elizabeth. "I'd better be going. I'll talk with you later tonight."

That was it! Ted suddenly remembered her. Terri Mann, parapsychology researcher. U.C. Davis. Or was it Irvine? He couldn't remember which. He'd seen her on TV, on one of those shows about unexplainable phenomena. What in the hell was she doing here? He knew better than to ask. The woman had the strong look and bearing of someone who would not reveal anything about a patient.

Terri shook hands with Andy, whose face was oddly dark and angry. Ted wondered why. Elizabeth walked Terri to the door and saw her out. When she turned back to him, he could have sworn he saw both fear and hostility in her eyes. These two were hiding something; he'd been convinced of that all along. He wasn't going to leave until he found out what the hell it was. Instinct told him it was an important piece in the enigma he faced.

"I'm sorry," Elizabeth said, her face brightening a little. "Won't you sit down? I warn you, we're all a bit tired and irritable around here."

Ted eased himself into the overstuffed cushion on the smaller of the wicker sofas. "Thank you," he said, trying to smile.

"I'm afraid, Detective that-"

"Let's not be formal. The name is Ted," he said, wanting to rid the atmosphere of the strong tension that had its grip on the room.

"Fine, Ted. What I was going to say is this...we've made up our minds that we have to get Dar away from here. He's definitely in danger."

Andy sat up and looked at her. "Lizzy, are you sure?"

"Positive!"

Andy nodded slowly. "Okay then, we'll find a safe place."

Ted raised his hand. "Wait a moment. As I told you before, we need to be able to reach you, in the event that we get a break in the case."

Elizabeth sat in the chair opposite Ted and looked at him with steely eyes. "There's nothing I can do to help. Both the men I saw are obviously dead. The only thing I can attest to is that Dar and I were abducted."

"Your abductors might have said, or done, something that might reveal who's behind this," Ted said. "You told me they admitted to working for someone else."

"There's nothing more than what I told you," Elizabeth insisted.

From somewhere upstairs, Ted heard a soft wail of a young child. Elizabeth started to get up, but Andy motioned for her to stop.

"I'll get him, honey. You're exhausted." Andy went to the stairway and disappeared upstairs.

"Where would you go?" Ted asked. You can't just take off and hope to find someplace that's safe. I'd prefer to put you under protective custody rather than have you do that."

Elizabeth looked toward the sliding door as if watching the waves folding against the sand. "We have some money put away. We could rent a place. Not tell anyone where we are."

Ted thought about it for a moment. It might be better to go along with her idea. If he could convince her that he could be trusted, she might at least let him know their whereabouts

"Tell me something, Elizabeth. Why do you think your child is still in danger? After all, the kidnappers are dead. If there's someone else involved in this, what makes you think he'll try for Dar again? Why wouldn't he go after another child? Much safer for him. Aren't you being a little paranoid? I can understand that, considering what you've been through. But I really don't think they'd be stupid enough to try for Dar again, do you?"

"Yes!" Elizabeth cried. "I know they will! I'm not being paranoid. Dar is...." She stopped suddenly and got up.

"Dar is what?" He knew he was close to something. Could he shake her up enough to get it out of her?

She walked to the sliding door and opened it wide, letting in gusts of warm wind. They blew the drapes about, but she didn't appear to care. She looked up and down the beach. From where he sat, he could see no one except one of the patrolmen who had been stationed there, and a lone fisherman who looked to be asleep in his beach chair, his fishing line tugging gently against the surf.

"Elizabeth?" he said. "Dar is what? Why do you think someone is still after him? Is there something about Dar? Something that you and Dr. Mann were discussing? Come on level with me here. Let me know what's going on."

"Nothing is going on!" Elizabeth refused to look at him. "Nothing at all. I just feel uneasy. We can't stay here. Too much has happened."

Ted got up, went to doorway, and stood beside her where he could see more of the beach. "Is there something more besides the abduction?"

"Isn't that enough?"

Ted heard Andy's footsteps on the stairs. He turned to see him carrying a smiling Dar.

147

"I think he's hungry," Andy said sitting on the sofa with the boy. "Are you hungry, Dar?"

"Fruit oops," Dar said.

"In a little while," Andy said.

"Dar go potty," Dar said with a touch of pride in his voice.

"Good boy," Elizabeth said turning away from the window.

"What were you looking at on the beach, Lizzy?" Andy asked. "Is that damn fisherman still there? Jesus, I don't think he's ever caught anything that I know of."

"He was there when that dog attacked us. And he didn't do anything to help," Elizabeth said with a tone of anger in her voice.

"Jerk!" Andy snapped.

Ted felt a sting of alarm go off. "Fisherman? Has he been there long?"

"Only about a year. Too young to be retired. Must be out of work." Andy replied. "I see him whenever I walk Dar. He sits in different places up and down the beach. Always wears the same stupid baseball cap. Nothing ever bites. Sometimes I wonder if he uses any bait."

Ted thought about it. Christ! A year with someone possibly staking out the house? Maybe checking on the kid! That'd be a hell of a long stakeout. Still, he'd better look into it.

Elizabeth moved away from the glass door and went to sit beside Andy, taking Dar on her lap.

Ted slid the door open and walked out onto the decking where the policeman sat reading a paperback novel. He leaned down so his voice wouldn't carry. "What's your name?"

"McWhirter, sir." The man snapped the book closed. "You're the dick they call Teddy Bear, aren't you?"

That struck Ted funny. "Yeah, I'm that dick. Listen, McWhirter, I've got something for you to call in. I need some assist ASAP. You see that fisherman over there?" He explained what he wanted, then went back into the house, and closed the sliding door behind him.

"Do you think that fisherman might have something to do with what happened," Andy asked.

"I have no idea, but it's worth checking." Ted sat back down. "Okay, now. Let's see if we can make some sort of deal. You want to go someplace safe. I need to know where you are. We should be able to manage that." Suddenly he knew what to do. He wondered why he hadn't thought about it earlier. "I know just the place for you. I own a little cabin in the mountains near Julian."

"Julian?" Elizabeth looked blank.

"That's fairly close to San Diego. It's gorgeous country. The place isn't large, but it's comfortable. Very remote. You need a four-wheel drive to get to it sometimes. It's not likely anyone would find you there."

Andy and Elizabeth looked at each other. Andy appeared to approve of the suggestion, but Elizabeth looked wary.

"What about Dar? Would it be okay for him there?" she asked.

"Yes, of course. Wonderful place for a child. Besides, it would only be until we can nail down the person who is after your son. That is, if anyone still is."

Elizabeth's eyes narrowed suddenly, as if she'd shut a door. "No!" she said firmly. "I don't think so. I don't want anyone knowing where we go. Not even you."

"Now look," Ted started, feeling his blood pressure climb.

"No, you look!" Andy growled. "It's not your child who's in danger. If Lizzy doesn't trust the situation, then the answer is no."

"Ah, Christ!" Ted stood up, ran his hand through his hair, and heard it crackle from all the static the hot wind had generated. He felt as if the static had invaded his nerve endings too. He wasn't in a mood for this. He was stuck with this case and needed a little help. Just a little, damn it! Well, if he had to, he'd get a court order for this family to stay put. He wasn't going to argue the point. He'd put them into protective custody if he had to.

When he turned to look at the couple, he saw that the child had a strange look on his face. "I'm sorry; I didn't mean to upset the boy. I'm just tired. And I know you two are also."

"It's okay, Dar," Elizabeth said soothingly.

"Prickles," Dar said.

"No Dar, he's a nice man," Elizabeth urged.

"If I can't reason with you, I'm afraid I'll have to put you in custody. I hate to do it, but . . ." Ted looked at the boy again and felt something like an electric shock. Then an odd, uncomfortable, squeezing sensation, gripped his chest. Little pulses of pain, like hot rivets, tore at his lungs. Good God Almighty was he about to have a heart attack?

❦

CHAPTER SIXTEEN

Ted clutched his chest, felt the breath go out of him. He legs turned rubbery and he struggled to stay upright. Looking at Andy and Elizabeth for help, he saw a mixture of horror and bewilderment on their faces. Christ! Didn't they recognize someone having a heart attack when they saw it? Why didn't they call 911? He tried to say something, but didn't have enough breath. Pain wrapped around him like a tight rope.

"Dar!" Elizabeth's voice broke the silence. "Stop!" She looked at the boy on her lap and gave him a rough shake. "Do you hear Mama? Stop, now! He's not going to hurt us. He's here to help."

Why in the hell, he wondered, was she talking to the child instead of getting help? His legs buckled. Like a piece of burning paper, he crumpled and sank to the floor. He tugged at his shirt collar as if opening it would pump air into his lungs. The pain pulsed harder. "Ahhh, damn!" he managed to say. He thought about Maddy and how little time he'd had with her. Not yet! He cried silently. Please God, not yet! A few more years! He thought of a thousand things he'd done and might never do again. Blue-black shadows of the past flowed by him, swerved into sight, and then moved away. The fragrance of summer dust, sunshine on blue water, rumbles of thunder. From what seemed like far away, he heard the wind blowing, knocking on the old house. A death rattle?

Cold gray fog invaded his brain, vaporous at first, then opaque. His heart jangled like a tambourine. Faster. Faster. Icy droplets of sweat rolled off his skin.

"Dar, stop right now!" Andy shouted at the boy. "Don't hurt him!"

Through the fogginess, Ted struggled to understand why the two of them blamed the boy for what was happening. Ted knew that had great significance, but the thick fog choked him mind and he couldn't comprehend the significance. Was his heart attacking him? Or was the boy exerting some sort of...power? That was the only word he could think of. If it was the kid, the son-of-a-bitch was compressing him like a fucking trash compactor. The pain circled around his entire body, burning, pressing, and invading. He let out what he thought was a tortured scream, but heard nothing. Silence rang in his ears. He felt something warm on his face and reached to touch it. His nose was bleeding! Holy Christ! Paralysis gripped him and he knew he had to do something to break its bonds.

"Dar," he finally managed to gasp. "I won't…hurt you…or your parents. *Please!*"

It seemed to Ted that time hung suspended. Even the erratic jangling of his heart ceased. Then, miraculously, the terrible suffocation began to subside. His blood pulsed in his veins again. His regular heartbeat returned. He listened to the rhythm of it pounding in his ears. Its erratic jangles gradually eased into a gentle lub-dub, lub-dub. The quintessential sound thrilled him.

"That's right, Dar. Good boy. Stop the wiggling." Elizabeth stroked the boy gently, soothingly. "It's okay."

The fog in Ted's brain dissolved. He looked at the child who was now snuggled against his mother, his lower lip trembling, tears welling in his eyes. Ted's pain drained away, like water emptying down a drain. He mopped the sweat from his face with the sleeve of his coat. He felt as if he'd been stuffed into a blender and whipped. His entire body buzzed and tingled. Good Christ Almighty! It was the child! What he'd done or how he did it, Ted had no idea. But he was convinced the boy had been responsible, as crazy as that seemed.

"Are you okay?" Andy said as he helped Ted to his feet. "I'm sorry. We don't have much control. Thank God he could stop. I don't think he understands what he's doing. Here, sit down." Andy braced him and led him to wicker chair. "Are you sure you're okay? Your nose is bleeding. Should we get you to a doctor?"

Ted took out his handkerchief and wiped his face and nose. The bleeding had stopped. He shook his head and sat down. "I'm okay. At least I think so. Give me a few minutes." He opened his shirt further and felt for the pulse in his neck, and then put his hand on his chest. Lub-dub. Lub-dub. It labored steadily. Thank God!

Some of his strength returned and as it did Ted felt a rush of anger. "Shit!" he roared. Then, looking at Dar, he thought better of his outburst. "Sorry. But that was one hell of a nasty experience!" He took in several long slow breaths. The pain was mostly gone. He could breathe easier. The buzzing sensation eased, however, his body felt as if a python had hugged it. A little more squeezing and he was certain every vein and blood vessel in his body would have burst. "Okay you two," he said, careful to keep his tone of voice low and calm. "Would one of you please explain to me what just happened?"

Tyree stood at the bar in her living room, stirring her daily dose of Sunshine into a bloody Mary with a piece of celery. Boo, perched on a stool behind the bar, sipped his large Mary. Tyree noticed how fatigued he looked. Dark crescent shadows loomed beneath his eyes. Despite the lines of fatigue, she thought him to be the handsomest man she'd ever known. She had fallen deeply in love with the tall, slender man, when she met him twenty years ago. After eighteen years of marriage, she still felt as if she were on her honeymoon. Boo's thick black hair framed a perfectly oval face and fair complexion. Nothing marred his skin except for a tiny heart-shaped mole on his left cheekbone. Although he attracted other woman, she never worried. He was the type of man who made a commitment and kept it.

His fatigue worried her however. He'd worked far too many hours the past month. She had to do something to stop his compulsion to continue perfecting Sunshine. "What say we take a trip as soon as things settle down with the Rosemonds?" she suggested.

"A trip? Where?"

"Oh, I don't know. Hawaii maybe. The weather's glorious, the ocean's warm, and the food's delicious."

Boo took a long sip of his drink. "I hate pineapple. It makes my mouth burn."

"Oh, stop being such a grouch. That's the problem. We need to get away, relax. I mean, you've been working night after night, for heaven's sake. You're exhausted. Anyone can see that."

"This is a crucial time for Sunshine." Boo refilled his glass from the pitcher on the bar. She saw his eyes narrow, darken. "A very crucial time."

"I thought all our problems would be behind us, now that the money people are in place. The drug's being tested. Why is it so crucial?" Tyree felt an alarm go off. "Don't tell me the Sunshine tests show something negative!"

Boo put his glass down and looked away, staring into space. "No. The tests for the FDA are going just fine."

Tyree's alarm increased. "If it's not the lighter version of Sunshine, then has something gone wrong with our version, the one we're taking?"

Boo shook his head, his black eyes appearing unfocused. "No. No. It's not that either."

"Then what?" Tyree demanded. "What problem do you have that's so crucial you have to work a twenty-hour day to solve?"

Boo turned to her and gave her a grin. "Hey, lighten up honey. You're taking this too seriously. You know I'm a workaholic. Always have been. It's just a pesky problem that's hard to explain. I'll get a handle on it. Not to worry."

Maybe she was making too much of it. After all, she'd never known Boo when he wasn't involved in problem solving. He thrived on it, and withered only when he didn't have some perplexity in his life. He could spend hours, days, on one of those little metal ring puzzles, or Rubik's Cube type things, unable to set it down until he'd solved it.

"Well," she said. "Okay. But, make me a promise. When you get this taken care of, we take off and have some fun."

"It's a deal. Hawaii sounds great. Pineapple and all." Boo picked up his drink. "Cheers," he said, lifting the glass.

Impulsively she reached out and touched the side of his face with her hand. "I do love you, Beauregard Rattigan," she said.

He took her hand and held it to his face. "I hope so. I know I leave you alone too much, and my work gets in the way of a lot of things. Sometimes I'm torn between you and my work. But I do love you the most. I hope you know that."

"Oh!" she said, remembering something. She pulled her hand back and picked up her glass, and took a gulp of her Bloody Mary. "I almost forgot. I had a talk with Foxhoven today."

He looked at her oddly. "Why?"

"I was worried, about Andy and Elizabeth. Or rather, about Dar."

"Well, after what happened the other night with Sarah Zipper, I'm not surprised."

"No. It's not just that. But because of what Dar can do, I've had this terrible fear that…." She peered into her half-full glass of Bloody Mary. "Well, that maybe Barry Brownstone was Dar's father considering the rape." She looked back at Boo and shook her head. "But Foxhoven assured me that the DNA tests showed that Andy is definitely his father. Thank God!"

Boo stared at her for a moment, lowered his drink, and then set it down. "Foxhoven actually told you he did a DNA? Despite a doctor's oath not to reveal anything?"

"Well, yes, in a clever roundabout way."

Boo got up and came out from behind the bar. "That's odd. Because we discussed this whole thing right after Dar was born. Given the genetics involved, and Sunshine, I wanted to know the same thing. However, Foxhoven told me he didn't plan to do a DNA. He was convinced Andy was the father without it."

"Obviously, after you two talked he decided to do the test after all."

Boo looked around, as if trying to locate something. "Have you seen my Reeboks?"

"What? Are you going somewhere? Damn it, Boo, can't you stay home for even a short while?"

"We are going somewhere," Boo said firmly. "You and I are going to talk with Foxhoven." He looked at his watch. "He should be in his office now."

"But I just saw him!"

"There they are. My shoes. Under the coffee table. Come on Tyree, please, let's go."

As he tied each shoelace with careful precision, she shook her head in wonderment. Boo seldom came out of his world of genomes and medical drug culturing so she might as well take advantage of it. What he hoped to gain by seeing Foxhoven, she couldn't imagine. At least they would be doing something together. Perhaps she could at least persuade him to stop on Lido Isle for some lunch. That would be nice.

❦

Ted sat quietly in the Rosemond's living room. He sipped the glass of Brandy that Andy had poured for him, savoring its pungent bite. He hadn't said a word since the young couple had explained more about Dar, and his frightening abilities. The whole idea of a child having the power to pulverize just about anything without touching it, didn't compute, even though Ted had experienced a taste of that power first hand. He began going over the ramifications of such ability. Then he considered the consequences. He could only think so far into the subject before it faded from his mind, as if his internal batteries had gone dead.

Elizabeth had fed Dar and taken him upstairs. Ted had to admit that he felt a hell of a lot more comfortable with the child gone. Andy sat across from him on the sofa with his feet tucked up, his arms hugging his knees. The young man kept sighing. His glances darted around the room as if he were looking for some hidden enemy. Ted had to admit the poor guy had good reason to be edgy. With a son like Dar, it could become a dangerous world, in a thousand ways. Just the thought of a child you could never discipline for fear he'd turn on you, a child whose tantrums could kill, were enough to give Ted a piercing chill. Christ on a crutch! This wasn't possible! Nevertheless, he had seen it, felt it, and knew it was terrifyingly true.

A sudden rap on the glass of the sliding door made him jump. When he looked over, he saw the face of young officer McWhirter peering in. When McWhirter saw Ted, he slid the door open and poked his head inside.

"Sir, that guy on the beach? The fisherman you were concerned about?" McWhirter said. "He's gone. Just packed up and left. Your partner, detective Ajax, called to say one of the officers on the alley side of the house saw that person go to his car. Got the license number. They're checking it now."

"Did anyone follow the guy?" Ted asked.

"Yes sir, but they lost him. He took off down coast highway toward Laguna. At Bluebird Canyon Drive he made a fast left turn and they lost him somewhere in the hills."

"Sounds as if the guy knew he was being followed. Okay, thanks." A strong gust of hot wind swept in through the open door and whipped the drapes about. Christ! Weren't the damn winds ever going to stop? "Are you okay out there?" he asked the officer. "It's blowing pretty hard."

"I don't mind. It's not cold. In fact, it's too damn hot, coming in off the desert. Where I'm sitting shields me from the worst of it. Looks like we're in for another night of Santa Ana winds."

"Sure looks like it." Ted swallowed the rest of his drink, unconcerned whether the officer saw him drinking on duty or not. He was going to retire soon anyway. McWhirter slid the door closed and went back to his patio chair and picked up the book he'd been reading. Ted felt sorry for the guy. Sand was kicking up all over the beach.

Andy shifted his position on the sofa and put his feet back on the floor. "Do you think that guy, the fisherman, has something to do with what's been going on?"

"Wouldn't surprise me at all. Either he loves fish, or he's up to something. And you said he never catches any fish."

"No. In fact, I don't remember ever seeing any bait in his bucket when we've walked by him."

Ted went to a wicker chair and sat down. Elizabeth was right. The child could certainly still be in danger. It appeared that someone had been following Dar's progress, his actions, and waiting for the right time to nab the kid. Obviously, they'd decided the boy was worth the risk of their being involved with a kidnapping.

"Andy," Ted said. "You have to convince your wife that it's safe to go to my place in Julian. At the very least, it will buy us some time."

Andy leaned forward, his face flushed with color now, his eyes no longer darting, but fixed on Ted. "I've been going over everything in my head. I have to accept the facts. Dar is…different and because of that, we're in serious trouble. I hate the situation, but I can't ignore it any longer. I've been acting like…well anyway; it's time I took charge. Lizzy has enough on her hands, working with Dar. I've decided to take up your offer and go to that cabin in Julian. That is, until we decide what else we can do."

"When?"

"Now," Andy said firmly.

"Okay, great. I need to make some phone calls." Ted felt a sense of relief. Doing something, anything, was better than just sitting, trying to understand the incomprehensible.

"You aren't going to tell anyone where we're going, are you?" Andy's shoulders straightened.

"No. No one. Trust me."

Andy nodded. "I'll go up and tell Lizzy. We'll get a few things together. It won't take long."

After Andy left the room, Ted picked up the telephone and dialed Maddy's number at the bakery. It took a few rings before she answered.

156

"A Little Bit of Heaven," Maddy's voice lilted. "May I help you?"

"Maddy, it's Ted. How busy is the bakery?"

"Umm, not very. What did you have in mind?"

"Any chance you could close the bakery? Or get someone to cover for you?"

A long pause at the other end of the phone.

"Maddy?" he said.

"I was just thinking. Jayne is here, doing the cake decorating. I'm sure she wouldn't mind sticking around. Will I be gone long?"

"Yes."

"Okay."

"You've got a Bronco, don't you? Is it running well?"

"Sure. You wanna use it?"

"Yes, please." Ted cleared his throat. "Do you feel adventurous?"

"Always, why?"

"How about a trip with me and some...cousins of mine?" Not only did he want Maddy to come along with him, but it would also look less suspicious. Less like he was escorting the Rosemonds somewhere, more like some friends or family just taking a ride.

"Sure."

Under his breath, Ted blessed the woman. She didn't ask questions, she trusted him, and she was open to most anything. He thought he was probably falling in love with her.

"Wonderful! I'll tell you what; let's meet at my condo. I'll leave the department car there and Ajax can pick it up."

"Is your car on the sick list?" Maddy asked.

"No, but you've got four-wheel drive."

"Ah, I see. This is going to be fun. Shall I pack us something scrumptious to eat? A picnic sort of?"

"That would be fantastic. Enough for four and a half of us? Is an hour okay."

"Sure. See you then. Oh, by the way, what should I wear?"

"Comfortable," Ted said.

"Good," she said and hung up.

Ted went to the window and looked out. The two patrol officers would have to know that they were leaving. He'd tell them they were heading for the station so he could take some statements. He checked in his pockets for his own car keys, and then looked over the bundle of keys for the two that opened the cabin in Julian. Being that they were the only two bright brass keys on the ring, they weren't hard to locate.

He began to plan. He'd take them to the cabin and open up, get the lights and water turned on, and make sure he'd stocked enough food. He didn't want to make any stops on the way, if he could help it. He didn't have fresh milk for Dar, but he always kept a canister of powdered milk. They'd have Maddy's picnic, inside the cabin if Julian was getting the wind. Maybe help Dar to feel at home there. Then he'd secure the place, and he and Maddy would come back down. Maddy didn't have to know the details. He knew he could trust her, if he asked her not to talk to anyone about what or where they'd been. It would work. It had to. At least until they found the slime that was after the boy.

Ted had no idea how long he'd been standing at the door when he heard someone on the stairs. It was the three of them. Andy carried two suitcases while Elizabeth carried Dar, and a blue and white checkered bag for his things.

"We go bye-bye," Dar chirped, clapping his hands together.

"Yes," Ted said. "We're going on a picnic."

"Pig nic, Mama," Dar said.

"Yes. It'll be fun." Elizabeth gave Ted a tenuous look. "I guess we're ready."

"Red dee!" Dar said with a lopsided grin.

Ted looked at the boy, at his chubby pink cheeks and golden curls. On the outside, Dar resembled one of those overly cute cherubs on a Victorian greeting card. What did that bright mask disguise? Ted wondered. How deadly could a child be who looked so damn angelic?

CHAPTER SEVENTEEN

Brady Twigs suspected the police might be onto him. He had lingered on the beach outside the Rosemond house looking for a chance to get inside and grab the child. He seriously wanted to keep Victor happy. Unfortunately, several uniformed police, and what appeared to be a detective, had the house well covered. His idyllic life as an angler had ended. It was time go home and change his appearance. He left the beach and walked to his car parked several houses down the alley. Another car pulled out not too far behind him. He wasn't sure if it was an unmarked police car that followed him, but he could take no chances. He drove down Pacific Coast Highway and then made a point of circling through the Laguna Beach Hills. When he was certain he'd finally lost the car following him, he headed back to Coast Highway. He started thinking about how he could get past the police at the boy's home. He hated the whole idea of kidnapping the kid, but his fear of Victor loomed far greater than his fear of getting caught.

He decided to go home and change clothes, get rid of his scruffy look, shave off his mustache so he wouldn't be recognized as the fisherman on the beach. Then, with his new image, he could go back with his tranquilizer gun the doctor had given him for the baby. He could also use it to zap the cop on the deck. It wouldn't hurt to use a little of it. Victor's guy had given him plenty. After taking care of the lone cop, he'd get inside the house, silently use the tranquilizer gun on all three, and then take off with the kid. He'd never used a tranquilizer gun before, but figured it was pretty much like using a regular gun. The gun was silent and had a night scope, so he would be able to see his target in the dark.

He had to give Victor credit. He thought of everything—could supply you with anything. With as much money as Victor had, you had all the power you needed. As soon as he got the child to Catalina, and collected his money from Victor, Twiggs knew he'd have the power to get away from this whole mess and start over.

It took him a half-hour to get to his apartment in Costa Mesa, shower, shave off his mustache, and change clothes. He decided to wear a blue-and-white tourist shirt with the outline of sailboats on it and the words NEWPORT BEACH across the back and front. Since dozens of people visiting the Peninsula dressed like that, he would hardly be noticed. He slicked his scraggly hair back with water and then inspected his image in the mirror. Pretty good. He rather liked the clean-shaven look. He put on a pair of brand new white tennis shoes with a pair of white socks. His beloved baseball cap lay on the end of the bed. He was tempted to put it on. He felt quite naked without it. Nevertheless, he resisted the temptation. The little mistakes could get you in big trouble.

Ted was relieved to find that all five of them fit easily into Maddy's blue Bronco. Ted drove, with Maddy up front and the Rosemonds in back. Dar rode comfortably in his car seat between his parents. Ted had introduced the Rosemonds to Maddy as his cousins from back East who were going to use his cabin for a while. Maddy, as usual, chatted effortlessly with them, not asking too many questions. Her holiday mood seemed infectious. Watching the young couple through the rearview mirror, he was pleased to see an occasional smile.

The drive took longer than Ted had anticipated. Strong winds battled him the entire trip. He decided not to use the old fire road. Although shorter, it was much rougher. Even with four-wheel drive, he figured there was no reason to make the trip uncomfortable. He took Interstate 78 all the way into Julian and then branched off and onto Willie's Ghost Road. Willie's was rough, but not as rough as the fire road.

It was close to five p.m. when they reached the cabin. Dar had fallen asleep during the last half hour of the trip. Elizabeth picked him up from the car seat without waking him and he continued to sleep in her arms as she carried him toward the cabin.

"This is it, folks," Ted said as he opened the car door and got out. "Such as it is." The sight of his cabin cheered Ted. It was something he'd always wanted. He'd paid for the place with the money he and his wife had saved over the years. The money had been for their retirement, but the cabin had seemed more important. After all, when he sold the condo, he'd have a lot more cash to enhance his golden years.

"Oh, Ted, it's wonderful," Maddy cried. "I had something entirely different pictured."

"Oh, yeah? What did you expect?" Ted asked.

"Golly, I thought it would be a…well, a sort of…shack. This is charming."

Ted agreed. Hand-carved pine logs formed the outside, with a heavy tile roof to protect against forest fires, and an ornate pine front door with an antique brass doorknob. A round stained-glass window picturing a dolphin completed it. The cabin sat on two acres of mountain land filled with pines, scrub oaks, and wildlife. Deer trailed through the area morning and evening looking for handouts. The trees were over-run with gray squirrels who threw pinecones at anyone who ventured beneath them.

"It's really very nice," Elizabeth ventured. "The air smells so sweet here."

"It's the pines," Ted said. A guest of wind curled around them and went past, moaning its way through the trees.

Inside, Ted showed them the large living room with its huge beams supporting the ceiling, and massive fireplace. He pointed out the small kitchen and the one bedroom. Elizabeth put Dar down on the bed and left the bedroom door open so she could hear him if he woke up.

"Well, I don't know about you people, but I'm starved," Maddy said. She put her basket of food down on the small wooden bar that separated the kitchen from the living room.

"I'm kind of hungry myself," Andy said looking more chipper than Ted had seen him. "Anyway, it's actually about suppertime."

"Good," Maddy grinned. "Then I think we should all gather around that gigantic table in front of the sofa right now and enjoy our picnic."

Foxhoven's office nurse looked up at Tyree and Boo, a surprised tilt to her left eyebrow. "I'm sorry, folks, but the doctor's left for the day."

She picked up the appointment book and glanced over it. "You didn't have a late appointment, did you?" She looked back at Tyree and frowned. "You were in earlier today. Are you feeling worse?"

"No, no," Tyree said. "I'm fine."

"We're close friends of the doctor," Boo added. "Can you tell us where we might find him?"

The nurse pinched her mouth together, as if straining to think. "He canceled all of his afternoon appointments, which is unusual for him."

"Maybe he had an emergency at the hospital," Tyree offered.

She shook her head. "No, I would have known about that. He just came out of his office and said to cancel his appointments for the rest of the day. Maybe he wasn't feeling well. You know how men are about admitting that." She smiled at Tyree, who smiled back at her.

"I guess we could try him at home," Tyree said.

"I don't think he's there. His wife called a few minutes ago wanting to talk to him."

"Damn!" Boo said. "We really need to see him."

"The tennis club maybe? But I don't think he'd cancel appointments for that," the nurse said. "Besides, it's pretty late for him to go there.

"I guess tomorrow will have to do." Tyree sighed.

"I'm sorry," the nurse said.

"If he calls in, please tell him the Rattigans need to talk with him."

Outside, Boo stopped and turned to Tyree. "I have a gut feeling that Foxhoven is at the Sunshine lab. He's been spending more and more time there, going over test results, checking out the refinements we've been making in the drug."

"I know he has some money invested in the company." Tyree said

"Some. Come on, let's take a ride down the coast, and check out the lab." Boo turned on his heels and strode off toward the parking lot.

Tyree frowned. What was going on here? Something was definitely rotten in Denmark! "Wait for me!" she yelled after Boo. Whatever was going on, she would make sure she was there. She didn't want to miss a thing.

Maddy unpacked a meal of little rolls stuffed with seasoned pork, a garlic pasta salad, chilled baby carrots in orange sauce and a thermos of lemonade. For dessert, she produced what she called her 'decadent chocolate cake. The four of them sat on the floor around the huge oak coffee table. Dar, wandered around the room exploring everywhere and inspecting everything. He wandered back to the table for a bite of food now and then, and then went off roaming again. Ted was relieved to see him acting like a normal toddler.

"You three should be comfortable here," he said to Elizabeth and Andy. "Unfortunately, there's no phone and there's no cell service in this area. However, I'll be back first thing in the morning. Best thing for all of you is to get a good night's sleep." Ted formed his words carefully so as not to tip Maddy off to the real reason the young couple were staying in the cabin. "Lots of food in the fridge and cupboard. Books are in that shelf over there if you like to read. Deer come by every evening but don't let Dar feed them. They get a little...ahh, feisty I guess you could say. They kick sometimes. Don't want Dar to get hurt. But it's fun to watch them at the salt lick a few yards down the road."

Elizabeth smiled. "Just what we need, some rest and quiet. This is really very pleasant."

Dar ambled back to the coffee table and picked up a small chunk of chocolate cake. "Dar like," he said, grinning.

"Not too much, Dar," Elizabeth warned. "You don't want a tummy ache."

Dar shoved the cake into his mouth. "Otay," he said through dark crumbs. He wiped his hands on the sides of his shirt then turned toward Ted. "Tank you," he said. "Dar like."

"Thank Maddy here," Ted said. "She brought the picnic."

Dar walked over to where Maddy sat on the floor at the table, her peach silk shift flowing around her. He reached out and ran his fingers over the soft material. "Petty," he said.

"Dar, you'll get Maddy's dress all chocolaty."

"Oh," Dar said.

"Honey, don't worry about it. It's washable silk." Maddy extended her arms, inviting Dar to sit with her. He grinned widely and accepted the invitation, plopping down beside her.

Ted blanched. Even though everything had gone perfectly so far, he hoped Maddy didn't accidentally do anything to upset the child. It probably wasn't fair of him not to tell her the seriousness of the situation. Putting her in danger without her knowledge suddenly seemed wrong. He could trust her, he knew. He decided that on the way home he'd fill her in on all the details, as unbelievable as they were.

"Is it okay with your mother if you have more lemonade?" Maddy asked Dar.

Dar turned to Elizabeth and lifted his eyebrows. "Otay, Mama?"

"Sure," Elizabeth assured them.

Maddy reached out for the thermos of lemonade but as she did, she accidentally knocked it over. It hit the tabletop with a resounding thump. Gold-yellow streams of lemonade spewed out across the table.

"Oh!" Maddy cried. "I'm sorry!"

"Dar fix!"

"No, Dar!" Andy shouted, but his warning came too late. The yellow pools of lemonade began to twist and churn.

"Dar!" Elizabeth tried to scramble to her feet, but Dar's actions were too fast.

"Upsy-daisy," Dar chirruped. A moment of silence held the room. Even the wind outside abated for a few seconds. A veil of blue light curled its way around Dar. Ted looked at Maddy whose face had suddenly gone as loose and shapeless as a wet paper mask. A soft crackling replaced the silence. Ted's scalp tingled and he expected his hair to suddenly stand on end, the way the hair on one's arms did when exposed to static electricity. The palms of his hands itched, as did the arches of his feet. He looked back at Dar, and he could have sworn his eyes were made of blue glass.

With a clatter that echoed metallic around the room, the thermos suddenly stood upright, wavered for a moment, and then settled silently on the coffee table. The churning lemonade began to flow uphill, along the sides of the container, and then slid like molten gold into the mouth of the thermos. Four or five last drops hung at the edge, gleaming, before disappearing.

Ted realized he had been holding his breath for quite some time. He exhaled, and then noisily gulped in some air. Elizabeth, who had gotten to her feet, sat back down. Andy sat still, mouth open and closing without a sound. The firmness slowly crept back into Maddy face, bringing with it a rosy flush.

"It otay now," Dar said clapping his hands together. He turned and looked up at Maddy. "All bet ta," he smiled.

Maddy looked at the thermos, then back to Dar, then back to the thermos. "My," she said in a breathless whisper. "What a clever boy you are!"

CHAPTER EIGHTEEN

Tyree believed SunTech Inc., where they manufactured and tested Sunshine, was the most stunning laboratory in the world. It was once a posh hillside restaurant with cascading waterfalls, panels of blue tinted glass, and a Koi pond lined with hand-painted tiles. The restaurant owner, after skimming more than profits from the business, had skipped the country. Sunshine's conglomerate had picked up the property at a short sale from the bank. The real money went into converting the inside into a laboratory.

Tyree and Boo arrived at SunTech at six p.m. to find the lobby empty and the receptionist gone for the day. Music streamed softly from the sound system.

"I'll only be a minute," Boo said. He dashed off, leaving Tyree standing in the lobby, and then disappeared down the corridor. She could hear his shoes smacking the silvery gray tile floor as he went.

"Hey!" she yelled after him. Her voice echoed through the hallways. She shrugged and seated herself on the leather sofa where she could see the sweep of ocean and bay through the wide windows. On the horizon, a blazing sunset stained the western sky and stippled the ocean with scarlet whitecaps.

Lulled into a pleasant reverie by the music and the view, she was suddenly startled by loud voices at the far end of the corridor. She recognized one of them as Boo's. He sounded angry. Was the other one Foxhoven's? Curiosity got the better of her. She got up and walked down the hallway in the direction Boo had gone. The voices faded. She moved closer to the small office that she knew Foxhoven kept there. The door to his office was slightly ajar. She pushed it open and stepped inside.

"We've got to find out what the hell is going on!" Boo said, lowering his voice. The other man wasn't Foxhoven; it was Benji, the head of genetics at Sunshine. The small man's face was flushed a mottled pink, not only his cheeks, but also his smooth baldhead. He pressed his mouth into a tight straight line. However, when he saw Tyree, his expression changed from one of determined stubbornness to a pleasant smile.

"My, I haven't seen you in a long time, Mrs. Rattigan." Benji walked over and took Tyree's hand in his. His fingers, as round as sausages, felt soft and warm. "Maybe you should come more often and keep this husband of yours from borrowing trouble." He turned and gave Boo a warning look. "Just be careful, that's all I ask. I think you are...well, never mind what I think. You'll do whatever you like, as usual." With that, he squeezed Elizabeth's hand, dropped it, and then abruptly left the room.

"Damn!" Boo spit out. "That's one ornery man."

"What's going on?" Tyree asked. "Is Foxhoven here?"

"He was, but he left." Boo paused a moment then straightened his back and lifted his head, as if he'd made a decision. "Do you have a nail file or anything like that?"

Tyree gave him a quizzical look. "Whatever for?" She opened her purse and felt around on the bottom. "I always carry the Swiss Army knife you gave me for our first Christmas," she said with a slight laugh. "Here," she handed him the red-handled set of knives.

"I knew that would come in handy one day," Boo said. He moved to Foxhoven's desk, sat down in the chair and bent over the top right-hand drawer. He opened one of the knives and began fiddling with the lock on the drawer.

"Whoa, wait a minute Beauregard! What are you doing? That's Foxhoven's desk. You can't break into it!" Tyree looked at Boo, aghast. "All we wanted to do was ask him whether or not he actually did a DNA test on Andy and Dar."

Boo didn't respond to her, but continued to jimmy the drawer lock. Tyree wanted to reach out and stop him, but since it was so out of character for him to be breaking into someone's desk, she hesitated. Had he flipped out? Foxhoven could probably press some kind of charges against him for what he was doing. Tyree heard a sharp metallic click.

"Ahhh," Boo said. "That's got it." He pulled the drawer open and pulled out a bundle of file folders.

"Boo! You can't do that!" She went to him and put her hand on the pile of folders. "What are you thinking of? We can talk to him tomorrow. You don't have to do this!"

Boo looked up at her. "I haven't lost my mind, Tyree. Please. Just let me look through these. I assure you, I have a good reason."

Tyree stared at him for a moment then withdrew her hand. She went to the visitor's chair and sat down heavily. "We're both going to end up in jail, Boo. If Foxhoven should walk in here...."

Boo ignored her and began to thumb through the papers in the folders. Tyree fell silent. Her heart raced and her hands turned sweaty. Boo set one folder aside and returned his attention to the others. After what seemed like hours, he finished the last folder, set it on the desk, and leaned back in the chair. He looked at her, his eyes dark and penetrating. Something bad was happening here, she told herself. Something she really didn't want to know about.

Boo lifted one of the folders and handed it to her. Reluctantly, she took it and opened it. For a few seconds, she was afraid to let her eyes focus on what was on the paper in front of her. When she finally did, it was as if she'd been shot with a dose of adrenaline. She let out a gasp.

"Oh, my God, Boo!" she cried. "This can't be!"

"That's not all of it," Boo said. "There's more."

The folder fell from Tyree's hand, but she didn't bother to pick it up. "Let's just walk away from it, Boo. Let's just leave and pretend we don't know. Please!"

Boo's dark eyes locked with hers. "You know we can't do that, Tyree. We have to do something."

Tyree closed her eyes to avoid Boo's stare. "Yes, I know," she whispered, then started to cry. "I know."

Twigs ditched the van, the one he'd stolen earlier that day, and picked up another car, this time a late model Acura Legend. He liked the way the Acura drove. Very smooth. Maybe, when Victor finally paid him for this job, he'd get his own Acura. He'd like that. The idea made him feel a little better about the job he had to do.

When he reached the Rosemont's house on the beach, he found that the two policemen who had been assigned to the alley side of the house were still there. He parked the car a few houses down the alley and got out. Taking the path between the houses, he made his way onto the beach and then walked through the sand to the Rosemonds house.

"Hi there," he said to the cop sitting on the deck.

The cop, startled, started to stand up. However, Twigs fired the tranquilizer gun and within seconds, the man went down. There hadn't been time for him to alert the cops on the other side of the house.

He moved quickly, checking the sliding glass door. He couldn't see anyone inside. The door was unlocked. He quietly slid it open just enough for him to get through. There was only one light on in the living area. All he could hear was the ticking of a Grandfather clock near the stairs.

"Son of a bitch!" he grumbled. "This is too easy. What's wrong?"

He quietly searched everywhere downstairs, and then started up. His fear was that he'd meet someone coming down, so he loaded the tranquilizer gun again and held it ready. It seemed too early for everyone to be in bed but maybe they had gotten ill or something. He checked each bedroom and what looked like an artist's studio and found no one.

"Damn it! They're gone!" he snarled. Would they be back, or had they snuck away, under the radar? He let out a long anguished sigh. How could he explain this to Victor? He'd been sloppy and taken too much time cleaning up. Now he was certain they had left and secreted the boy away from everyone. Well, he would find them, no matter where they'd gone, and get the child. If he didn't, his life wasn't worth a hill of beans. Victor would see to that.

Back in the car, he fumbled in his pocket for his cell phone. There was a way to find out anything. Finding out things was his specialty. He was good at it. He quickly dialed the number for the Newport Police and waited while it rang.

"Police Department," a young woman's voice said. "Is this an emergency?"

"No," Twigs said. "I'm trying to get in touch with a certain detective. The one I met on the peninsula today. Can't remember his name. He was at the Rosemonds. They're neighbors of mine. I may have some important information for him."

"Concerning a case?"

"Yes, that's right."

"Okay, please hold while I see what I can do."

He heard a click as she put him on hold. It wouldn't take long and he'd be off to find the child. He smiled to himself, reached into his pocket and took out a pack of Spearmint gum. He unwrapped a piece, and popped it into his mouth.

After Ted and Maddy left the cabin at ten p.m., Elizabeth took some blankets and pillows from the bedroom. She decided they would all sleep in the living area next to the fireplace instead of in the bedroom. The double bed wasn't large enough for the three of them. She knew that Andy would be happy to sleep on the sofa so she and Dar could share the bed, but she wanted them all together. It felt safer that way. She made a cozy spot for each of them. Andy kept yawning and she knew that he was as exhausted as she was. They would sleep soundly tonight. Outside, the wind sang through the pine trees and howled around the eaves of the cabin making a rather unearthly duet. Elizabeth was glad for the sound. It had been a long time since she'd gone to sleep without the rumble of surf in her ears.

"Should we leave the lights on?" Andy suggested.

"No," Elizabeth said. "We don't want anyone to know someone is staying here. It's better if it's dark."

"I think one of us should stay awake…just in case." Andy went to the door and locked it, then put the chain in place. "I'll take the first shift. You get some sleep. You really need it."

"Oh Andy, you're just as tired as I am."

"No I'm not. Don't argue."

Elizabeth nodded, thankful for Andy's mandate. Her entire body ached from fatigue as well as from the terrible time she'd had on the boat. She wasn't certain how much longer she could manage without a good night's sleep. She crawled under the quilt she'd spread on one of the two sofas. Dar was already asleep on the other one. Andy settled down in a leather recliner.

She didn't fall asleep as quickly as she'd expected. Thoughts and ideas about what they should do next and where they should go tumbled through her mind. Her parents had moved to Seattle the year before. She knew the three of them would be welcome there. However, that would be too easy for someone to trace. No, they had to go somewhere that no one would think of. Maybe Oregon, find a little place in the forest area. Or Hawaii. She wondered if Andy would be able to keep on writing. Maybe using a different name. Her thoughts became ragged, and it wasn't long before she found herself being sucked into a dark, dreamless sleep.

Ted fought the increasing wind as he and Maddy drove along the mountain road toward Pacific Coast Highway. Every now and then, he felt it lift the car slightly, and he worried about losing control. He slowed his speed. No need to have the car overturn, or maybe get pulled over for speeding. Besides, he enjoyed having some time with Maddy. He'd decided to retire soon, possibly after this case was over. He hoped he could persuade Maddy to move to the cabin with him. Maybe they could open an apple pie shop in Julian. He'd bet that together they would make the best-tasting pie on the face of the earth. He smiled at the thought.

"Such a nice young couple," Maddy said. "I think they really liked my picnic."

Ted realized it was time for him to explain what had happened earlier with the lemonade. Maddy had taken it in stride, as if things like that happened every day. He knew she wouldn't ask about it, but he owed her an explanation.

"Yes," Ted agreed. "I guess by now you've figured out they aren't really my relatives." He glanced over at her and saw her anxious face in the dim light. Still, she didn't say anything. "They're part of a case I'm working on. It's very involved, so I won't go into all of it. What I will tell you is that yesterday someone tried to kidnap the child. They took the mother also and attempted to kill her. Thank God, the kidnapping was thwarted."

"So, you put them in your cabin for safekeeping."

"Basically, yes." Ted wondered how in the hell to broach the subject of Dar's abilities. She'd seen a small example of it herself, but explaining it was something else.

Maddy solved it for him. "I assume they wanted the child because of what he can do."

"Yes," Ted said, relieved.

"Can he do more?"

"A lot more!" The wind eased some, for which Ted was thankful. "I should have told you about the boy. It wasn't fair of me to keep what he could do a secret."

"Don't be silly. I'm sure you didn't expect him to...perform like that."

Ted felt a lick of shame. "Well, actually, I should have expected it. I had just had a very nasty experience with what the child could do. Take my word for it! He can be dangerous!"

"That little angel! I don't believe it!"

"Believe it," Ted said. "I shouldn't have put you in danger without your knowledge. I just didn't want to make this trip alone. I wanted to be with you."

"Thanks, I think." Maddy gave a rumble of a laugh. "Okay, so he's psychokinetic. And dangerous."

"You know about that stuff?"

"A little. I've read some things. Poltergeists and all. Quite interesting."

A sudden bleeping sound caused Ted to brake the car. He looked at the control panel to see if any of the dash lights were on. "Maybe we're low on oil or something?" He pulled the car over to the shoulder of the road.

"No, no! That's my cell phone. It's in the glove compartment," Mandy explained.

"I'm surprised there's service here. Although we almost to Julian now.

"Maybe it's Jane at the bakery. She's the only one I know of who'd think to call me on the cell phone. I like having it for safety, in case I get stalled somewhere alone at night." She reached into the glove compartment, pulled out the phone, and punched the on button. "Hello? What? I can't hear you." She put her hand over the mouthpiece. "The signal is bad. Doesn't sound like Jane, though. A man I think. Probably a wrong number." She gave the phone a shake, as if that would solve the problem. "I'm sorry, what? Say it again, please. Oh. Yes. Okay." She took held the phone out to Ted. "It's for you!"

Ted blinked at her, unable to comprehend how someone could be calling him, on Maddy's cell phone. He took it from her and held it to his ear. "Bearbower," he said. He did what Maddy had done and gave the phone a shake. "I think it's Ajax, my partner but I can't make out a damn thing he's saying. Ajax, if you can hear me, give me thirty minutes and call back." Ted hung up the phone and handed it to Maddy. "How the heck did he get your number?" He pulled the car out onto the road, anxious to make his way down the mountain as fast as possible.

"He probably talked with Jane. Earlier, did you tell Ajax you were with me?"

172

"Yes, actually I told him we had a date." He grinned at the word 'date'. "That must be it. Christ! I hope we don't have another bizarre homicide on our hands." He let out a long sigh. "They're beginning to pile up."

As Ted maneuvered the car around the twists and turns of the mountain road, he realized how dark it was. With no streetlights, houses or other cars around, he felt as if he were driving through a black hole. He didn't like the feeling at all. He had the eerie sensation that the darkness could grasp him, hold him, and never let go. Mountain road, or no mountain road, he pressed his foot against the accelerator and made his way as fast as possible toward civilization.

Brady Twigs put a fresh piece of chewing gum in his mouth, and then leaned back against the black leather seat of the Acura. The car practically steered itself. He drove with his left hand and ran his right over the soft leather seat beside him. Such luxury. The drive along the I-15 freeway had been a breeze. He'd done ninety most of the way, with not a police car in sight. Now here he was zooming along on the twists and turns of Highway 78, and marveling at how well the car took the curves.

It had taken him exactly ten minutes to find out where the detective had taken the child and his parents. Like chain links, he'd gone from one person to another at the police department until he had enough links to make a whole chain. The chain led to Julian where the detective owned a cabin. After that, finding the location of the cabin was a snap. The good detective hadn't told anyone where he was going, or that he had the Rosemonds, but the links fit together flawlessly.

He stopped feeling the leather and reached over to the passenger seat and picked up the tranquilizer gun. He had six rounds, enough to put down an elephant. He had to make certain he got the child first; otherwise, he'd be in danger. At least that's what Victor had told him.

"If the child's awake, you'd better think good thoughts," Victor had said. "And keep your mind a blank, which should be easy for you. From what we know, the child can sense danger from quite a distance. So don't pose a threat to him until he's tranquilized."

Think good thoughts, Twiggs told himself. Use your mantra. He'd long been into meditation. His hadn't been part of the hippie generation, although he wished he had. He loved their motto of smoke a joint, say your mantra, and mellow out. Only this time he wouldn't have the help of any pot. Well, he'd better start now. He wanted to have a quiet mind before he reached the child. He put his Eternal Om DVD into the Acura's player and turned it on.

"Ommmmmm," he intoned quietly along with the tape. "Ommmmm." He liked the way the mantra resonated around the interior of the car. When this business was done, he'd buy a new Acura and travel across the country—driving and meditating. The thought of that made him feel almost lightheaded. It wouldn't be long now.

CHAPTER NINETEEN

The night seemed darker than usual when Dar awoke. He'd become used to the nightlight on his chest of drawers at home. He missed it. He lay on the long sofa listening to the wind outside the cabin. It sounded much different than it did at home. He missed his crib and the colorful blocks that hung over it. Even so, he really liked the cabin. So many new places to explore.

He tried to decide if he wanted to get up and do more exploring or go back to sleep. But he wasn't at all sleepy so he got up and padded over to the other sofa. He found Mama sleeping there. Even in the dim light, he could see that her mouth was slightly open. She had a pale green blanket spread over her. He patted her arm gently. It would be bad to wake her. After that, he walked carefully around the dark room until he found Daddy sleeping in a chair, his head tilted back. Daddy always made a soft rasping sound that Dar loved to hear. He touched Daddy's arm. Daddy lifted his head and Dar was afraid he'd woken him. He didn't mean to. He could feel how tired they both were. But Daddy just turned his head another way and kept sleeping.

He wandered over to the window of the small living room. It was a different kind of window than he had at home. He wasn't tall enough to see outside. A wooden chair sat next to the window and he thought he could climb up on it and be able look. He had to tug the chair a foot or so to position it. Then with great effort, he managed to haul himself up onto the wooden seat of the chair and stand up.

"Oh," he whispered, peering outside. "Dark!" He couldn't remember ever seeing anything as dark before. When Dar looked out his bedroom window at home the ocean always glowed slightly, illuminating the edges of the sand. But here it was like looking into a great emptiness. He was about to climb down off the chair when he realized he was now seeing a few dark forms. Trees bending in the wind. Some huddled rocks.

The dark night was full of all kinds of things now that his eyes had adjusted. He pressed his face against the glass, eager to see more. He heard the wind howl, a much different howl than it made at home.

After staring through the window for a long time, discovering more and more shapes in the darkness, his eyes felt heavy and he rubbed them with his fists and yawned. "Sleepy now," he whispered to himself. He yawned again and was about to climb down off the chair when he felt something. Uncomfortable little prickles were jabbing at him. He rubbed his stomach and chest, hoping to get rid of the feeling, but instead, it grew stronger. He sat down on the edge of the chair seat. He mustn't pay attention to the pinchys and prickles. He wasn't supposed to do anything about them. He dangled his feet trying to reach the floor and finally managed to slide off the chair.

He crept his way back to the sofa where he'd been sleeping. He heard Mama and Daddy both move slightly and settle into new positions. He crawled back under the blanket and pulled it up around his chin. It felt soft and comforting. He closed his eyes. The pinchys didn't get any worse, but they didn't get any better either. He tried to figure out where they were coming from, but couldn't. Too far away. He turned on his side, determined to ignore the awful feeling. He would sleep and the pinchys wouldn't bother him.

It seemed like a long time before he finally felt sleep tugging at him. As he drifted off, he was only slightly aware that whatever was causing the painful pinching was moving closer and closer.

When Ted and Maddy finally reached the tiny town of Julian, Ted pulled the Bronco over to the shoulder of the road. He reached into the glove compartment and pulled out Maddy's cell phone.

"I know I told Ajax to call me back, but I think I'd better try and reach him," he said. "It sounded urgent."

Maddy smiled at him and nodded.

He tapped in the phone number and waited. Outside, a gust of wind buffeted the car roughly.

"Is that you, Ted?" Ajax's voice rang in his ear. "We've got trouble!"

"So what else is new," Ted growled.

"I mean real trouble!"

Ted looked at Maddy and rolled his eyes. "Great," he grumbled.

"Listen, Ted, I don't know where you are or what you're up to. All you said was that you were going somewhere with Maddy. Later, someone called the department trying to locate you. Said they had some info on the homicide on the peninsula. I don't know which homicide they meant. The guy on the deck who bled to death, or the dead transients who looked as if they'd been hit by a vampire. They transferred the call to me, but he wouldn't tell me anything more. He only wanted you. I told him you weren't available, but he kept at me. I think I goofed! Bad!"

"How's that?" Ted asked, feeling a sharp-edged curl of apprehension.

"Well, the more I thought about it, the more I realized the guy wasn't on the level. But I didn't realize it soon enough…before I told him about…. Well, anyway, all he wanted to do was find you."

"Ajax! You're driving me nuts! What did you tell him?"

"That you might be at your cabin in Julian."

"Ah, Christ!" Ted closed his eyes and took a deep breath. "What in the hell made you think of that?"

"I don't know. You're always talking about retiring there. You mentioned something about you and Maddy living there, maybe opening a pie shop. I guess I just put it together with your spending the afternoon with Maddy. Tell me I'm wrong. Please!"

It wasn't Ajax's fault, he realized. He had gone on and on about the cabin. "No. You're not wrong. What else did you deduct?" he said in a level voice.

"I didn't tell him where in Julian or anything like that. But the words just came out and I couldn't take them back. I tried to divert him after that. I told him it was more likely you were at the bakery, or a movie, or a bunch of other things. Maybe he didn't pick up on Julian. Anyway, I hoped that he wouldn't know how to find the cabin."

"Don't bet on that," Ted said. Ajax was silent for a moment. Ted heard his labored breathing.

"I'm sorry Ted, I realize now that you used Maddy as a cover and took the Rosemonds to your cabin. Christ! I hope I didn't put the wrong person onto it."

"Listen, I should have trusted you and let you know what I was doing. My own fault." Ted sat for a moment staring into space. He knew he had to jump into action, but felt completely paralyzed. He'd promised the young couple they'd be safe, and now it was evident they might be in worse jeopardy than they would have been at home.

"By the way, Captain wants us off the kidnapping case," Ajax said. "And he wants us to switch to investigating the transient deaths instead. Says you're the one most familiar with this vamipirish kind of thing.

"Lucky me!"

"He said the FBI would be stepping into the kidnapping soon."

"Yeah, well we can't wait for soon! We need to act now, or the boy will be gone, probably without a trace. So, arrange for some SWAT teams up here ASAP, and seal up the whole area. I'm going back to the cabin. Let's pray I can beat whoever it was that called you."

"Okay, will do. But...that's not all of it."

"What!"

"Well, the good news is that that Brownstone guy you had me check out, he's not only merely dead, he's really most sincerely dead!" Ajax said in a melodious tone. He's gone where the goblins go, Below - Below - Below!"

"You're positive?"

"Positive. I talked to the coroner, and the funeral director. They said he was now just ashes, which were buried in a regular plot. Seems some group of people in Newport Beach paid for everything."

"Good, now get to work Ajax, my little tarantula!"

"Yeah, okay I'll take care of the SWAT teams. I hope the Captain isn't too angry."

"Fuck the Captain!" Ted felt his adrenaline take over. It bit him, hot and nasty, but he was glad for it. He clicked off the phone, sucked in a deep breath, and looked over at Maddy. "I need to drop you somewhere, fast!"

Maddy shook her head. "No way! I'm with you. Don't waste time finding a place to drop me."

Ted frowned. "I've already put you in too much danger," he argued, but saw by the expression on her face that it was useless. "Okay, is your seat belt fastened? Right. Then hang on! It's going to be rough. I'm going up the fire road, the back way. It's shorter. I need to get those kids out of there."

The Bronco's tires squealed like pigs being slaughtered as Ted pulled out onto the highway and made a wide U-turn. He wasn't about to let anything happen to the Rosemonds or the child. He sure as heck didn't need that kind of guilt hanging around his neck for the rest of his life.

Brady Twigs swung the Acura around the mountain curves doing seventy. At this rate, he'd be in Julian in a few more minutes. The cabin was only a short distance up Willie's Ghost Road. He grinned, feeling pleased with himself. He had looked up Bearbower's address in the phone book, quickly driven there, and then easily broke into the condo. The place had been a burglar's delight. Stupid police detective! The kitchen window had been left slightly ajar. He'd slipped the screen off, pushed the window wider, and crawled in. It took him less than a minute to find Bearbower's desk and the address book with the address of the cabin.

As he drove the mountain road toward the cabin, Twigs checked the passenger seat where the tranquilizer gun lay. He hoped that the darts would be enough. He carried a regular gun, but he'd never killed anyone. He refused to take a life, even if it made Victor angry. Actually, even the idea of kidnapping was aberrant to him. His specialty was surveillance. He loved a stakeout. He didn't mind breaking and entering.

He hated his job tonight. However, he'd promised, and he knew that if he pulled it off Victor would be impressed with his skills. He had to keep his mind on the money, on the future, and not fret over what he had to do.

As the car sped around the mountain road, Twigs went back to reciting his mantra. "Ommmm," he intoned, enjoying the soothing vibrations from the ancient sound.

Andy felt a dull ache in his back and suddenly realized he'd been sleeping in a recliner chair. He opened his eyes and looked around, wondering where in the hell he was. The darkness around him was complete. He stretched his arms, trying to get rid of the tingling in them. Then he remembered. They were in a cabin in Julian. The thought soothed him. He yawned. He was supposed to stay awake and guard the place. But the past few days had caught up with him. He got up and stretched his back, feeling the ache dissolve. He felt his way to the end of the longest sofa. He could just make out Dar's gold curls. He gently pulled the blanket up around the boy, then stretched out on the opposite end of the sofa and covered himself with an afghan that Elizabeth had left there.

No one knew where they were except Bearbower and his lady friend. The cabin was safe. No reason he couldn't get a decent night's sleep. After all, in the morning they had some tough planning to do. Where would they go? What could they do about Dar? Impossible questions, but ones they had to find answers for. Andy yawned and almost instantly fell asleep again.

Dar tossed in his sleep, dreaming about spiders. One large one crawled closer and closer, and Dar found he was unable to move. He wanted to run. He tried to call Mama.

The spider was going to bite him. Dar tried to cry out, but no sound came from his mouth. It took every effort to finally flail his arms about. The effort woke him. He sat up, feeling his small heart thump violently in his chest. His body filled with pinchys. The spider, he told himself. It must have been the spider that caused them. He lay down and closed his eyes. He really didn't want to go back to sleep and dream about more spiders. But he didn't want to stay awake either, feeling the awful pinchys. He thrust his thumb into his mouth and let it soothe him. He had to control himself and not let the pinchys get to him. He had to be a good boy and make Mama happy. With some effort, he managed to push the pinchys away. When he fell asleep again, his dreams were about rainbow-colored soap bubbles, the kind the Zipper sisters made for him when he went to visit them.

CHAPTER TWENTY

Twigs parked the car a short distance from the cabin. He was certain no one could hear the engine over the howl of wind. Great dark pine trees swayed around him as if alive. He picked up the tranquilizer gun and loaded it with one of the darts. The others he put in his jacket pocket. He checked the night scope to make sure it was secure. With the scope, he would be able to spot his target in the dark. First, the child. He wasn't sure what kind of things the child could do. "Tranquilize the boy while he's sleeping," Victor had warned him. "That way you'll be safe."

Twigs couldn't imagine why he wouldn't be safe, but an image of what had happened to the dog on the beach, as well as all the seagulls, gave him a worrisome warning. He hesitated a moment before getting out of the car. Maybe he should just back away from all this, get in the Acura, and drive to Las Vegas. There he could get his savings out of the bank and disappear somewhere. Someplace where Victor couldn't find him. Only problem was, the money he'd saved wasn't enough. Not really. No, he needed the bonus money from Victor. Then he'd be set until he found a regular job.

Twigs opened the car door and got out, the tranquilizer gun in his hand, and made his way to the cabin's small wooden porch. He didn't have to worry about being quiet with the wind making such a racket. He moved to the window and looked in. Inside the cabin it was even darker than outside. He raised the gun and looked through the infra-red scope. He could make out the back of two sofas, some chairs, and a table. If there were people in there, he couldn't see them. Most likely they were asleep in the bedroom.

He leaned the gun against the side of the cabin and took a pack of lock-picks out of his pocket. It took him several seconds to trip the lock on the front door, only to find a chain barring his way.

"Son of a bitch!" he muttered. He picked up the gun and made his way around the cabin, checking windows. All of them were tightly locked. Frustrated, he moved back to the front porch. He fumbled in his pocket for his glasscutter. He hated using it because it made too much noise. With the wind's sound as a cover, he set about cutting out part of the round stained glass window in the front door. He had difficulty cutting through some of the leading. It took him longer than he'd planned. Finally, with enough glass carefully removed, he was able to reach in and slip the chain off the door. By then he was sweating and under his jacket, his tourist shirt clung wetly to his back.

Inside, he slowly walked through the living room toward what he thought should be the bedroom. It was only by chance that he turned and looked down at the two sofas. The sight of three people asleep there made him jump. His heart pounded so loudly in his ears that if it hadn't been for the wind, he was certain the sound would have woken them.

He lifted the gun and sighted the child. The first dart in his gun was the one for the child. The rest were adult doses. His shot hit the child exactly where he wanted, on the fleshy area of his arm near his shoulder. The boy made a small jerk, but that was it.

The sound of the gun, a dull clank, caused both the sleeping parents to jump. The second dart caught the woman in the shoulder as she started to sit up. She didn't make a sound, as she slumped back on the sofa. However, the noise of the second shot aroused the man enough to get him to his feet. Twigs felt more sweat break out as he reached into his pocket and loaded a third small dart. His fingers felt thick and twice the size as usual, as he attempted the maneuver. The man let out a yell and started toward him just as Twigs got off his third shot. The dart hit the man on part of his upper arm. The effect took a few seconds to take hold. The man didn't let the dart's impact stop him. He leapt forward and lunged at Twigs. Twigs stepped aside and gave the man a whack on the head with the barrel of the gun. That did it. The man went down.

Twigs fumbled for a light, found a lamp which he switched on, then looked at the unconscious trio. He checked each of them to make certain they were really out of it. Boy, he thought, that stuff is great! Victor said it should last at least a half hour on the adults, maybe longer on the child. He spotted a blue and white checkered bag sitting to one side of the sofa, picked it up and looked over the contents. Good, a small blanket, a baby bottle and what looked like a bottle of juice. With the child tranquilized, he probably wouldn't need them, but he took the bag just in case.

He quickly bundled the child in one of the blankets and picked him up, hoisted the bag over his shoulder, then grabbed the tranquilizer gun. It was a handful, but he managed to get everything back to the Acura. He placed the child in the back seat, wondering if he should put a seat belt around the boy. If the child got hurt, Victor would have his head. Besides, he wasn't the type of person who would hurt a kid. He reached around, found the two ends of the seat belt, and carefully fastened them around the child.

He'd left the engine running so it was easy to pull away from the cabin and head down the mountain. He'd take Willie's Ghost Road back. It was smoother then the fire road, and wouldn't juggle the child about so much. He had to get to Newport Beach and the chopper pad so Victor could fly the kid to Catalina before anyone realized he was missing. He switched on the overhead light and glanced back to make certain the boy was secure. Staring back at him were two bright blue eyes. A sudden feeling of dread filled him. The boy was awake!

Elizabeth lay on the sofa wondering why she felt so odd. A strange dream, she told herself, that's what it had to be. She had no idea where she was, but the whole place was undulating. For a second she thought she was back on that awful boat with those men. The idea of that gave her a violent chill. She felt her teeth chatter and her body shake. Then the movement eased somewhat, and she realized she wasn't lying in a boat, but on the floor of Detective Bearbower's cabin. The light was on in the room. Her vision was blurred somewhat. Her shoulder ached and she rubbed at it with her fingers. She felt a strange object, her eyes flew open, and she tried to see what the hell it was. Even with blurred vision, she could tell it was some kind of metal dart, but not like one any she'd seen before.

"Andy?" she tried to say, but all that came out was a hoarse whisper. Her lungs felt depleted of air. "Andy," she tried again, just a slight bit louder. "Dar?"

She pulled the dart thing out of her shoulder and tried to sit up. The room moved around her, and she had to grip the sofa cushion to stay upright. Her tongue felt too large for her mouth. Something familiar about that sensation. She'd felt it before. Shit! She remembered! It was on the boat. Whatever they'd drugged her with that time, they had used again. She blinked and looked around, trying to clear her vision. It came back to her, slowly. They'd come to a safe place, but it wasn't safe after all. Whoever wanted Dar had found them again. She let out a low wail, almost a keening sound as she forced her body to move, to find Dar, to find Andy.

Andy wasn't in the chair where he'd been when she fell asleep. In addition, Dar wasn't on the long sofa! Maybe Dar was with Andy. Maybe he was okay. Hanging on to the edge of the sofa, she made her way around it. The floor felt like spongy rubber under her feet, but she kept going. Then she saw Andy lying on the floor just a few feet from her.

"Andy!" she screamed. This time her voice echoed throughout the room. "Oh, my God! Andy!" She dropped to her knees and crawled to him, feeling for his carotid artery. He had a dark bruise on the side of his forehead and a swelling bump. But his chest was moving, his heart beating, and his carotid pulse slow and even. She let out a groan of relief. He'd obviously taken a bad blow to his head, but otherwise he seemed okay. She saw the same type of dart thing she'd been hit with lying on the floor beside him. Maybe he'd hit his head when the dart's sedative took effect. How long were they unconscious? Panic struck her! Where was Dar? He wasn't in the room as far as she could see. She got to her feet and went to the bedroom. He wasn't there. She felt a low aching pain in the pit of her stomach. The son-of-a-bitches had her child again! Whoever the hell they were, they'd made a bad mistake. They'd left her alive, and as long as she was alive, she would find them, and find Dar. When she did, she wouldn't hesitate to kill them if she had to, to get Dar back.

At first Dar thought he was dreaming again. Everything around him kept turning as if he were inside his toy top and watching things go round and round. The face of a strange man whirled by him and disappeared. Dar's ears rang with a high-pitched whine that made him turn his head from side to side. This was not at all like his usual dreams.

He tried to sit up, but something tight across his tummy held him down. The spinning sensation eased. He blinked his eyes hard, trying to focus on his surroundings. Too dark. He blinked again. Nothing. The ringing in his ears slowly stopped and he heard a rumbling sound. It sounded like the engine that ran his daddy's car. That was it! He was in a car, in the back seat. With his tiny fingers, he began exploring the area around him. A blanket. Soft, smooth seats. No car seat. A belt thing, that's what was holding him down. He studied it for a minute, and then deftly pressed the release button.

He looked at the back of the head of the man who was driving. It wasn't his Daddy. He didn't know who it was. Neither Mama nor Daddy were in the car. He was alone with this strange man. The man drove the car fast around all kinds of turns. Dar kept sliding about on the seat and he was almost sorry that he'd taken off the belt. He wanted the car to stop. His stomach would be sick if it didn't.

He could wiggle the insides of the man. But if he did that, the man would stop, but maybe the car wouldn't. Besides, he promised Mama that he wouldn't wiggle anyone again. He thought about it for a while. He could wiggle the engine, but wasn't certain what that might do. Maybe the car would crash. Then he remembered something that had happened when he was driving with Mama and Daddy not too long ago. He'd heard a loud pop and his daddy had said "Damn!" and pulled the car over to the side of the road and stopped it. "Flat tire," his daddy said. Flat tires made a car stop.

He thought about the tires, all four of them. He had no idea which one he should make flat. Maybe all of them. Wiggling something that he couldn't see, like the bad man outside the house that night, which was much harder than wiggling something he could see. It had been hard for him to stop the man from coming inside. But he'd done it. The man was going to hurt him. Hurt Mama and Daddy.

He quenched his eyes closed and pictured the tires in his mind. Round, black, and spinning around. He knew what they looked like inside because he'd looked at them after his Daddy had the flat tire. He could remember how the other three tires looked inside, but he couldn't remember what the flat one looked like. All he could do was try. He began to wiggle the tires in his mind. He wiggled the strings and ribbons he saw in his mind, that were inside them. Mix up the strings, move them around and change them. With his eyes closed like that, he almost fell asleep, but he told himself he had to keep wiggling. Had to stop the car so he could go and find Mama and Daddy.

The tires didn't pop the way the one had when Daddy was driving. But he heard a strange grating sound. The man in the front seat slowed the car.

185

"Goddamn!" He heard the man yell. "Damn it to hell!"

It was working, Dar realized. The car was stopping. As it did, it made him slide around even worse than before. His teeth banged together and he bit his tongue. It hurt, but he didn't stop the wiggling. He kept on doing it until the car wasn't moving anymore. Then he pushed the thought of the tires out of his mind and opened his eyes. He looked at the man who was now looking over his shoulder at him. The man was frightened. Dar felt his fear. He didn't like the feeling and wished it would go away. But it was better than the awful pinchys he had felt earlier.

"Damn it, kid! How the hell did that shot wear off so quickly?" The man picked up something, but Dar couldn't tell what it was in the dark. "Maybe the shot wasn't strong enough for you. Guess I'm going to have to give you another one."

"Dar no need shot!" Dar said. He looked at the man's insides. Ribbons, strings, maybe he could just tangle them, not change them much. Maybe that would stop him. But he wasn't supposed to. "Dar no want shot!" he cried.

"Sorry," the man said.

Dar felt a stinging bite hit his arm. He tried to make the man's insides wiggle, but he couldn't do it. Everything around him began to spin again. Round and around. He closed his eyes, waiting for the spinning to stop. But it didn't. Instead, it made Dar feel as if he were being sucked into some long dark tunnel, into a place where he wouldn't be able to get out, a place where there was no Mama and Daddy, no strange man, no one but him.

Tyree put the phone down and then picked up the stack of papers she'd gone through several times. She looked over at Boo, who was sitting on the sofa, staring at the wall of paintings that adorned the living room. "Foxhoven's still not home," she told him. "His wife hasn't heard from him, and she's pretty worried."

"I'm glad you didn't tell her about what we've discovered. No sense in scaring her at this point." Boo ran his hands over his face as if trying to rub away the awful fatigue that showed there. "We need to find him first, and find if it's true. If everything in those papers are the

Dorothy McMillan

true facts then what the hell do we do? Who do we tell that Foxhoven has actually resurrected the Brownstone version of Sunshine? What the hell could he have been thinking? It was apparent from the files we found that he thought he'd changed it enough to make it safe. Idiot!" Boo growled. "If so, then just like Barry, he may have already tried it on himself.

"What did he hope to gain by doing it?"

"Maybe he was hoping to create genius in himself and that he would be able to control the killer craving it caused in Brownstone.

"I don't understand what he was thinking," Tyree said.

"Why on God's earth would he want or need more than what our version of Sunshine gives a person."

"Human nature has always been greedy. Even our little elite Sunshine group wasn't happy with the version that's being tested nationwide. We take a stronger one, with faster results and better results."

Boo got up and walked over to her. "Right now Tyree we need to figure out how the hell do we deal with Foxhoven?

Tyree closed her eyes and sighed. She felt as fatigued as Boo looked. "How could Foxhoven have been so stupid?" she said, opening her eyes and look at Boo. "And how did he get hold of the original version?"

Boo just stared off into space. She could have sworn that his face had turned ashen. All of this was almost making him ill, she knew.

"Boo? Did you hear me?" she said. "Where did he get it? The raw version of Sunshine? I thought after Barry and the horrible things he did, you got rid of it."

Boo slowly moved to the bar and stood surveying the bottles there. "I could use a Mary right now, but we need to keep our heads clear. We've got to find Foxhoven."

"Boo, please."

"Of course we kept some of it, Tyree! It was flash-frozen and put in a vault. Just in case."

"In case of what?" Tyree went to the bar and sat on one of the stools. She fingered the stack of papers in her hand. They had taken the time to photocopy Foxhoven's files so they could take them home. She looked at the papers, thinking about all the horrible things that were written there.

"It's the parent of the Sunshine we take," Boo said. "If

something goes wrong with any of the later formulas, we can always go back to the source. It's a safeguard."

Tyree gave a brittle laugh. "Some safeguard!"

Boo sat on the stool opposite her, his eyes dark but darting and alive. "It doesn't matter how he got it. What matters is that he is says in the papers that he used himself to experiment with it. No wonder he's been at the lab so much lately."

Tyree flipped through the pages. "Look here! According to these notes, he hoped by taking it, he could use his own DNA to study its effects. To find out what caused the grisly effects it caused in Barry."

"Because of Dar." Boo shook his head, a look of disbelief on his face. "He did all of this because of Dar."

"Yes, because we now know Dar is actually Barry's son," Tyree said. "We know he lied about the DNA tests. But why would that make Foxhoven take the drug that made Barry insane? He knew even with his few changes it could still lead to disaster."

"I suppose," Boo said, "That he feared Dar would inherit some of the same horrible traits that his real father had. Maybe he wanted to find a way to avoid it causing poor Dar the same behavior."

Boo was silent. She knew he was thinking of a way to fix this horrendous mess. But she could see no way out except straight through it. She'd read through Foxhoven's notes several times, hoping somehow that they would read differently, that she'd misinterpreted them. But the notes were clear-cut. Foxhoven had discovered early on that Barry was Dar's father, but he hadn't told Andy and Elizabeth. "For the boy's sake," Foxhoven had written. "Nothing could change the fact of his parenthood, so why muddy things?" He'd followed Dar's progress carefully from the time the child was born, having known even then that Barry was the boy's father. He'd monitored every aspect of the child's growth and behavior which was relayed to some unnamed person. Foxhoven had only called him V in his notes. Foxhoven had been the one who had passed on information to this V person. Once Dar showed his unusual abilities, he was to be whisked away from his parents. When the child was safely housed in a laboratory somewhere, Foxhoven was promised he would be the boy's physician.

Was it money, Tyree wondered thinking about all the skullduggery that had gone on? Or was it the prospect of being in on a scientific discovery as spectacular as Dar and his abilities?

Whatever the hell it was, Tyree couldn't imagine any reason being good enough to warrant what Foxhoven did, taking the raw version of Sunshine, and facing the possibility of becoming a monster like Barry.

"I don't believe it was altruistic," Tyree said.

"What?"

"Foxhoven's concern with Dar. I don't think he really did it for the child. I think he stood to gain something by helping this V guy. Something big! Maybe he expected one day to win the Nobel Prize for chemistry or genetics, or something. But what that man did had nothing to do with protecting Dar or Andy and Elizabeth."

Boo nodded. "The Nobel may have been what he had in mind. However, I can't believe that he didn't realize his efforts could never become public. Not when it concerned a kidnapped child. You're right, he really is crazy!"

"We have to find him!" Tyree exclaimed, hearing the sharp edge of her voice. "I'm certain he knows where this V person is, and where they planned to take Dar. If we stop them, they won't be able to try again. And we have to find Andy and Elizabeth. Tell them the truth about Dar…and Barry."

Tyree thought about telling the young couple. Did they really have to know? It would devastate them both. Still, they had a right to know. A right to be forewarned about what Dar might become. Well, she would decide about that later. She had other things to do right now.

"We should turn it all over to the police," Boo said, a note of finality in his voice.

Tyree thought about it. Maybe Boo was right. Besides, if Foxhoven had taken the raw drug, who knew how long it would be before he got a taste for human blood, the way Barry had? Tyree closed her eyes and wished she could just melt away into the blackness she saw. Maybe Foxhoven had already begun seeking out blood the way Barry had, unable to take nourishment any other way. Hadn't she read something in the paper about a recent similar killing not far from them? She forced her eyes open. It didn't do any good to speculate. They had to do anything and everything, not only to stop the cycle from starting again, but to protect Dar.

"Okay, I agree. Let's call the police and turn Foxhoven's notes over to them. Let them do what they can. At the same time, we should try to find the good doctor ourselves. He wasn't at his office, the lab, or at home. Where else might he be?"

Boo picked up the telephone. "I don't know yet. But after I call the police, we'll turn over every stone we can. Somewhere under one of them we're bound to find that low-life piece of shit."

CHAPTER TWENTY-ONE

The Bronco traveled the rough terrain extremely well. Only a short distance to go. Ted prayed he'd get there in time, and that the couple and the child were safe. The thought made him press even harder on the gas pedal. Maddy, despite her seatbelt, bounced rather wildly about in the seat beside him, but didn't complain.

The wind become even heavier and Ted felt its resistance against the car. Jagged branches from pine trees and bundles of scrub oak twigs continually flew across their path. Some of them hitting the windshield. Ted hoped to God none of them would shatter it. This was a wild night in a lot more ways than one.

When they finally reached the cabin, Ted was alarmed to see the lights on. The three Rosemonds had planned on going to sleep right away. He looked at the clock on the Bronco's dashboard. It was close to midnight.

"The lights are on," Maddy said. "Something's wrong."

"Let's hope it's just that the child got them up." Ted swung the car into an open place in front of the cabin. He scrambled out of the car, giving Maddy a sign that he wanted her to stay there. He drew his revolver and raced to the door. His heart rattled erratically when he saw the pieces of stained glass from his window lying on the porch. "Goddamn!" he said hoarsely. He looked through the window opening and saw Elizabeth and Andy sitting on the couch. He scanned the rest of the room, but saw no one else.

"Andy," he yelled and saw the young man turn toward the door. "It's Bearbower. "What's happened?"

Andy opened the door and Ted strode into the room. As he did, he caught a glimpse of Elizabeth's face. Tears streamed down her cheeks. He could see her shoulders convulse with sobs. "Ah, Christ!" he cried. "They took Dar! God damn it to hell!"

"They found us," Andy stated simply. "How did they find us?"

Ted shook his head. "How long ago?"

"I...we don't know. Not too long ago I guess. Whoever did it, hit us with a tranquilizer." Andy held up the two syringes. "Probably did it to Dar too, or else Dar would have stopped him."

"We're going to find him!" Elizabeth said in a violent tone. "Now! We're going to find him."

"Yes, we are," Ted told her. "You can damn well bet your life on that!" He holstered his revolver and went back to the car hoping Maddy carried a flashlight in the glove box. The first thing they had to do was find out the direction the kidnappers had taken. It would be tough, with the wind scouring everything, but Ted knew he could do it. Had to do it. If the kidnappers got off the mountain, they might never see the boy again. Elizabeth followed him out, wiping at her face with the back of her hands.

In the light from the car headlights, Ted saw the resolve in her face and in her walk. Even the strong wind couldn't sway her from her path to the car. She climbed into the back seat and buckled herself in. Andy came after her and sat beside her, struggling to close the door against the wind.

Maddy, anticipating his needs, handed him a long-handled flashlight with strong batteries. He took it and began inspecting the area around the cabin for tire marks. They had to be there, somewhere. It only took him ten minutes before he found them. Fresh and deep. The wind had not yet eroded them away.

❧ ❧

Twigs knew there was nothing else to do but abandon the car. With four flat tires, it would be impossible to get down the mountain. Afoot, Twigs found the going extremely difficult. He was afraid he might stumble in the dark and drop the boy. He'd bundled the tranquilized child in a baby blanket to protect him from the violent gusts of wind and. It seemed to Twigs that Dar grew heavier with each step. Twigs pulled out his cell phone, but it read "No Service". He had to find a cabin or house where he could use a land line telephone, or else abandon the child and get the hell out of there. It wasn't the fear of Victor that kept him going now. It was the fact that he couldn't leave the child in the middle of nowhere and run. That would be cowardly. No, he was made of better stuff than that. Even Victor, as cruel as he could be, did not intend to harm the boy.

He'd already passed several small weekender cabins which had been dark and had no telephone lines. He began to realize just how undeveloped the area was. Fear nudged him. What if he couldn't find a phone? What if he became lost and unable to walk anymore? The

Dorothy McMillan

muscles in his legs screamed from the unaccustomed exertion. He
wondered how long he could continue before total exhaustion set in.

He stopped for a moment and pulled back the blanket from the
unconscious boy's face. He worried that he'd given the child too
much tranquilizer, but for some reason it hadn't affected the boy the
way it should have. It must have had something to do with the child
being special. He could just make out the soft curves of Dar's face.
At least the boy was breathing normally. Why in the hell had he
agreed to this? How stupid he'd been to even consider Victor's offer
of a surveillance job of the Rosemont place. At least it was almost
over. He pulled out his cell phone again, but still no service. He had
to get a call to Victor fast, have him send his chopper, and that would
be that.

He pulled the blanket over the boy and began battling the wind.
His legs felt like melting rubber. He forced them to keep moving.
Several times the wind buffeted him about so roughly he almost
dropped the child. But he managed to keep his footing and continued
stumbling through the darkness. After crossing a deep ravine, he saw
a massive dark formation not far from him. At first, he thought the
looming object was a steep bank, but as he approached, he realized
that it was a house. He felt some of his fatigue drain away when he
saw it was large, with two stories, several wooden decks, and a
fireplace. He hoped that a house of this size would be someone's
permanent residence and would have a landline telephone. The place
was dark and he wondered if the occupants were asleep, or not there.
Well, it didn't matter. If there was a landline, he'd find a way to use
it.

He took the boy to the main deck and laid him down in a
sheltered corner by the front door, making certain he was well
covered by the blanket. After that he walked around the outside of
the house checking for telephone lines. Only a few yards away, he
found them. Now, if only they were connected and working. He
explored the area around the house carefully, trying to spot a car, but
found nothing. He hoped that no car meant no occupants.

He decided that the direct approach was best. He banged on the
front door, making sure that if the owners were at home they'd be
able to hear him over the roar of the wind. After a few minutes and
no answer, he banged again. Nothing. His heart did a little skip as he
began to realize that luck might finally be with him. He tried the

193

doorknob, but the door was locked. He began checking the windows, looking for one that might be open just a little. However, they were all tightly secured. He noticed the slanted cellar door. He hadn't thought about it the first time around. Cellars were a rarity in California. This time he stopped to inspect it. It swung open easily, and he found himself peering down into the darkness of the basement. He picked up Dar.

"Son of a gun!" he muttered to himself as he went down the wooden steps carrying Dar. He laid Dar down on an old patio chair inside the basement and fumbled for a light switch. To his delight, the electricity was on. Flooded with light, the place took on a friendly appearance with its shelves of canned food, a washer, dryer, and an assortment of old bicycles. In one corner, he found the steps to the upstairs and actually held his breath while he tried the door. It opened! His relief was so great that he let out a whoop. He heard Dar stir and make a small sound. He couldn't be waking up! Not yet! But after moving about a little, Dar returned to sleeping soundly, or at least he appeared to. He easily found the telephone, lifted it to his ear, and prayed that he would hear a dial tone. He did.

Ted drove carefully as they battled the sharp curves of the road. By now, Ajax would have the SWAT teams in place so no one could get off the mountain unless they walked. Even so, he hoped the guy hadn't thought about the fact that he might have to find an alternative way out of the area. They had found the guy's tire tracks leading from the cabin to the main road, not the fire road, so he was looking for anything that might let him know if the guy had deviated.

"Are you sure we're taking the right road?" Elizabeth asked, as if reading his mind.

"Doesn't matter," Ted said. "With the SWAT teams in place, there's no way he can get out of here."

"Yeah," Andy growled. "Sure. Just like there was no way, anyone would know we were staying at the cabin last night."

Ted felt his face flame at the words. "Okay, so I made a serious mistake. It happens. I'm very sorry about it. Nevertheless, we'll find Dar. I promise you!"

Maddy reached over and put her hand on Ted's knee. Her fingers were warm. She patted his knee for a moment, a gesture of what?

Sympathy? Assurance? He wasn't certain, but the touch of her hand made him feel better. Then suddenly, he felt her stiffen.

"Wait!" Maddy shouted. "Look! There!" She pointed to the far side of the road. "Between those two huge trees."

Ted squinted through the darkness to see what it was she'd pointed out. Then he saw it. A car! He slammed on the brakes. The Bronco skidded some but he quickly controlled it and brought it to a halt. He backed the car up and then pulled off the road, so his headlights somewhat lit the dark car. "It could have been there for some time," he said. "Everyone stay here. If it is the kidnapper's car, he may be armed. Doesn't look as if he's around, though. And something seems to be wrong with the car wheels."

Ted got out of the car and drew his gun. The wind whipped trails of dried leaves around him. The air crackled with their movement. "I need the flashlight," he said to Maddy. She nodded and handed it to him. He moved cautiously to the parked car and flashed its light in the windows. Empty. He opened the driver's door and looked in, checking to see if there was any evidence of its being the kidnapper's car. A small tranquilizer gun lay on the passenger's seat along with a pack of Spearmint gum. In the back seat, he spotted a blue and white checkered bag. He reached over the seat and picked it up. It contained a baby bottle and a few other things. Outside, he walked around the car to see if he could spot anything else. That's when he noticed the car's tires. They were shredded, and the rims had collapsed. All four of them.

Back at the Bronco, he held the bag up for Elizabeth and Andy to see. "I found this. Is it yours?"

Elizabeth gasped and reached for the bag. "Yes! It's Dar's bag! He's got to be close." She opened the door on her side and got out. "Let's go find him."

"Wait," Ted said. "We have no idea which way they went. We can't all go wandering around in the dark with the wind blowing like this. Christ! We can't help Dar if we get lost!"

"I'm going to find my child!" Elizabeth cried. "We can't wait for the SWAT team to find them. We have to do something, now!"

Andy and Maddy got out of the car. Andy put his arm around Elizabeth. "Honey, we have to get some idea of which way they might have gone. This is a wilderness area."

Ted turned off the Bronco's headlights. "Okay, listen up. It appears the tires on the car are totally shredded. This is a rough road, but I can't imagine it would do that much damage."

"It's Dar!" Elizabeth cried. "It has to be! He shredded the tires!"

Ted shook his head. "It's a wonder he didn't shred the kidnapper."

"I told him never, ever, do that to a person again. I guess I got through to him."

Elizabeth gave a weak smile.

"Okay, here's what we're going to do," Ted said. "All of us will surround the car and move outward. See if we can find some trace of them. Footprints, whatever. It won't be as easy as it was to find the tire tracks. People walking when the ground is this dry don't leave much of a trail. And what tracks there might have been, have probably been swept away by the wind."

"I can't believe Dar's out in all this wind. It's so dark. He must be terrified,"

Elizabeth said.

"At least it's not cold," Maddy said, reassuringly. "We can be thankful for that."

The four of them took places around the dark car. It was unlikely they would find anything, but he had to keep them busy, keep total panic from setting in. He had the only flashlight so he swept the light from his back and forth, hoping for a miracle. Just one tiny piece of something that would point toward the way the kidnapper had gone, that's all they needed. However, his real hope was still with the SWAT team.

The wind, already fierce, increased. It yowled around pines and oaks, and blew stinging dust into Ted's eyes. Even with the flashlight, he could barely see the ground in front of him. The wind had turned the mountain terrain into a moving, living creature that fought them at every step. They wouldn't be able to stay outside very long. Not unless the wind let up. If it was this bad for them, Ted knew it had to be terrible for the boy.

"Damn!" Andy shouted from a few yards away from the car.

Ted saw him lean down and lift up his shoe, look at the bottom of it.

"Stepped in something. Chewing gum I think," Andy said. "Just what I need!" He started to try and scrape the gum off his show against a small rock.

"Wait!" Ted yelled at him. "Let me see it!" He raced to Andy and held up his foot so he could see the gum. He leaned down and smelled it. "It's Spearmint!"

"So what?" Andy grumbled.

"So there was a pack of that kind of gun in their car." Ten gave a rough grin. "They must have gone this way, into the pines." He waved for the others to join them.

"Are you sure?" Andy asked.

"It's all we have." Ted forged ahead of the group, hope surging inside him.

"Let's go!"

The four of them joined together and began moving. Even if they were moving in the wrong direction, Ted knew they were at least keeping busy and not getting hysterical over the fact that Dar was gone. None of them seemed to realize the futility of searching in the violent wind and darkness. Even the SWAT teams might not be out in force if the object of their search hadn't been a child.

Ted felt as if he were leading a band of troops into battle. As he forged ahead of Maddy, Andy and Elizabeth, the words of a song marched uninvited through his head. "Over hill, over dale, as we hit the dusty trail...." Try as he might, he couldn't get rid of the damn words. At times, he felt himself whistling it. Obviously, he was losing his marbles, which might be just as well, considering the circumstances.

He prayed they were moving in the right direction. The possibility of getting lost and needing a rescue team themselves was great. That event would make interesting headlines in the evening paper. Ted's breath came in short, painful gasps. At his age and weight, the last thing he should be doing was marching up steep hillsides and trudging across deep ravines. Shit! His heart could attack him at any minute! The thought of it didn't stop him. Death might be better than insanity. More peaceful.

They reached the plateau of a tall hill, all four of them struggling to breathe. Elizabeth sat down moaning. Andy sat beside her. Maddy came over to Ted and took his hand.

"You okay?" she asked.

"Yeah, just out of breath," Ted said.

"Me too. Let's sit," Maddy suggested. We can't keep going like this much longer. It's useless, this kind of searching, isn't it?"

197

"It may be," Ted agreed. "The SWAT team will find them, though."

Maddy nodded, then looked around, found a smooth spot and sat down. Ted sat beside her, feeling his legs ache fiercely as he bent them.

"We'd better go back," Ted shouted to the young couple. As he did, the wind dropped. His voice boomed and echoed around the hillsides. The four of them sat there in silence for a moment, waiting for the wind to return. But it didn't. Above them, the night sky glowed with so many stars it looked as if someone had spilled silver glitter across it. Ted had forgotten the way the stars looked up here. In the city, you could hardly make out more than a few hundred. But here, the sky was like a huge window to the universe.

Maddy looked up at the sky too. She sucked in her breath as she viewed the sight. "My lord! Isn't it something!" she said.

One of these days, he would propose to Maddy, after this case was taken care of. In addition, he sure as hell wasn't going to take on the Vamipirish cases. Been there, done that. Did not want to do it again. Fate had a sense of humor, didn't it? Never lined anything up. Life was completely filled with squiggly lines.

"It's almost impossible to find any sort of trail up here at night." Andy said.

"Andy!" Elizabeth started to protest.

"Ted's right, Lizzy. We have to leave it to the SWAT team. What we need to do now is to go home and wait. Be ready for when they find Dar."

Elizabeth looked at Ted with a plaintiff expression. He saw her face lit by starlight and wondered why someone so young and vulnerable had to go through so many terrible things. Fate again, he supposed. However, she was strong. That much he knew. Otherwise, she would have broken long ago. The rape and attempted murder by Barry Brownstone would have done it.

"I guess you're right," she said finally. "We should be there when they bring Dar home."

The four of them sat in silence awhile, resting. The absence of wind cheered Ted, but he wondered if his legs would work when he tried to get up. He marveled at Maddy, who gave no appearance of having felt the awful climbing and walking. Suddenly, an odd sound broke the silence. Not the wind, he knew, but something familiar. It echoed from one hillside to another. It grew louder, vibrating the ground under them.

"What the devil!" He scanned the area, unable to see much of anything in the darkness.

"What is it?" Andy asked

As the sound intensified, Ted realized what it was. The turbo-throb of a helicopter rotor! The SWAT team? Ted squinted into the darkness. From behind the edge of the hilltop across from them, the chopper emerged. Its light flashed eerily across the dark terrain. The jagged shapes of pine trees appeared and disappeared as it moved past them. It wasn't a police chopper. Who in the hell would be dumb enough to venture into this area on a night like this? The chopper, flying low like some giant black grasshopper, went directly over them. Whoever was piloting it had obviously taken advantage of the break in the terrible wind. Ted could just make out several numbers on the side of the machine. He made a mental note of the numbers. Just as the chopper vanished into the darkness and its turbo-throb faded, Ted realized what he'd seen.

"It's the boy," he yelled. "Damn it to hell, they sent a chopper in here to get him out before the SWAT team found him."

"What?" Andy said jumping to his feet. "You mean...you think Dar was in that helicopter?"

"I'd bet on it! Come on, we have to find an area where there's cell phone service. Christ! We can track them if we're quick enough!" With that, he stood up on legs that almost refused to hold him up. Pain in his muscles bit at him as if they had long sharp teeth. He forced them to move anyway. All that mattered now was that they not lose the chopper.

Tyree closed her eyes and leaned her head back in the car as Boo drove. She tried to think of any possible place where they might find Foxhoven. He wasn't at home, which at this hour wasn't unusual for a doctor, but he wasn't at the hospital either, or any of the few places where he might have stopped for a drink. She knew he'd be driving his pearl-blue Maserati, which shouldn't be hard to spot. Even in Newport Beach, few people had the luxury of driving such an expensive automobile.

She'd called the police department, asking for Detective Bearbower, since he had been the detective in charge of the Barry Brownstone case, but was told he was unavailable. She had finally reached his partner, Alex, who was out in the field. The department patched her through to him after she refused to give the information on Foxhoven to anyone but Bearbower or his partner. The person she talked to seemed distracted but took the time to listen to her. However, it didn't give her much hope that the police would get going on the problem. She'd finally hung up, realizing that she and Boo would have to find Foxhoven themselves, talk some sense into him, and persuade him to go somewhere for treatment.

"Okay," Boo said. "Where do we look now? We checked all the places we know he might have gone."

Tyree looked out the window. "Let's do a sweep, starting at Peninsula Point, and cover the entire area. If we don't spot his Maserati, we'll go up on the hill around Hoag Hospital. Then…well, then…I don't know." She sighed.

Boo turned the car toward the point and drove slowly along Balboa Boulevard. It seemed to Tyree that it took hours to cover the entire peninsula, with no trace of Foxhoven. Discouragement began to nag at her. Foxhoven had probably realized he was in a no-win situation and had skipped. They rounded the last block on the peninsula and headed across Pacific Coast Highway and up Superior toward the hospital area.

"We might as well check out his office. Who knows, he might have gone back there late to take care of some things," Tyree suggested.

"Good idea," Boo agreed. They spotted the Maserati the moment they turned into the parking lot of Foxhoven's medical office building. The lights were on inside his suite, which gave Tyree hope. He had to be there! She wondered how he would take their confronting him.

"Boo, what if he has a weapon or something?" Tyree asked.

Boo parked the car and turned to her. "Let's hope not. He never was one to have a gun, not even for protection at home."

"He was never one for getting involved in a kidnapping scheme either. Or for using himself as a guinea pig for Sunshine research."

Boo hesitated a moment then got out of the car. "We're about to find out, I guess."

Tyree got out and looked toward the lighted office. "Maybe we should just call the police. Get someone out here. That would be the smart move."

The two of them stood there for a few moments. Tyree couldn't see any movement inside the office.

"We never were ones to do the smart thing, were we?" Tyree said finally.

On that note, they both started walking toward the building. Halfway down the walk, Boo stopped abruptly. "Wait a minute, let's check out his car, and see if the engine's warm. See if he's been here long. Maybe the car's been here some time and he's gone off somewhere else."

"With someone else, you mean?"

"Right. Maybe some of those people he's involved with."

Tyree hadn't thought about that possibility. They walked the twenty yards or so to where the Maserati was parked. Boo reached it first, started to put his hand on the hood, and then jerked it back suddenly.

"Oh my God!" he whispered. He turned back to Tyree and put up both hands in front of him, telling her to stop.

"What?"

"Don't come any closer. It's Foxhoven. He's in the car. I think he's...dead!"

"Oh, no!" Tyree said, turning away. Then, that morbid urge to find out what had happened, took hold of her. Turning back, she followed Boo to the driver's side of the car. She could see Foxhoven's silhouette through the window. Boo opened the door slowly and looked in. Foxhoven was sitting with his head back against the seat, his eyes, and mouth slightly open. A small trail of dark blood led from what appeared to be a single bullet wound in the middle of his forehead. Tyree winced and looked away, trying to erase the terrible sight. "Is there a gun?" she asked. "Do you think he killed himself?"

Boo shook his head. "Not likely. No sign of powder burns on his forehead around the wound."

"Maybe he wanted out of the deal, so they stopped him. Or maybe they found out what the raw Sunshine had done to him."

Boo nodded and closed the car door. "Let's hope whoever did this, didn't hang around. Come on, let's get out of here and phone the police," he said softly. "We can't do anything for him now. What about his wife, Ann? We should be the ones to call her, shouldn't we? Not the police."

Tyree walked back to their car, her whole body feeling as if it had turned into soggy cotton. It had been a long time since anyone she knew as well as Foxhoven had died. He'd not only been her friend for many years, but also her physician. To die that way! She began to shake. A surge of hot tears filled her eyes. She fought them back. Later she'd have time to cry. Right now, they had things to do.

Ted stood in the mountain meadow beside the other three. Elizabeth looked exhausted, dark circles ringing her eyes. Andy, his arm around her, appeared undaunted. Maddy gripped Ted's hand and she stood quietly, stoically, as if these kinds of things happened to her every day. They had moved quickly down the hillside and Elizabeth had spotted a ranch house isolated in the middle of a large meadow. They hadn't seen it when hiking up the hill because of the winds and blowing debris. The house was occupied and had a phone which Ted used, and then moved all of them out to the meadow area.

The police helicopter would meet them there, using the meadow as a landing site. The owner of the ranch house and meadow set up one of the high-powered lights he used for the yearly rodeos he held. The police helicopter would be able to spot them. Radar had already begun tracking the chopper that Ted believed held Dar. They'd get the son-of-a-bitch no matter where he went. In the distance, Ted could hear the police chopper. He thanked God that the wind was still at bay.

"I think we should go with you," Andy said. "Dar will be frightened. He'll need us."

"No way," Ted growled. "You three are staying here. Wait for the police car. The officers will take you home. The moment we locate Dar, we'll call."

Elizabeth finally nodded agreement. Maddy gave him a soft smile. Ted was relieved they hadn't argued much. No way could he allow them to go. Ajax would be in the chopper, along with several police officers. Another chopper was being fueled and readied with SWAT team members. One or the other of them would be on that other chopper, the one carrying Dar, like flies on a dead horse!

Dar heard a rumbling that hurt his ears. The rumbling seemed to echo throughout his body. Was he in the car? He tried to open his eyes, but couldn't. He fought off the awful sleepiness that kept trying to suck him back into that dark scary place. He'd never been so frightened. He wanted Mama, wanted her to sing "The Muffin Man" for him. He wanted to be snug and warm in her lap, rocking back and forth in the rocker by the window at home. Just thinking about those things changed the fear to anger. He felt it rise up in him like something burning hot. He didn't like the feeling, but it was better than the fear.

He was angry with the man who had taken him away from Mama and Daddy. If he saw him again, he'd wiggle his insides for sure, no matter what Mama said. He'd wiggle and wiggle until the man wasn't there anymore. He had stopped the car by wiggling the tires. He was certain he could stop anything, if he really tried hard. He reached out with his thoughts and began to wiggle everything around him. He'd wiggle until the rumbling stopped. He'd wiggle until someone took him back to his Mama.

"What the hell!" someone yelled.

Dar heard the voice although he still couldn't open his eyes.

"I can't control the damn thing!"

Dar tried to understand what the man was talking about. He eased up on his wiggling to listen.

"How far are we?" another voice asked.

"Not far, but the way the chopper is vibrating, we may have to ditch."

"Not with the kid. No way!"

Dar remembered the word chopper, but couldn't quite think of what it was. He strained as hard as he could and finally managed to open his eyes. He blinked and looked around, unable to understand where he was. Chopper, he said to himself. Then he realized what it was. He'd seen them on TV. Like an airplane, except it had a go-round thing on top. Dar felt the anger in him growing. He wanted to wiggle things even harder. Wanted them to turn this thing around and take him back to his home. But for some reason, no matter how hard he tried, he couldn't manage to wiggle things as much as he usually could. The sleepys kept tugging at him. He tried not to give in to them. He made a giant effort to wiggle the things around him again, but the effort made him so tired that he had to stop.

"Whoa!" one of the voices said. "Must be some bad down-drafts. But we are almost to Catalina. You can see Avalon lights up ahead. Only a few more minutes."

"Keep us out of the water," the other voice said. "Just get us to Victor's pad."

Dar was unable to keep his eyes open any longer. "Gotta wiggle," he said softly. "Can't sleep. Gotta wiggle." The anger and the sleep began to fight each other. A fierce battle. Dar hoped the anger would win, but it didn't.

CHAPTER TWENTY-TWO

Twigs climbed out of the chopper carrying a sleeping Dar. Victor met him at doorway of his Catalina house, took the sleeping Dar from Twigs, and carried him into the bedroom where the boy would stay from now on. Victor wanted him to live in the Catalina house with him like a normal child. He'd only make visits to the lab when necessary. Victor had seen to it that the bedroom was as home-like as possible. Besides the crib, with its multicolored paintings of various nursery-rhyme figures, a hand painted mural with fanciful animals, cars, and planes on it stretched around three of the walls. Shelves of toys lined the other wall.

Twigs followed him into the room and Victor noticed that the man was sweating profusely.

"We almost didn't make it," Twigs said, an odd quiver to his voice. "The damn chopper kept giving us a bad time. I think maybe it was a sign that this isn't such a good thing we've done."

"Well, you did make it." Victor tried not to be too curt. He wanted to keep Twigs calm until he was able to dispose of him. The last thing he needed was a case of remorse at this late hour. Foxhoven had been enough trouble.

Victor placed the boy in the crib and covered him. He turned to Twigs and realized that the guy's appearance had changed a lot since the last time he'd seen him. He looked reputable now, despite the heavy sweating. It was too bad he had to get rid of him. Twigs had done a good job in the end, even if he'd fucked up a few things along the way. However, it was necessary to rid himself of Twigs. Just as necessary as it had been to get rid of Foxhoven. The poor doctor had really fucked up. He'd not only used the raw form of Sunshine on himself instead of studying its effect on simians, but also had threatened to expose Victor if he didn't abort his plan to abduct the child. Foxhoven had become a bleeding heart at the last minute, overwhelmed by sentimental feelings for the parents. That kind of man never did great things in this world. Sentiment was the enemy of progress.

He would have to find another physician for Dar as fast as possible. He had only a short supply of tranquilizer left, and Dar would need to always be partially sedated until he became used to his new surroundings—and to his new father. Victor felt a surge of pride as he glanced back at the sleeping boy, his son. He'd already decided that the child's name would be Michael from now on. Michael after the archangel. An entity that had great power.

"It wasn't so hard after all, was it Twigs?" Victor said. "You did a fine job. Come on, let's go have a drink and let the boy sleep. With so much tranquilizer in him, he'll probably sleep for hours." Victor moved toward the door and motioned for Twigs to follow.

"I'm not so sure…about his sleeping," Twigs said, giving the sleeping boy one last look. "He's been in and out of it a number of times. That stuff doesn't seem to have the right effect on him. Maybe because of his genetics or whatever. Better keep an eye on him."

"Good old Doc Foxhoven provided us with a little something that will take care of that, if we need it.'"

Twigs followed him down the hall and into the living room. "Okay, good!" he said. "If you don't mind, I really don't want a drink. Just my money and I'll be on my way."

"Certainly. You don't mind if I have a drink, do you? Then I'll pay you and arrange for the chopper to take you back to the mainland." Victor saw Twigs pale slightly and wondered if he suspected that he was soon to be disposed of.

"No thanks!" Twigs said emphatically. "I know a guy on the island who's got a forty-foot ketch. He'll get me back. I don't like that chopper!"

Victor was about to pour a drink when he noticed something outside the large window that overlooked Avalon harbor. Some lights were moving in the distance. Too low for a plane, too high for a boat. Goddamn! It looked like another helicopter! He checked his watch. Almost three a.m. No chopper, except his, would be buzzing around Catalina at this hour. He watched the chopper as it moved inland, saw it curve slightly and head toward his chopper pad.

"Twigs!" he snapped. "Are you positive no one saw you when you took the child?"

"Yeah, sure. I completely tranquilized the parents. No cell phone signal there, so even when they came to they couldn't have called for help. Why?"

Victor stood at the window and watched the approaching lights. He wondered if he should alert the security crew at his laboratory. He really didn't want to involve them if he didn't have to.

He turned to Twigs. The man still looked pale. He might as well use the poor slob as much as possible until he could get rid of him. "Twigs, I've got one more job for you, and then I'll make out your check."

Twigs went whiter. The guy was about to wet his pants. He hadn't wanted to do more than surveillance to begin with. More involvement obviously scared the shit out of him. But if that was a police chopper, and if Twigs had fucked up royally, then he might be their target.

Victor went to his gun cabinet, opened it, took out a pair of Walther P38 pistols, and loaded them. He handed one to Twigs. "We may have some uninvited guests," he said. "Thanks to you." Victor gave him his most menacing scowl.

"What!" Twigs reluctantly took the gun. "Are you kidding?" He looked out the window toward the lights. "Holy shit! I can't believe it! How the hell did they track us? Look, Victor, I swear...."

Victor slipped his pistol into his pocket and held up his hand for Twigs to be quiet. "It doesn't matter now. What matters is that we get the boy and get out of here! Fast! First, I need to get my passport and some cash from the safe. We'll take the underground tunnel from here to the lab. I've got a Land Rover there that can get us around to Little Harbor. My boat will meet us and we can slip away before they get here."

"Where will we go?"

"For now, I've got a place in the desert. For that matter, I have a lot places. Places no one will find us. We have the child. And the child holds the key to the future."

Ted gripped the arm of his seat as the police chopper did an unexpected dip. He looked over at Ajax. The little tarantula seemed to be enjoying the ride. The chopper carrying Dar had been traced to Virtual Images, a computer program company based in Palo Alto, California. Virtual Images had an offshoot, Earth Dues Inc., in the Silicon Valley, which in turn had a small subsidiary with a lab on Catalina. Ajax had been brilliant in tracking it down so fast. Ted was beginning to like the little fellow a lot.

Ted looked at his watch in the dim glow of the helicopter's interior light. Ah, Christ! The thing wasn't working, as usual. It had to be close to two in the morning. He closed his eyes and wished he were back on the mainland in bed with Maddy, snuggled into her soft warmth. He could spend the rest of his life there and be completely happy.

"I hope we have enough force," Ajax shouted over the noise of the chopper. "If they're expecting us, it could get rough."

Ted nodded. He'd alerted the Catalina police. Outside of that, they had five uniformed police officers, plus himself and Ajax in this chopper, and eight SWAT team members in the other. That would have to do it. He hoped the kidnapper or kidnappers weren't expecting them. If they were, then Ajax was right. It could get bloody.

As they approached the area, Ted saw below him the helicopter that had taken Dar. It sat on a small pad next to a large sprawling house. Down the hill from it was a small squat building. The building appeared dark. The house however, had lights on in several rooms. If he was right, and he hoped he was, they'd find Dar in the house.

"There!" he shouted to the pilot. "Put us down on that side of the house. Tell the others to circle and find a spot as close as possible."

"Roger," the pilot replied.

As the chopper descended, Ted felt his stomach lurch. He wondered if it was the motion of the chopper, or his fear for the child. Maybe he was just hungry. His thoughts must have showed on his face because Ajax leaned over and shouted in his ear.

"We'll get the boy!" Ajax said. "Don't worry. We'll have him out of there and on his way home ASAP."

Ted gave him a grim smile. The sensation in his stomach increased. He recognized it now as a strong form of anxiety. It was more than just fear. More like a portent to death. He'd heard that people who were going to die had that type of sensation just before death. Ted wondered how they knew that, since the people who supposedly experienced it couldn't come back and tell anyone. He shrugged off the thoughts and the feeling. It was no time to get spooked. He had a job to do.

The grounds where the chopper landed were so dark it took Ted a few minutes before he could make out anything at all. Whoever was inside had to know they had arrived. After all, a helicopter wasn't the best form of transportation for sneaking up on someone. Ted had hoped to see patrol cars from the town of Avalon at the scene. As far as he could tell in the dark, they hadn't arrived yet.

"Ajax, you come with me. You two, what are your names?" Ted shouted at two of the uniformed men.

"Tate," one man answered. "Ron Tate."

"Jerry, sir," said the other. "Mullrue

"Okay Tate, Mullrue, you're with us. You three others cover the back and that little building below the house. No shooting unless it's absolutely necessary. The child's here somewhere. Our Swat chopper should be landing in a few minutes so we'll have backup."

"Do we need a search warrant?" Ajax asked.

"No. We've got probable cause. Boy, do we have probably cause!" Ted motioned for them to follow.

With his revolver drawn, Ted moved toward one of the lit windows of the house. He had to get the lay of the place fast, and determine the best way in.

Ted's cell phone gave a soft buzz. He clicked it on. "Bearbower," he said.

"This is chopper two. Had a little trouble. We clipped a tree branch on our way in." Ted recognized the voice as Castillano, one of the officers he'd often worked with.

"Ah, Christ! Is anyone injured?" All he needed now was a deadly crash.

"No, not really." Castillano said. "A few bruises. We were lucky. I swallowed my gum, is all. We'll get it together and be with you in a few minutes."

"Great," Ted said, feeling a surge of relief. "We're going to need you."

CHAPTER TWENTY-THREE

Dar opened his eyes and looked around. For a moment, he thought he was home in his crib. Then he realized that his colored blocks weren't hanging where they should be. The walls looked funny, pictures all over them. He wasn't in the cabin in the mountains either. He lay there for a while, wondering what to do. He still felt sleepy, but not nearly as much as before. He finally sat up, and then pulled himself to his feet. The crib was very different from his own. The side rails were a little lower, and had brightly colored balls on them. He gave one of the balls a whirl with his hand. His stomach rumbled. He was hungry. He wanted his bottle. Warm and soothing. He put his thumb in his mouth and sucked on it. He remembered that a while ago he'd been in a plane with a roundy-round thing on top. That had been awful and had made him mad. He felt the same anger scrunching up inside him again. He looked at the colored balls on the crib and began to wiggle their insides. Very quickly, they become soft and droopy looking, like melted candles. He began wiggling the rails of the crib. The wood made a crackling sound and for a moment Dar was afraid they might go bang, the way his blocks at home had done. Instead, they broke into long splinters and fell to the ground.

He found it easy to slip out of the crib with the rails gone. Padding across the room, he stopped to inspect the toys on the shelves. More toys than he'd ever seen. He pulled a truck off the shelf and spun its wheels. He put the truck back and picked up a brown teddy bear, which was dressed in a bright red suit. It looked almost like his teddy bear at home, the one he'd wiggled too much. He snuggled the soft bear with one hand, and thrust the thumb of his other into his mouth. That felt good. He wasn't quite so mad. Now, he had to go and find Mama. To comfort himself he began singing in a soft whisper so no one would hear him. "Do you know da muffin man, da muffin man?" He had a hard time saying muffin but he didn't care. He liked the tune.

He opened the door to the room and peeked out. There was just enough light to see the hallway. No one there. He heard nothing, not even the tick of a clock, the way he always could at home. He had a hard time deciding which direction he should take, then decided to go down the hall to the room where he saw the most light. Maybe his Mama would be in that room. He hoped so.

Ted led Ajax and the two uniformed men into the house through an unlocked side door. The door led to a storage room, its shelves stacked with canned goods. That room opened into the kitchen which was dark. Ted let out a sigh, relieved that they hadn't walked into a room filled with people. The next room was a large dining room, also dark, but an archway in one wall opened into the living room. He heard voices.

He moved silently into the dining room, flattening himself against a wall and working his way toward the opening into the living room. He had to see if Dar was there too. He didn't want any shooting if the child was in there. When his eyes adjusted to the light, he saw only two men. One medium tall and young, the other was older, Hawk-faced and tall. He scanned the room carefully. Good, only the two men, and no Dar.

"Let's do it," Ajax whispered. "Right," Ted said. With his revolver positioned in front of him, he stepped into the living room. "Freeze!" he yelled and saw the two men look up, startled. "Police! Where's the boy?" he bellowed.

Both of the men were silent. Time seemed to hang suspended for a moment. Ted felt his gun go slippery in his fingers. Ajax stepped out beside him, his gun also drawn. Tate and Mullrue, automatic rifles in hand, covered the rest of the room. With a sense of astonishment, Ted saw the tall hawk-faced man pull a pistol from his coat pocket.

Ajax moved forward, his gun aimed at the man. "Don't try it!" he bellowed.

It happened so fast Ted didn't see it coming. A loud report and bright flash filled the air. Ajax spun around like a propeller, his feet splaying out from underneath him. Ted fired from pure reflex; the men behind him echoed his fire. It was only then that Ted realized Ajax had been shot.

"Ah, damn it to hell! No!" Ted flung himself down on the floor beside his partner. Mullrue and Tate continued to fire, but the two

211

men in the living room had barricaded themselves behind a heavy desk. Ted wondered what in the hell had gone wrong. He'd had the upper hand, and then lost it in a split-second. He should have waited for the rest of the men. He'd been over-zealous to find the boy. Damn! He ran his hands over Ajax, desperately trying to find where he'd been hit.

"Ahhh, my side!" Ajax cried out. "The fucker caught me in the ribs!" He held his hand over his side. Blood seeped between his fingers. It was bad! Too low to hit the heart, but may have nicked a lung. He will be sucking air through the bullet hole in a minute if's that's what happened.

Quickly, he slipped off his jacket, pulled out his cell phone, then rolled the jacket into a firm ball and pressed it against Ajax's side. "Keep this on the wound. Press hard! I'm sure as hell not going to lose another partner, you little tarantula. I'm just getting used to you!"

A bullet zinged past Ted's head and he flattened himself against the floor. Maybe this was the reason for his earlier anxiety. He was going to die there on the floor, like some squashed bug. When he looked a few feet away, he saw that Tate was also down. He couldn't tell how bad he was. He fumbled in his pocket for his cell phone, found it and pressed the speed dial. "We need help in here!" he yelled at whoever answered. "Where the fuck are you guys?" Another bullet hit the carpet about two inches from his head. Time to pull back; get Ajax and Tate out of there. "We've got two men down!"

The shooting stopped for a moment and Ted a made mental note of the living room's layout. Then he crawled to where Tate lay and saw that he'd been hit but thank God, the bullet had just grazed his skull bone. Knocked the guy out. Mullrue jumped back into the corner of the dining room out of harm's way. Ted didn't blame him. Tate started to come to. He'd get Ajax out of there, and then come back for him.

He moved back to Ajax, put his arms under him, and began sliding him toward the dining room. The little runt must have weighed a lot more than he appeared to. He could only move him a few inches at a time. The two men behind the desk must have reloaded their weapons. Bullets began flying again. They sounded more like wayward mosquitoes than lethal pieces of lead. Their aim was off. Probably couldn't see much behind that huge desk. Thank God for small favors!

Between gunshots, he heard an odd noise. Then heard it a second time. When he looked up, he saw Dar standing in the doorway of the living room, a teddy bear clasped in his arms. The gunfire stopped. Ted expected his heart would too. Instead, it thundered inside his chest like someone beating on an empty barrel. Dar let out a low cry which didn't sound at all like a child. No, Please! Ted yelled silently. Go back Dar! Don't come in here, for God's sake! Dar looked over at him, a puzzled expression on his face. Then suddenly, like a snake striking, one of the men leapt out from behind the desk and grabbed the boy.

"That's it," the hawk-faced man said. "Put down your guns and stay where you are. I've got the boy. You wouldn't want your fire to hit him, would you?"

Ted put his head down on the floor, bitter tears behind his eyes burning like flames. "Shit, shit, and shit!" he hissed into the carpet. He let go of his gun and pushed it to one side. "Okay," he said. "No one wants the boy to be hurt. Just let me get these men out of here. They need medical attention." He lifted his head and looked at the man who held Dar. The man was smiling; an odd twisted smile that made Ted's heart beat even faster. The second man, a slender man who quivered nervously, came out from behind the desk. As much as he wanted the SWAT team to charge, Ted was afraid they'd hit Dar.

"Come on, Victor," the second man said. "You said we were getting out of here. Let's get going."

"Shut up, Twigs. Take your gun and put those three men out of their misery."

Twig's mouth fell open. "Are you crazy? I'm not going to kill someone. Not for you. Not for anyone."

"Well, okay then," Victor turned the gun on Twigs. "I guess it's bye-bye Twigs. Or, have you had a quick change of heart?"

Twigs stood looking from Victor to the three men on the floor then back to Victor. "If I don't…do it…you'll kill me?"

"That's right. You. Then them. Either way, I'm rid of them."

Ted looked at Dar. The child's eyes seemed huge. His breathing had become measured and slow. "Dar," Ted called.

"Shut up!" Victor screamed. "Don't talk to him. He's harmless right now. Had enough tranquilizers to numb an elephant." As if in

213

answer to that, Dar yawned.

Twigs looked at his gun and then at Victor. "Okay," he finally said. "Okay, I'll do it. But you gotta promise not to shoot me after I do it."

"Of course not. I really need you to help us get out of here." Victor gave him a mirthless grin. "After all, I'm sure they have more force coming."

Ted looked back at Dar. Something was going on with him. Ted hoped he was doing his special thing on Victor. It couldn't happen to a more deserving guy. But he'd have to hurry or it would be too fucking late. Twigs walked toward Ted, gun in hand. Was the guy really going to do it? Kill the three of them? Was he dumb enough to think Victor would really spare him afterward? Christ! Where the fuck was the SWAT team? They were cutting it way too close.

Twigs stood over Ajax who was panting, and writhing in pain. "Sorry, guy. Maybe it's better. You look pretty bad." He extended his arm and aimed the gun at Ajax's head. Ted closed his eyes. If he did anything to stop him, Victor might do the boy.

An odd renting sound filled the air. Ted opened his eyes. For a moment, he thought the Santa Ana winds had started again. The air in the room moved, as if blown by a giant fan. Air that grew warmer and began to curl into a dark funnel. Dar's face turned stony. A faint blue haze tinted the air, the way twilight does. Sparks fluttered around Dar like electric fireflies. Then a wild force erupted from him, as strong as a burst from a machine gun. Crazy arcs of light crackled around the room. Overhead, the timbers of the house began to scream.

Twigs and Victor stood motionless, their faces dumb and shiny from sweat. Victor slowly loosened his grip on Dar. The boy slid from Victor's arms to the floor and stood there in front of him, eyes vacant, looking at nothing. A loud booming echoed around the room as the guns exploded in Victor and Twigs hands. Twigs shrieked as he looked down and found his fingers missing on his right hand. Victor fared better. His hand had only been charred.

Ted sat up, reluctant to reach for his own gun. He expected to see the two men bolt from the room, but neither of them moved. They stood like concrete statues as if their feet were melted into the floor. Overhead, the ceiling timbers continued to scream. They twisted, writhed, and rippled the walls like paper in the wind. Tate, conscious now, staggered to his feet, looked around wildly, and began to back away from the scene.

"Get out!" Ted yelled at him.

"What the hell's happening?" Tate shouted. "An earthquake?"

"Just get out!" Ted looked back at Dar and held out his arms to him, but the boy didn't appear to see him. "Dar," he cried. "Enough! You can stop now." But the boy's face remained dull and expressionless. Ted looked at the shelves on the far wall and watched as the books suddenly caromed across the room. They pelted Victor and Twigs, but circumvented Dar. Guns from the gun cabinet broke loose and whined loudly as they slung themselves around the room. The large glass windowpane imploded with a screeching sound, sending shards of glass whirling about like gleaming propellers. A runaway of glass shards nearly decapitated Victor. Instead, it sliced off a thick piece of his jacket and shoulder, and flung it into the whirling melee. The destruction spread out from Dar in every direction like a fast growing spider's web. Bricks jumped from the fireplace. Two-by-fours, metal pipes, and electrical wires filled the air. A recliner chair convulsed and twisted into what looked like a giant Brillo Pad.

As if caught in a violent chain reaction, Dar's power grew. The air filled with plaster dust and bits of loose debris, choking Ted. The convulsing room smelled sharply sweet from melting paint. Water gushed from broken pipes. Carpet fibers went soggy beneath Ted. He tried to stand but couldn't find his balance. He had to reach the boy and stop him. He had no idea how far Dar could go, but he had no wish to find out. In minutes, Ted knew the entire house would crash down on them. Then he realized he had to make a choice between getting Dar, and saving Ajax. He might possibly be able to heft Ajax over his shoulder and make a run for it, leaving Dar and the two men. But if Dar's destruction widened, God knew where it would stop. Ted had to go for the boy.

He saw Twigs legs fold beneath him and he collapsed onto his knees, boards and bricks bombarding him. Ted watched as a silver-gray shaft of pipe, like a knight's lance, soared across the room impaling Twigs through the upper chest. Twigs looked around, astonishment on his face. He reached a hand in Dar's direction. Then lowered it and attempted to pull out the pipe. Nevertheless, it was no use. He gave a little cry and then his muscles began an involuntarily twitching. Ted looked away.

"Dar, please! You have to stop. You're going to hurt yourself!" Ted hoped to get through to Dar's sense of fear, but the boy only blinked and went back to staring into space. The wild rotating wind that filled the room blew Dar's golden curls into a gyrating halo around his head. A strange apparition. An angel in the eye of the hurricane.

Ted heard Victor yell. The yell turned into a moan. The man's eyes bulged, grew huge, and then grossly popped from his head with a terrible snapping sound, leaving dark vacant hollows in the man's face. Ted's stomach convulsed. Would he be next, he wondered? With great effort, he began crawling across the floor toward Dar. Some great sword of glass would probably slice his head off before he reached him, but he had to try.

"Come on, Dar. Stop it! Turn it off! Then you can go home to your mom and dad." Ted's voice sounded raspy. He coughed. So much plaster dust filled the air he could barely breathe.

Just as he reached Dar, Ted saw the boy's eyes look down at him. Christ, he hoped he recognized him as one of the good guys! Dar blinked several times and then his lower lip began to tremble.

"Please, Dar. Stop!" Ted pleaded.

Tears welled up in the child's eyes. "Dar not know how!" he said. "Dar can't stop it!"

Ted pulled the boy into his arms and held him. "Yes you can. I know you can." He felt Dar's tiny body begin to shake. He lifted him and, keeping as low to the floor as possible, carried him back to where Ajax lay.

"It go by self," Dar said. "Not stop!"

An overwhelming fear hit Ted. What if the boy had unleashed something that fed on itself? Something that mushroomed like an A-bomb? One atom breaking apart, hitting others and breaking those apart and on and on. How far could it go? Could anything stop it? The fear spiked him with a jolt of adrenaline. He grabbed Dar securely in one arm, and then reached for Ajax with the other.

"Get the kid out first," Ajax said. "You can come back. Or maybe I can walk."

Ted gave a growl and jerked at Ajax who moved agonizingly slow, but moved none the less. Ajax didn't feel as heavy as before. His adrenaline was probably spiking. "Shut up," he told Ajax. "It's all three of us, or none. This whole place is coming down fast. No time to come back. You'd be a mashed potato."

When Ted reached the kitchen, he found that room in as much turmoil as the living room. Cupboard doors, ripped off their hinges, flew around the room. One passed within inches of his head. He tried to shelter Dar against his chest and still drag Ajax. Dishes, utensils, everything loose in the room, even most of what had once been nailed down, seemed to have a life of their own. Ted heard a horrible wrenching sound. The house was ripping itself apart. Roof timbers wailed, and then crashed to the floor. One narrowly missed the three of them. As Ted reached the small storage room, the walls fell outward with a whooshing sound. The adrenaline spiked again and Ted made a leap for the safety of the outside. Behind him, the last timbers of the house collapsed.

He lay on the ground a few yards from the house, Dar in his arms and Ajax sprawled next to him. Ted felt as if he had a herd of thundering horses in his chest instead of a heart. He took in a breath, but it hurt. He tried it again, shallower. Better. The pile of rubble that had been the house gave off purple sparks that frolicked in the night air. Was it over? Or would the landscape around him begin the same dance of destruction? He lay there letting his heart slow. The more time that passed, the easier he began to feel. The implosion, or whatever it was, was stopping.

"I try stop." Dar said with a sob in his voice. "Bad, bad thing!"

"It's okay, Dar. It's stopping." Ted patted the boy, trying to soothe him.

"Dar want Mama," the boy said, still grasping the teddy bear. He thrust his thumb into his mouth.

"Yes. I know. We'll get you to Mama. I promise." Ted felt the boy begin to sob. Huge glistening tears rolled down his cheeks, but he continued to suck his thumb. "Go ahead and cry. You've got good reason."

The pile of rubble in front of them continued to spark. Small licks of flames jumped from one area, then another. Christ! Gas was probably leaking. Better get the hell out of there.

"Ajax…how you doing? Is it bad?" he asked.

Ajax moaned and tried to sit up. "Piece of cake," he said. "I've think I've stopped the leak." He lifted the jacket from his side and held it up to Ted. "Ya want your jacket back? It's kinda nippy out here."

Ted heard himself laugh. "Lie down. You move much, and you'll spring the leak again."

From somewhere below the remains of the house Ted heard a commotion. The SWAT team, the Catalina police, all of them converging on the scene. Tate and Mullrue were among them. Thank God, they'd gotten out okay. He wondered, though, if anyone else had been in the house besides the man called Victor and the one-called Twigs. If they had been, it was too bad. From the look of the rubble, they'd be about an inch tall at this point. The men reached him and stood gaping at the scene, mouths open.

"Well," he said to the men. "Where the fuck have you guys been?"

The chopper ride back to the mainland was smooth. They flew into the early morning light. The sun had not yet come up over Saddleback Mountain, but the sky had turned a pale slate blue and a sliver of moon was just setting into the Pacific. Dar slept in Ted's arms during the trip. Ted watched the child sleep. So adorable. So terrifying. Why had God allowed a child to be born like this? What kind of life would he have?

With his adrenaline depleted, Ted felt fatigue settle on him like a stone heavy quilt. He propped Dar so he wouldn't fall, then closed his eyes and let sleep capture him. It was a dark, dreamless kind of sleep that he welcomed.

CHAPTER TWENTY-FOUR

Ted curled himself around Maddy's warm body. He listened to her soft breathing and wondered if she'd fallen asleep. She smelled like autumn, spicy and sweet. They'd made love slowly, enjoying every touch. Ted couldn't remember when he'd felt so good.

He'd put in for retirement from the police department and in two weeks he'd be a free man. He and Maddy would move to the cabin in Julian as soon as possible. They'd agreed to think about a pie shop there, but would take some time off first. Thank God, there'd be no more similar cases like the Barry Brownstone murders, the new ones caused by Doctor Foxhoven. He knew he'd never make it through another one. He was just thankful that Ajax was recovering. He'd miss the little tarantula, but not the police work.

"Are you awake?" Maddy asked.

"Yes. You, too, I see."

"What cha thinking about?"

"About how long it is until I'm a free man."

Maddy gave a throaty laugh. "If you wanted to be free, you shouldn't have asked me to marry you."

"You, my love, are a part of my freedom."

"Are all your cases closed now?"

"Yep. Even those gruesome vampire kind. That stupid doctor started the whole thing all over again. He developed the same blood craving as the Brownstone guy after he took the raw Sunshine drug. Even after he'd made some changes to it. What he hoped to learn by experimenting on himself, I can't imagine. At least he was stopped early on."

"The doctor's dead?"

"Murdered by Victor Bryce, another stupid man."

Maddy was silent for a moment. "Was it frightening? All that happened on Catalina?"

Ted felt himself jerk slightly, an uncomfortable flashback to the scene. "More terrifying than anything I've ever experienced."

"That poor little child."

Ted gave a laugh. "That poor little child can take care of himself."

"Yes, but will he be okay?"

"I don't know. I hope so."

Ted snuggled Maddy closer to him and whispered in her ear. "I want to make love to you again," he said.

Maddy chuckled. "My God! Your lust for sex is even stronger than your appetite for food! How lucky can a gal get?"

Ted leaned over and kissed her. This, he told himself, was how he wanted to spend the rest of his life.

⟡

Elizabeth bundled Dar into his padded jacket. The air-conditioning in the airport felt as if it had been turned up to frigid. That seemed fitting, Elizabeth thought, considering where they were going. She looked at the little group of people around her and felt tears threatening. This was the hardest thing she had ever done.

Dar pointed at the wide sweep of windows, his face aglow with delight. "Dar fi, Mama?"

"Yes, Dar. You're going to fly."

"Big plane?" Dar asked.

"Yep, really big plane," Andy said.

"Dar like," he said, clapping his hands. "Ree go too? And Zips?"

Tyree grinned at the boy. "No, Dar. I'm afraid Boo and I have to stay here." "But we'll come visit soon," Boo assured him.

Mabel Zipper reached out and tousled Dar's gold curls. "Sister and I will visit too, one of these days."

Dar's mouth turned down. "Wan you come too," he said softly.

"I know, but my goodness, you've got your mommy and daddy, and Doctor Terri here. That's a lot of people," Sarah Zipper said in an unusual burst of words.

"Dat my Ter re," Dar said, pointing to Terri. "Dar's teacher."

"That's right," Terri said. "I'm going to be your teacher. However, we'll learn together, won't we Dar? You show me what you can do, and I'll teach you how to use it the best way."

Elizabeth drew in a long slow breath. For the first time in a long while, she felt almost at ease. Terri had explained that Dar's abilities were caused by the unusually strong electrical impulses he generated. Somehow, he could set up vibrations that had a physical effect on matter. The mind was a complicated organ. No one yet knew the extent of what it could do. According to Terri, most people didn't believe in things like telepathy or PK. But one proof she'd explained was that this type of power actually existed was the connection between identical twins. Even when some twins were far away from each other, they often felt each other's pain. They also knew when the other experienced something traumatic. The fact that this type of power could be demonstrated led Elizabeth to hope that one day the mystery behind Dar's abilities would be understood, or at least accepted.

"We see S-kim-O?" Dar asked.

"What?" Andy said.

"He means Eskimo, dear," Mabel said. "Don't you Dar."

Dar nodded his head. "In laska."

Elizabeth laughed. "Right, we're going to Alaska. Maybe you'll see an Eskimo, Dar."

"Cold dare," Dar said.

"Very cold," Sarah said.

Elizabeth looked at the people around her. She'd miss Tyree the most, even if she was a mother hen. And of course the Zipper sisters. In addition, it was Aunt Mary's house on the beach she might miss the most. She heard herself sigh. But maybe one day they could come back. One day when they were certain Dar wouldn't harm anyone. Until then, they would live in a very remote part of Alaska.. Tyree had arranged for a house there. A large house where the three of them could live along with Terri. Terri had volunteered to spend her retirement years working with Dar. Elizabeth would paint and send Tyree her paintings. Andy would write. Money would not be a problem. It was best, she knew, to keep Dar isolated until he could control his abilities. Besides that, it would be a deterrent to anyone who might try to get at Dar again. It would be an adventure, Elizabeth kept telling herself. To get to Isolat they would take a small plane from Anchorage, then a car to where they would catch a riverboat that would take them the last miles to the tiny town. No television, no telephones, no internet. Only radio contact with the outside world. The Zipper sisters had promised to send them DVD's of the latest movies.

The airport's loudspeaker shattered Elizabeth's thoughts. "Global Airlines flight 169 to Anchorage, Alaska, now loading at gate seven."

"That's us," Andy said. "Time to go."

Dar clapped his hands and squealed with delight. "Bye," he said, waving to the small group. "Dar fly now."

Tyree watched the four of them as they boarded the airplane. Mabel and Sarah stood next to her, both of them wiping their eyes with lace edged hankies.

"Oh my, I hate to see them go," Mabel said.

"Hate to," Sarah said with a little sob.

"How about a Bloody Mary, ladies?" Tyree suggested.

"Oh, that sounds dandy," Mabel sniffed.

"Dandy," Sarah echoed.

"I saw a nice little place just down the corridor," Boo said.

"Mercy me, we'd better go fix our faces first, sister," Mabel said.

"Yes, fix them," Sarah said.

Tyree smiled at them. "Go ahead. We'll meet you at the restaurant."

The two women nodded and set off at a brisk pace toward the ladies room.

Tyree looked at the plane that had begun to taxi toward the runway. "There they go, Boo. I'm going to miss them terribly!"

"I know. But we'll see them before long. I promise I'll take time off from the lab for an extended visit."

Tyree moved closer to the window so she could watch the plane as it took off. A few minutes later, the silver and blue craft seemed to leap into the air and began to soar higher and higher. Tyree reached over and took hold of Boo's hand.

"Maybe we should have told them after all," she said.

"Told them?"

"That Barry Brownstone, not Andy, is Dar's father."

Boo shook his head. "What good would it do?"

Tyree felt a small tear escape her eye and trickle down one cheek. She wiped it away with her fingertips. "None, I suppose. Just think about it. All of this happened because of Sunshine. We struggled so long to make life better for everyone. Mabel and Sarah's lives have become whole and useful because of it. Nevertheless, Barry and Foxhoven's lives were lost, as well as that of their victims. So much good. So much evil."

"So then, does that make Sunshine a blessing or a curse?" Boo said

"I believe that only God knows the answer to that." Tyree looked up at him. "Come on Boo, I really do need that Bloody Mary!"

END

About the Author

Born in Pasadena, California, Dorothy McMillan now lives in Riverside, California, with her husband, Al, her two widowed daughters, a grandson, two dogs, two cats and a variety of raccoons and possums that have made the trees next to her home, their home. When she isn't penning suspense thriller novels, Dorothy is busy creating a wide variety of items using polymer clay.

Books by Dorothy McMillan

Deadly Urges

Soul Crossed

Vile Acts

Blackbird (with two film options)

The Gray Green Underground

Creative Ways with Polymer Clay (as Dotty McMillan)

Artful Ways with Polymer Clay (as Dotty McMillan)

The Devil's Bell

The Dark Horse